Breath of Heaven

BOOK 3 OF THE CAMFIELD LEGACY

Deborah Raney

RANEY DAY
PRESS

Praise for Beneath a Southern Sky

2002 RITA Award Winner • ACFW Book of the Year finalist •
Holt Medallion Finalist •
Faith, Hope & Love Inspirational Readers Choice Award •
Romantic Times Reviewers' Choice Best Inspirational Novel

"Forget the movie of the week. *Beneath a Southern Sky* reads like a dramatic film, but has substance of eternal importance. Six months after reading it, I'm still digesting what it means to me. Everyone will be talking about this book!"
—Lisa Tawn Bergren best-selling author of the Full Circle series and *Midnight Sun*

"There aren't many novels that keep me awake reading into the wee hours of the night, but *Beneath a Southern Sky* did. Nathan, Daria, and Cole slipped from the pages of this book and into my heart. I experienced all their heart-wrenching emotions, agonized over every decision they had to make, and rejoiced as they triumphed by God's grace in the midst of an impossible, hopeless situation. Bravo, Ms. Raney!"
—Robin Lee Hatcher best-selling author of *The Forgiving Hour*

"In *Beneath a Southern Sky*, Deborah Raney reminds us that God's ways are not our ways...but His paths lead to fulfillment and joy."
—Angela Elwell Hunt author of *The Note* and The Heirs of Cahira O'Connor series

"*Beneath a Southern Sky* captured my attention on page one and held me in its grips to the last page. Deborah has written an incredible tale of passionate love, tragic mistakes, and second chances. Write faster, Deborah Raney!"
—Denise Hunter author of *Reunions*

"*Beneath a Southern Sky* has magnetic qualities! I just couldn't seem to put it down! In her normal, five-tissue fashion, Deborah Raney has created an impossible situation for her heroine, Daria Camfield. As I read, I thought I imagined all the ways Raney could tie her book into a neat little bow. Not so! The poignant ending of this thought-provoking novel took me unaware and lingered in my mind for days afterwards. You definitely won't be disappointed."
—Lisa E. Samson best-selling author of *The Church Ladies*

"Deborah Raney dug deeply into my heart with this story of sacrificial love. No reader could walk away from this novel without a clearer, more personal picture of the love of Christ. I thank Deborah for reminding me that, even though life's choices aren't always easy, God is always there to help us make them."
—Hannah Alexander author of *Sacred Trust, Solemn Oath*, and *Silent Pledge*

Breath of Heaven
Breath of Heaven is the third book in the Camfield Legacy series by Deborah Raney, following *Beneath a Southern Sky* and *After the Rains.*

Published by Raney Day Press

Cover design by Ken Raney

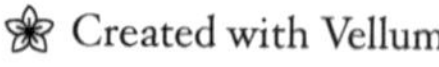 Created with Vellum

*In loving memory of Terry Stucky.
It's still hard to imagine
a world without you in it, dear friend.*

I will lift up mine eyes unto the hills, from whence cometh my
help. My help cometh from the Lord, which made heaven and
earth. He will not suffer thy foot to be moved: he that keepeth
thee will not slumber. Behold, he that keepeth Israel shall
neither slumber nor sleep. The Lord is thy keeper: the Lord is
thy shade upon thy right hand. The sun shall not smite thee by
day, nor the moon by night. The Lord shall preserve thee from
all evil: he shall preserve thy soul. The Lord shall preserve thy
going out and thy coming in from this time forth, and even for
evermore.

Psalm 121
King James Bible

PROLOGUE

Bristol, Kansas

The sanctuary still wore its holiday finery on this Saturday after Christmas. A copse of artificial trees twinkled with white lights on one corner of the stage, and tall lanterns adorned with ivy lit the aisle beside each pew. The effect was magical, despite the fact that Natalie always imagined she'd be married in the spring, outdoors on her parents' farm.

"Because David and Natalie have exchanged solemn vows before God and these witnesses, because they have pledged their commitment to each other and have sealed that commitment with this exchange of...er, with these *rings*—" Pastor Vickers cleared his throat and looked pointedly at the ornate tattoos encircling the ring fingers of her and David's clasped hands.

Natalie suppressed a giggle and David shot her a stern look that said, *Don't you dare get me started!*

Pastor Vickers raised his voice, looking solemn. "Now, by the authority vested in me, I pronounce that they are husband and wife. Those whom God hath joined together, let no man put asunder."

Natalie had dutifully given her full attention to her parents' pastor through his rather long and—if she were honest—*boring* remarks. But now she turned to David—her *husband*. *Finally*, her husband. She didn't even try to hold back her smile.

"You may kiss your bride." The pastor nodded as if David needed permission.

Her groom seemed even more somber than usual today. A twinge of worry went through her. She prided herself on having brought David Chambers out of his shell over these past months while they'd been falling in love. But he'd made it clear that he saw their marriage as a supremely serious matter. They'd weathered more than a few arguments because David was afraid she didn't understand what she was getting into, marrying him and committing their lives to the mission field in the Republic of Colombia. Leaving the luxuries of America that she'd grown accustomed to these last few months while she was home recovering from malaria. He didn't think she understood the isolation their little home—more accurately, a hut on stilts —in the tiny village of Timoné promised. Especially now that her father was gone, and it would only be her and David in Timoné.

But she did understand. She'd lived in Colombia for almost a year before she and David decided to marry. And she was not afraid of what lay ahead for them, even though she knew it would be hard at times. Even dangerous. After all, they'd chosen tattoos in lieu of wedding rings because they were heading to a place where thieves might chop off limbs to steal jewelry.

But she loved this man with all her heart. And she would follow him to the proverbial ends of the earth if that's what it took to be with him.

David's jaw tensed, then relaxed, and his gaze softened as he bent and took her face between his palms, his touch profoundly tender. "I love you," he whispered, his lips barely moving, ensuring no one could read them. He brushed a hand lightly over her vintage birdcage style veil, as if to stroke her cheek. For a minute, she thought he was going to try to lift her veil—unnecessary since it barely skimmed the tip of her nose. Instead, he bent and placed his lips on hers. A kiss far too dispassionate for her taste.

He'd never been one for public displays of affection. It might have bothered her had she not quickly learned that what he hid in public, he made up for when they were alone together. Not that he'd ever violated the boundaries they'd set for themselves, what they'd agreed to wait for until after marriage. But in the rare moments when they were alone, she loved the urgency of his kisses and the promise of what they had to look forward to as husband and wife.

She still smiled when she remembered his proposal. An invitation to share the comfy bed she'd envied in his hut back in Timoné. He'd forgotten the "Will you marry me?" part until after he'd already blurted out the "I want you in my bed" part. She loved when friends asked how he'd proposed. David would groan and blush beneath his neatly-trimmed beard. And she would give him her orneriest smile and launch into the story with great enthusiasm. He would never live it down. And she didn't think he minded too much.

Now, she reached up and put her arms around his neck, making sure her sisters got the wedding kiss they'd been waiting to witness. He pulled away but not before Nikki and Noelle whooped in celebration. On cue, the strains of "How Sweet It Is To Be Loved By You" came over the little church's sound system.

David gave her a sideways glance that said, *That is* not *the hymn we agreed on*. But his smile said he'd already forgiven her. He pulled her to his side and ushered her down the aisle as the little congregation rose and cheered.

As she sashayed past the pew where Mom and Daddy sat, a lump formed unexpectedly in her throat. Dad—Nathan Camfield, her birthfather—should have been here. And if heaven had balconies, he *was* here, looking over the railing, cheering them on.

So much heartache their family had endured. So many losses and tragedies. Some of their own making, some for reasons no one would likely understand this side of heaven. But she'd spent too much time on her makeup today to let herself get teary-eyed now.

She pushed the thoughts aside and forced a smile. Today was not a day for reflection. It was a day for looking to the future, for celebration.

And celebrate, they would.

Eridanus:
River

❧ I ❧

Dwight D. Eisenhower National Airport, Wichita, Kansas
"Is this everything?" Cole Hunter hefted the last suitcase from the bed of his pickup truck and set it on the snowy curb in front of the airport.

"It better be." Frowning, Natalie eyed the small mountain of luggage and heavily taped cardboard boxes they had to get checked in before they could board their flight.

David clicked on his phone, pointedly checking the time, his breath hovering in a cloud on the chill air.

"Well, I guess this is it." Natalie willed her voice to remain steady as she hugged her two sisters, who'd come with Mom and Daddy to see them off at the airport. "We'll FaceTime when we can, okay?"

Nikki and Noelle nodded soberly.

"You'd *better* FaceTime, Natalie Joan!" Her mother shouldered her way between them for a hug. "And you let us know the minute you get there, you hear?" Tears welled in Mom's pale blue eyes and she let out a low wail. "Now I know what I must have put *my* parents through."

Natalie laughed. "Don't worry, Mom. Everything will be okay." But her laughter faded at the thought that everything had *not* been okay when Daria Camfield Hunter had flown to Colombia twenty-six years ago with her new husband. Mom had returned two years later, a grieving widow, just beginning to suspect she was pregnant with Natalie. Nate, Natalie's birth father, had been thought dead, "killed" in a tragic fire in a jungle village where he'd gone to offer medical care. But when Natalie was just a toddler, Nate Camfield had been found alive and had returned to the States to find his wife remarried and expecting the child of her new husband.

Only since her own marriage had Natalie begun to truly understand the agony her parents' situation must have caused.

"We'll text you the minute we have a signal," David reassured his new mother-in-law.

Natalie slid from Mom's embrace. "But remember, we won't be able to let you know about Timoné until—"

"I know. I know. Just...let us know as *soon* as you can." Her mother swiped at her cheeks with the back of her hand.

When had those crow's feet etched the corners of Mom's eyes? A stab of guilt came with the thought and Natalie swallowed hard. *She* was responsible for most of them. "We will, Mom. I promise. David won't let me forget."

"Good for him. I'm just so thankful you guys have internet now."

"We do when the server isn't down. Or the sun doesn't shine so the solar won't charge." David's gentle reminder was meant to ease her mother's anxious fears in case they couldn't get a message through right away.

"Oh...wait! Take my coat." She shrugged out of her winter coat and handed it to Mom. "I won't need it after today."

Mom took it, then turned to David, her voice wavering. "You take care of my baby, you hear?"

He embraced her, then stepped back and placed his hand over his heart, his eyes never leaving Mom's face. The gesture was the Timoné equivalent of an American handshake, but with far more of a promise attached. A forever one.

Her mother's face crumpled with emotion, and Natalie's heart welled with love for this thoughtful man who knew how much his gesture would mean to a woman who'd left so much of her heart in Timoné.

She gave Mom one last hug before turning to her dad. This was the goodbye she dreaded most. She tilted her head and offered a comical frown. "'Bye, Daddy."

Cole Hunter gave a sharp nod of his chin. He swallowed hard and pressed his lips into a firm line, pulling her into a bear hug.

She fell into his arms, trying to memorize the feel of his embrace—this man she shared not a drop of blood with, but who had been the only father she'd known until she'd met Nathan Camfield when she was barely two years old. And of course, she didn't remember that meeting. She couldn't remember a time when she hadn't known her parents' story. She still had newspaper clippings that told the tragic tale. But Nate had been more like a legend to her when she was younger. She'd gotten to know him better as a teenager, and had grown to love her birth father deeply when she'd gone to Timoné to work with him after the tragedy that changed the trajectory of her entire life.

She swallowed back a knot of grief as the memories assaulted her... *Her hands gripping the steering wheel of the Camry Grandpa Camfield had bought her that summer, Sara beside her in the passenger's seat.*

For a minute Natalie felt as woozy as she had that fateful night when too many beers had clouded her judgment and she'd climbed behind the wheel of her car, ignoring Sara's pleas. Sara, her best friend, who'd never been rebellious a day in her life. And in a flash, everything had changed.

It would forever break her heart to think of all she'd put her parents through back then. Never mind the anguish of Sara's family. Sometimes it still seemed wrong that God had forgiven everything and allowed her to have a life full of joy, full of people who loved her and who'd also forgiven her. Daddy, maybe most of all.

She leaned back to study her dad's face. When had those lines appeared across his forehead? And the permanent crinkles in the corners of his eyes? The threads of silver in what was left of his hair? Cole Hunter was still a handsome man, but Natalie hadn't realized until this moment that he was growing old. Daddy was in his fifties now. Older than Mom, though Natalie didn't remember either of them celebrating landmark birthdays. Those must have happened while she was overseas the first time.

She'd missed so much. Torn between two worlds, trying to make up for the pain she'd caused.

She shook off the weight of the thoughts. She'd been forgiven. God had redeemed the mess she'd made of her life. She wouldn't dwell on the mess. Wouldn't waste these last precious moments with her family on thoughts of what could not be changed.

She kissed her dad's cheek, then pulled away and wrinkled her nose at him, which produced the smile she'd hoped for.

She said a last goodbye and turned away before Daddy could see her tears. Or she his.

❧

"Wait... Do you have my tickets? David?" As they waited in line to check their luggage, Natalie dug through the massive canvas bag she was using as a carry-on, panic rising when she didn't find the envelope where she'd tucked the printed boarding passes.

"Settle down, you crazy woman. You gave them to me, remember? For safekeeping." He patted the thick sheaf of folded papers that protruded from his shirt pocket. "Besides, you have our boarding passes on your phone, right?"

She gave a little gasp. "My phone! What did I do with it?"

"Natalie. Settle down." He looked pointedly at her cell phone protruding from the breast pocket of her shirt. Right where she'd put it moments ago.

Her eyes burned with unshed tears and David hurriedly slipped the bulging backpack from his shoulder and piled it atop the mountain of luggage between them on the shiny tile. He gripped her shoulders then ran his hands down her arms. "We have everything. You do remember your phone won't even work once we get on the river?"

"Yes, but we need it to make the satellite phone work. You do have the sat phone, right?"

"Right here." He hoisted his backpack where they'd stowed the expensive satellite phone her parents had insisted on buying for them as a wedding gift. The service plan for the phone cost them almost sixty dollars a month, but since it would save them a couple of trips to Conzalez each month, they'd decided it was worth it. Mom and Daddy had offered to pay the service fees too, but David insisted they could fit it into their budget. They could, if they didn't lose any supporters or if they didn't have any unexpected expenses—both of which were not at all sure things.

"Take a deep breath, love." David looked down at her, waiting until she raised her chin to meet his eyes. "We have *everything* we need."

She'd always loved that at six-foot-five, he was almost a head taller than her. She'd always felt safe with him. And not *just* physically. The kindness in his eyes now warmed her.

"And if we did forget something, Nat," he continued, "we can buy it in San José before we get on the river."

She inhaled deeply, warming to his endearment. She wasn't sure why she was so nervous and unsettled. When they'd hugged her family outside only minutes ago, she'd felt sad, but a little relieved that the day of departure was finally here, and she and David could soon resume the life they'd thrived on, working among the Timoné people on the Rio Guaviare. It had been fun showing David her stomping grounds in Clayton County, Kansas. Sweet to have him get to know her family and for David and her to have time to get to know each other apart from their life in Colombia.

They'd learned things about each other they may never have discovered had they not spent some time away from Timoné. She'd seen a more vulnerable side to David than the confidence he usually wore in his role as a Bible translator. Ironically, he'd seen a more confident side of her. She was in her element with her friends and family. She suspected David disliked the bolder aspect of her personality as much as she liked seeing him with his defenses down a bit, not so cocksure of himself for a change.

They'd weathered the challenges of exploring their relationship in a different culture. But they agreed: they were best together in Colombia. And she was eager to get on with it.

Forty minutes later, they boarded the plane, and David motioned for her to take the window seat.

"Are you sure?"

"Of course. As long as I can use your head for a pillow."

"Maybe we'll luck out and get a row to ourselves."

"Maybe." He looked skeptical.

She loved David's selflessness, and she resolved—for the dozenth time since they'd said "I do"—to do everything in her power to be more like him in that way.

After their layover in Houston, she slept most of the flight to Panama City. And two hours later, the now familiar lights of Bogotá El Dorado International twinkled beneath them. David hadn't wanted to have to take a cab to a hotel after dark, but there weren't any other affordable options.

Their friends, Hank and Meghan Middleton, would pick them up in the morning and fly them to Conzalez where they'd get on the river. She could almost smell the Rio Guaviare's fusty, fishy scent. One that would make her sisters turn up their noses, but that smelled to her like the path home. Only this time, home would be an *utta*—a hut—she shared with David. And a bed shared with him this time too. With the blessing of Gospel Linguists, they'd moved into the larger hut that had been Dad's, with two small bedrooms, what passed for a kitchen, and a screened porch on stilts that was like the treehouse of every child's dreams.

David's bed, the one she'd envied so while she slept on a *mittah*—a grass mat—on the floor of Dad's hut, would now be *their* bed and would wear the colorful, thin coverlet she'd stuffed in her luggage, sacrificing space for several skirts in the bargain.

She smiled, already daydreaming about where she would place the treasures she'd brought with her from Kansas—things she hoped would blend her life with David's and make the *utta* a home. *Their* home.

♪

TIMONÉ, COLOMBIA, SOUTH AMERICA

"Is that the last of it?" David surveyed the hut cluttered with boxes and luggage. There was no way this would all fit in here. Not if he was going to have a home office like they'd agreed. He swallowed back an unkind comment.

"You got that red duffel bag from the boat, right?" Natalie was already unpacking a soggy cardboard box, casing the room for where she could put the trinkets she'd brought back with her. Just more things to dust and to worry about whether they might be stolen every time they left the hut.

There was a thief in Timoné, and though David had his suspicions, he couldn't prove who had pilfered the seemingly random items that had gone missing from his and Natalie's huts and from one of their neighbors' last fall before he'd left for the States. Nothing of great value had been taken, but it was disconcerting to know someone had come into their homes and taken things without asking. Worse, precious pencils and pens had disappeared from the *oficina misión,* his former *utta,* now serving as the new mission office. He'd brought new office supplies back with him. This time he would keep them locked in the rickety file cabinet or in the safe in the *utta* he and Natalie now shared.

Before traveling back to Kansas, they'd locked everything of value in the new mission office, and he'd asked a couple of the Timoné men he trusted to keep an eye on things. Tados had met them at the dock this morning and proudly reported that everything was safe.

Before David and Natalie had left Timoné for their wedding in the States, they'd had a room built on to Nate's hut for their master bedroom, one that would accommodate David's height better than the seven-foot ceilings of the rest of the *utta*.

They'd also moved most of Nate's office furnishings out to David's old hut. The plan was that his former hut would be an off-site mission office with a bedroom where Natalie's parents, Hank and Meghan, or other visitors could stay short-term. The former office in Nate's quarters had become the kitchen and living area, and Nate's old bedroom would serve as David's office.

That was the plan. But at the rate Natalie was cluttering up the space with her knickknacks, he'd be surprised if there was an inch left for that home office.

"Do you want this in your office?" Natalie held up an ornate clock.

"What's wrong with the one that's in there? Don't *you* want this one?"

She looked sheepish. "I'd love to have it here in the living room, but I don't want to hog all the pretty stuff."

"Oh?" He gave a short laugh. "I was under the impression that I would have use of the living room too—at least occasionally."

She laughed and set the clock on the bench that served as a coffee table. She crossed the room to where he was standing and tiptoed to plant a kiss on his mouth. "Of course you will! That's not what I meant."

"I know it's not, love." He kissed her again. "Now if it's the kitchen we're talking about, that one is all yours."

"You do remember it's an eat-in kitchen?"

"Oh. Ouch. I take that back. I'll definitely eat in. But the *cooking* area, that's all yours."

"Fine. Until it's time to do dishes, then I'll happily share."

He gave a playful groan. "This conversation is going south fast. And why are we speaking English?"

She glared at him. "Because that is our native language, Mr. Chambers. Please don't tell me you're going to make me speak Timoné when it's just the two of us."

"How else will we learn?" He arched an eyebrow at her. "Never mind. We'll talk about that later. I don't want to fight. Not on our first day in our new home."

"English could be like our secret, intimate language we speak, just the two of us, when we're alone togeth—"

He put a gentle finger over her lips. "Shh... I said I don't want to fight." He removed his finger and kissed those lips.

"What? That wasn't fighting."

"Oh? What would *you* call it?"

"Persuasion?"

Her coy grin won him over and he took her in his arms, desire and elation filling him at the realization that this woman would share his bed tonight and for a lifetime of tonights. That the delights they'd discovered together those evenings—and mornings and afternoons—in the Airbnb where they'd honeymooned were theirs till death did them part.

Natalie could be difficult, but she was a gift from God, plain and simple. And she was worth every hiccup she'd brought to his formerly uncomplicated life.

What he wouldn't tell her was that after a month in the States, a month speaking English exclusively, he was almost afraid he'd lost half of what *he'd* learned. Nate Camfield, his mentor, had always said he'd never seen anyone learn a language so quickly or use it so instinctively as David. Languages and everything about linguistics did seem to come naturally to him. It was one reason he'd chosen to do this work of translating after he'd been ousted from his teaching job at the college. After Lily.

But he didn't think Nate had known how hard he'd worked at learning, not just the Castilian Spanish spoken in most of Colombia, but the peculiar Timoné dialect which was a unique blend of Portuguese and Spanish with a smidgen of Swahili thrown in the mix. He'd been relieved when the words came rushing back to him this morning as he spoke with Tados while they carried things over from his *utta*. No, from the *oficina misión*. The mission office. He would have to get used to calling places by the names of their new function.

He and Natalie gravitated to different rooms, finding a rhythm, and before they went to bed that night, most everything had a place, and the empty boxes—the ones that survived the trip on the river anyway—had been stored away in the clinic. Nathan Camfield's clinic.

It was hard for David to even walk into the clinic now that Nate was gone. Just opening the door brought the memories tumbling back. Nate's crumpled body on the floor, dead of an apparent heart attack. No warning, no time to prepare for the loss of his friend and mentor.

The mission still used the clinic, though more for storage now and sometimes as a first aid station, a place for kids to come and get scraped knees bandaged or have a sprained ankle wrapped.

He'd made his desire to have a new doctor in Timoné known to Nate's sending organization and to his own, Gospel Linguists, since they often coordinated with other mission agencies. And of course, he'd made his desire known to God. But so far there was no word of such an assignment in the making. Of course, Nate hadn't been gone even a year yet, and things happened excruciatingly slowly in the world of missions.

He missed his mentor and friend as if he'd lost a limb. He was acutely aware that shared grief over Nate had been one of the things that had cinched Natalie's love for him. And if *he* felt the loss of Nate so heavily, how much more must Nate's daughter?

He closed his eyes and visualized words, in the Timoné dialect, writing themselves onto his heart in a flowing script font—a practice that helped him turn away dark thoughts. *Whatsoever things are true, whatsoever things are honest...whatsoever things are lovely—*

Well, that was easy. *She* was lovely. Natalie Camfield. No. Natalie Camfield *Chambers*. The reminder lifted his heart and made him smile. This was his first day in the home he shared with his wife. The first day of their real life together. He wasn't going to ruin it with melancholy musings.

❧ 2 ☙

"**A**re you planning to sleep your life away, love?"

David's voice interrupted Natalie's dream, one she couldn't remember but could guess at from the heavy cloak it had cast over her. She rolled onto her back and stretched, relishing the cool breeze that blew through the open windows and the deep timbre of her husband's voice. They'd been in Timoné for over a week now, but she still thrilled at the realization of his presence with each new morning. "What time is it?"

The sun painted saffron patches across the floor of the hut, filtering through the gauze of mosquito netting that swayed above her. She eased her feet over the side of the bed and swatted away the netting.

David winked. "It's only ten after eight, but that's late for you."

"Oh, goodness, it is!" She unfastened her hair tie, tucked in some wayward strands and redid her ponytail. "I blame you."

"Me?" He placed a steaming mug of coffee in her hands, looking genuinely puzzled.

She took a sip of the aromatic brew and fluttered her lashes at him. "Somebody kept me up way past my bedtime."

He leaned to kiss her. "I take full credit. That's why I let you sleep in."

"And that's why I love you."

"You're too easy, woman."

"I'll remind you of that next time you're complaining about how complicated I am." She took another sip of coffee and moaned her pleasure at its herbal, almost fruity notes so unique to this part of the country. Coffee—*cazho*—was her favorite Colombian thing. She'd only tolerated coffee before coming to Colombia, but armed with a college roommate's lessons in coffee grinding and brewing, and a constant supply of fresh, true Colombian beans roasted to perfection by the villagers, she'd become a fan.

David retreated to the office, and she retrieved the steaming kettle and padded to the tiny bathroom with its makeshift "plumbing." Thanks to David, they did have cold running water in the kitchen, and he'd rigged up a hose to fill a porcelain basin in the bathroom.

The "bathroom" was little more than a small table with a pitcher and basin to wash up in, a mirror, shelves that held their toiletries, and in the corner, a large lidded basket that concealed a plastic bucket, with a lidded toilet seat, which served the purpose in the middle of the night.

They did have a *poucochet*—an outhouse—a few yards from the house, but she refused to use it when it was dark outside. She'd grown accustomed to the spiders and lizards and other creepy crawlers of this dense jungle, but not enough that she was willing to risk meeting up with them in the dark of night.

She filled the basin and heated the water with the kettle. After washing up, she dumped the wash water into the corner bucket, then quickly dressed and went to find her husband.

He was poring over a thick book, his laptop open beside it with a document full of notes that looked like a word list and definitions.

"Have you had breakfast?"

"I had some fruit. I left you half a mango if you want it." He pushed the book away and turned to regard her. "Will you be talking to your students' parents today?"

She stopped short, recognizing a not-so-subtle hint and the tension in his jaw. "Today? We *just* got back, David. I was hoping to get the house back in order and get the rest of the supplies put away. Maybe make some bread."

They'd brought groceries and other supplies back from San José on their return from the States, but the house was dusty and cobwebbed, and though the cupboards were full, there was nothing substantial ready to eat.

He managed an anemic smile. "I suppose it wouldn't hurt to wait until Monday, but we don't want to let it go for too long. You know the kids will have already forgotten their good habits. And these mamas need plenty of warning. Remember what we learned in our training."

"I know, David. This isn't my first rodeo."

He gave a humorless laugh. "I didn't say it was. I just don't want to let the school slide for too long. We're already behind."

"You mean *I'm* already behind."

He scooted his chair closer to the desk and turned back to his book. "Do whatever you think is best."

Her ire rose at his condescension, and she shot up a prayer that she would hold her temper. Being selfless in their marriage —putting his needs before hers—was turning out to be more difficult than she'd expected.

She worked to keep any hint of anger from her voice. "I thought I would take some bread to Meena and see how she's doing. I could bake today and make the rounds first thing on Monday. Or maybe I could take bread to church and talk with anyone who's there."

David slowly pivoted his chair toward her. She thought she detected apology in his eyes. "Monday would be fine, Nat. It's a good idea, in fact. The bread. But maybe we shouldn't take it to church since there might not be enough for all."

He was being optimistic thinking there'd be more than a handful at the little church tomorrow. There rarely was since her father's death and she knew that fact rankled David. But maybe she should be more optimistic herself. "Okay. I'll take it around to the students' families on Monday."

A soft answer turns away anger... She smiled to herself, grateful that Mom and Daddy had instilled that truth into their daughters. It would come in handy with this too-serious husband of hers.

❧

NATALIE SANG QUIETLY IN THE KITCHEN AS THE HEAVENLY smell of yeast bread wafted through the *utta*. The happy tune his wife sang—the same chorus over and over—filled David with a sense of peace and gratitude he'd never dared hope for. After everything that had happened with Lily, he'd never expected to have a life with one special woman, never expected to be a husband.

David had enlisted some of the men of the village to help him move Nate's *fogoriomo* onto the enclosed alcove that served as a kitchen. Natalie was giddy at the thought of having a stove in the house. And though Nate would not have approved, believing they would gain more credibility with the Timoné people if the missionaries lived as they did—cooking in the open air, sleeping on mats on the floor—David hadn't been thinking of Nate when he'd helped move the heavy stove. He'd done it for Natalie. His wife.

It was simply a matter of practicality. The issue of whether to adapt fully to the native ways had been possibly the only thing he and Nate had ever strongly disagreed on. And while he'd never voiced it to Natalie, he'd reveled—a little too smugly perhaps—in being able to reason out the decision about the stove without Nate's interference.

He lost himself in the translation of a difficult passage and startled when Natalie set a small plate beside him, the scent of warm bread drizzled with olive oil wafting to his nose. "Mmm, that looks amazing. Thanks, love."

"You'd better enjoy it. The rest is going to Meena and the other school families."

"Uh-huh," he said over a bite of the melt-in-your-mouth delicacy.

"Hola!" a little voice called from below the window.

Smiling, Natalie went to peek over the windowsill. "*Hollio*, Lele!" She waved and looked past the girl. "Where is your abuela?" she called in Timoné.

Lele's giggles faded down the trail in the direction of the *utta* where she lived with her mother and her grandparents.

Natalie came back to David's desk, looking perplexed. "Lele was all by herself! Do you think I should make sure she gets home safely?"

"You can't keep tabs on every kid in the village, Nat. She's not your responsibility. She'll be fine."

"You don't know Lele's story, do you? Why isn't Gabrielle raising her?"

He knew Natalie tried not to play favorites, but she couldn't deny the fact that little Lele had taken a special place in her heart. Though the girl was only three or four years old, her grandparents, Jamos and Meena, had brought her to Natalie's school almost since she could walk. The Timoné couple's daughter and her child lived with them, but they seemed to be the ones raising Lele.

David struggled to look away from his notebooks and concentrate on Natalie's question. "Her story?"

"What happened to Gabrielle's husband? Don't you think Lele looks...Caucasian? With those hazel eyes and the lighter streaks in her hair? I asked Dad once and he said he'd tell me someday, but then of course, he never got the chance." Her voice broke and she swallowed hard.

David never knew how to respond when she teared up over

her father. She was still grieving, of course. He wouldn't expect any less. He still grieved Nate himself. But he couldn't bring him back and he wasn't sure how to comfort her.

He gave her a look meant to sympathize and took the cowardly option of ignoring her emotions, and instead, answering her question with one of his own. "So, what did your dad tell you about the situation?"

"Just that Lele's father wasn't in the picture. Did you know him?"

"I...met him. Well, at least I met who I *think* is Lele's father. Gabrielle was never married to him." He hesitated, not wanting to withhold what he felt sure to be the truth, yet if he was wrong... "Let's just say I have my suspicions."

"Really? Who is it?"

"No one you know. Someone who was only here for a short time."

"Here in Timoné?" Natalie pulled a low stool over and sat beside him at his desk, keen interest in her expression. "Where is this guy now? And why do you suspect it was him?"

"Mostly because Lele was born about nine months after this guy went back to the States."

She gave a wry smile. "Good guess. So, her father *is* American? I thought so. What's the story? Were they in love? Him and Gabrielle?"

"She may have thought so. Personally, I think he took advantage of her. And sadly, I speak from experience."

Natalie closed her eyes.

"I'm sorry." He took her hand and squeezed it briefly. "I know you don't like to think of that part of my life."

She shook her head.

He'd hidden nothing from her about his shameful past. How he'd had an ongoing affair with one of the students at the college where he taught. Lily was only three years his junior, but he'd violated a position of authority by assenting to her advances. And although she'd been the initiator and had consented in every regard, he never should have allowed it to happen. His actions had been immoral and unethical.

But that wasn't the worst of his sins. When Lily became pregnant, her father threatened to withdraw his sizable support of the college where David taught and to ruin his reputation if he refused to pay for Lily's abortion. He did so, willingly, and not only did that end his and Lily's relationship and his employment, but it left him with a load of condemnation and shame too heavy to carry. He thought he *had* loved Lily—as much as his immature, degenerate self knew how to love back then.

It had been a long road to finding forgiveness, but if there was one redeeming grace about all that had happened with Lily, it was that his experience and his journey to faith in Christ had enabled him, years later, to help Natalie finally forgive herself for a sin that was far less premeditated, but with equally grave consequences.

After the horrible accident with Natalie behind the wheel, she'd spent forty-eight hours in jail and several weeks of community service for driving under the influence, a badge of shame that still burdened her.

Sara's family had readily forgiven her, an amazing gift. But like David, Natalie had struggled mightily to forgive herself. He'd merely showed her the lesson he'd learned himself: If we truly believe God has forgiven our sins and made us new creations, then we throw that gift back in his face when we refuse to forgive ourselves.

"It's okay, David," Natalie whispered now, reaching across the desk to take his hand again. "What were you saying? You knew Lele's father? You would have been here in Timoné four years ago, right?"

"I was here. A father and son team—an American pastor and his college-age son—came to help us with building the school during the pastor's sabbatical. Your dad always suspected the sabbatical had more to do with getting a rebellious son away from bad influences than with the man's own need for a respite.

But anyway, they came. Pastor Hilton was a hard worker and I could tell your dad was really blessed by their conversations. But the kid, Lee, was as lazy as they come. Nate and I didn't know what to do. It was hard to say anything when his dad was here with him. We both felt any discipline should come from his father. The kid worked as little as possible and then if we pushed at all, he suddenly came down with some mysterious symptom and took to his bed."

"So, you think he fathered Lele?"

"We have no proof, of course, but Jamos and Meena had become believers shortly before this happened. In their Bible study classes, Nate had been teaching about the gift of hospitality. It apparently took root because when he told Jamos about the team coming to help build the school, they insisted on taking the two into their home, offering their own bedroom. Unfortunately, half the time they were here, Lee was supposedly sick in bed. But I saw him and Gabrielle coming back from the river one of those days he was supposedly suffering from a headache, and I had my suspicions they were messing around."

"How old was Gabrielle then? She's still just a teenager now, isn't she?"

"I don't really know. She was...old enough. She was flirting, that's for sure. But I suspect he took advantage." He wished they could change the subject. He knew all too well how easy it was to take advantage of a young woman who had her sights set on you. Regretful thoughts of Lily flitted uncomfortably close.

Natalie shook her head. "Gabrielle's a beauty. I can see why he would pursue her. Do you think they had a thing for each other?"

"Maybe. As much as you can have a 'thing' for someone in two weeks' time." He drew air quotes with his fingers. "But whether they did or not, he had no business letting it come to... what it seemingly did."

Natalie shook her head. "Wow. Dad never said any of that. Never even hinted at it."

"He probably didn't want his innocent daughter to have to think about such things."

He expected her to tear up again, but she winced. "I wasn't that innocent. So, what happened with Gabrielle and this guy? Did they send him home? Does he even know he has a child halfway across the world?"

"I'm pretty sure he doesn't. Your dad and I talked about it, but aside from requesting that they send supplies—the only child support that would be worth anything here—what could they do? And to be fair, the pastor was already supporting the mission financially. But there was no way Lee was going to stay here and be a father to that child."

"Lee? You said his name was Lee? Well, that pretty much proves it, doesn't it?"

"Lee Hilton was his name. Why?" David nodded, not sure where she was going with this.

"Lele. Gabrielle named her baby after her father."

His breath caught and he shook his head. "Some linguist I am. That never even crossed my mind. For whatever reason, your dad spelled her name L-E-L-E…maybe an Americanized spelling? Even though her family definitely pronounces it with long E's." He shrugged. "But I'm still not sure that proves anything. Gabrielle could have gotten pregnant by someone else and just named Lele after Lee Hilton. Because he was her first crush. Or whatever you want to call it."

"Maybe. But if I had to guess, I'd say it was him. Her hair has those caramel-colored streaks in it. And didn't you say that Gabrielle gave birth to Lele almost exactly nine months after the Hiltons left Timoné?"

"I don't remember the exact math, but I remember your dad saying it added up. So, am I detecting that you think we should have told Pastor Hilton? Or maybe told Lee privately? He was in college after all. An adult."

She hesitated. "Maybe. I mean, how would *you* feel if you had a child you didn't even know about?"

He hung his head briefly. "Think about it, Natalie. I could have had a child. If Lily hadn't gotten rid of it...the baby," he corrected quickly, recognizing his almost unconscious distancing from his role. It was a shifting of blame, and he didn't like what it said about him. "Lily could have left school and never told me she was pregnant."

"And you'd be okay with that?"

"I can't answer that, Natalie. I don't think a person can really say what they'd do until they're in that position."

The look she threw him held challenge. "You're the one who's always telling me to put myself in someone else's shoes. So, what if that *had* happened. Lily had your baby and didn't tell you. And say you found out years later that you'd missed out on your child's life. Would you be okay with that?"

"No." He thought for a minute. "I wouldn't be. But what I would do from there would depend on the circumstances. If she'd married someone else and the baby had a good dad, maybe it would be a better thing if I *wasn't* in his life. For him."

"Him?" She looked stricken. "Do you know that your baby was a boy?"

"No. Of course not. She was only a few weeks along. I didn't go into the...room with her. We weren't together by then. But I'm sure she didn't know. They wouldn't have told her at the clinic whether it was a boy or girl. I was just—"

"Imagining having a son? A little David Junior?" Her soft smile didn't fit the conversation. And what it *did* fit was not a conversation he was eager to have.

"No, I was just using the generic 'he,' that's all. Anyway, it—"

"Don't you ever wonder what *our* children will look like? Will they have your gorgeous dark curls?" She ran a hand through his hair, then cradled his neck. "Or my blue eyes? They'll be tall for sure, between my five-nine and your six-five." Her eyes swam with that dreamy look he'd sometimes seen in his students' eyes. *Lily's eyes.* How had their conversation taken this turn?

"That's pure speculation," he hedged. "We couldn't know. Even if we were ever to have children."

"What do you mean *if?*" She looked startled.

He hesitated. "What else would I mean?"

"Da-vid." She dragged out the syllables. "You make it sound like you think we couldn't have children or something."

"Not couldn't. Just...shouldn't. Well, at least not if God continues to call us to serve here. And I can't imagine why he wouldn't."

"Me neither. But what does that have to do with whether we have kids or not?"

"Think about it, Nat. Where would they go to school? Or to the doctor or dentist? Who would they marry?"

"They'd go to school right here." She swept her arms to encompass the office. "I've always thought I'd homeschool. Whether I was in the States or here. I mean, Nikki homeschools, and that little Emily is smart as a whip."

"You're a great teacher. And...you'll get your chance to use those skills right here."

She took a step backward and studied him. "David? You're serious, aren't you? You don't think we should have kids."

"It's not that I don't think *we* should, love. It's the circumstances we're in. I know I've said this to you before."

"Said what? That you don't want kids? Believe me, I would have remembered that."

"Natalie. It's not that I don't want kids. I love kids. And that's exactly why it wouldn't be the loving thing to do to have them here, under these circumstances."

"What circumstances? A beautiful home in this lovely corner of God's creation? These wonderful children for playmates? Two parents who love each other deeply and only want the best. Parents who would raise them for Jesus? Those circumstances?"

He'd never missed Nate so much. And he realized for the first time what a buffer Nate had been between him and Natalie.

And they desperately needed a buffer. "Can we not have this conversation right now?"

"I don't understand why we haven't had this conversation *until* now!"

"Natalie, we *have* had this conversation. More than once. We talked about it during our missions training. And whenever the subject of Lily has come up. I've *told* you how I feel about having kids."

"But...that was because of Lily. That you didn't think you deserved to have kids. This feels like you're punishing *me* for your sin."

He flinched as if she'd struck him. Indeed, it felt as if she had.

Tears welled in her eyes. "I'm sorry. I shouldn't have said it like that, David."

"How *should* you have said it?" Anger boiled up inside him. "Natalie, we've discussed this. And I don't think—"

"No, we have not discussed this. Not like you're implying. Believe me, I would have remembered," she repeated, her voice quavering. "Because it would have made a difference in my decisions." She burst into tears and fled the room.

＊   3   ＊

"**Y**ou look pretty."

Natalie hadn't heard David come into the room, but when he brushed a hand down her bare arm she bristled despite his attempt at smoothing things over.

She mumbled a thank you and turned away, the shock of last night still stinging. Surely today—before he preached a sermon—he would apologize, tell her he hadn't really meant what he'd said about how they shouldn't have children. That wasn't even biblical. The Bible said to be fruitful and multiply, for heaven's sake! Maybe he'd had trouble translating that verse. If so, she'd be happy to straighten him out.

"Do you want me to wait and walk over with you?"

"I know where the church is." She attempted a smile to cover her barbed comment.

But he wasn't having it. "Natalie. Stop it. Sarcasm doesn't become you."

And idiocy doesn't become you. She bit back the words before they could actually form. She hated this gulf between them, but she was determined to be mature about this.

She took a deep breath and steeled herself. She would reason with him. Her husband was a reasonable man.

"I'm sorry." She offered a genuine smile. "I shouldn't have spoken that way." *Or thought that way.*

"Forgiven." He kissed her temple. "I'd really like to get there a little earlier than usual. I have some visual aids I need to set up before anyone arrives."

She was tempted to tell him *he* was forgiven too. But that would have been a lie. "I'm almost ready. I just need to get my highlighters and find the bug spray."

"It was in the bathroom last I saw it."

"Be right back." She hurried to the bathroom and quickly spritzed the precious bug spray on her neck and on her ankles beneath her skirt, then hurried to the screened porch where she kept the highlighter pens she used in her Bible. The pens were an expensive brand that had been a Christmas gift from her sisters, and she'd carried them, wrapped and taped, in her bag from the moment they boarded the plane in Wichita. The markers weren't in the drawer of the little desk where she did her devotions each morning. Sometimes she took one or two to her nightstand, but she wouldn't have taken the whole set. She should have put them in the safe.

With a little growl, she searched her backpack. The pens weren't there either, but she reluctantly gave up the search and returned to the living room, lest David think she was making him wait out of spite. "Okay, I'm ready. Can I carry anything?"

"I've got it." He patted the worn briefcase he used for his translation notebooks and papers.

"You haven't seen my highlighters, have you?"

"They're not in your desk?"

"No. I can't think where I put them."

"Do you want to go search? I can wait." But his demeanor said he was getting antsy.

"No, it's okay." She waved him off. "I'll look later."

His sigh gave away his impatience. He arranged the length of red ribbon they'd taken to putting on top of the doorframe in a way that would disclose if someone tried to open the door while they were gone. He started down the steps. "Any guesses on how many will be in services?"

She laughed. "Probably the whole village will be there just to see the newlyweds."

"I hope you're right."

"Is that why the visual aids?" She looked pointedly at his briefcase.

"It is. Is that terribly opportunistic of me?"

"I think it's terribly smart of you."

They walked in silence along Timoné's streets that were actually nothing more than footpaths worn smooth by the villagers who traversed them daily. The birds sang in a high-pitched cacophony Natalie had always found rather pleasant. The breakfast fires were dying out by now, but the savory scents of sausages, onions, and roasted corn made her stomach rumble, despite the bowl of fruit she'd eaten for breakfast.

Yesterday's puddles had mostly dried, leaving the streets spongy but passable. In the inlet where villagers fished, water lilies were in bloom, their pale pink buds and white flowers putting on a spectacular show. With each breath Natalie caught the faintest whiff of their citrusy scent. Growing up in Kansas, she'd never dreamed she would someday live where flowers bloomed in January.

Fifteen minutes later, the little open-air pavilion came into sight. The commons area served as a church on Sundays and a classroom during the week—at least when it wasn't raining. The shelter's thatched roof had been crafted for shade, not rain, and worked about as well as a sieve in the infamous Colombian torrents.

As long as she'd been in Timoné, they'd rarely had more than thirty or so in church, and after Dad's death, attendance had dropped to twenty or fewer. On more than one occasion, it had been just her and David, little Lele and her grandparents, and

Tados, the Timoné man who helped David with the translation work.

Zari and her mamá would be here if Zari's papá allowed. Sometimes he did, but if his mood turned foul, he forbade it. Dr. Nate had saved Zari from an allergic reaction to a bat bite when she was four years old, and Natalie suspected the girl's mamá came to church out of gratitude to Nate more than a genuine belief in God. But as David said, at least they were there. Believing came by hearing.

Tados was waiting in the pavilion, and David left her side and went to shake the young man's hand. Apparently, David had enlisted his unofficial assistant to help with the visual aids he'd planned for the morning. David opened his laptop and gestured at the keyboard.

Natalie noticed a mass of spiderwebs and the attendant spider under the thatched canopy in the corner where two grass mats joined to form walls. She went to find a palm branch to brush the webs away but before she could do so, she spotted Jamos and Meena coming up the path with Lele.

To her surprise, Gabrielle was with them too, lagging a few feet behind.

When the little girl saw her, she broke into a run. "Miss Natalie!"

Natalie laughed and went to receive Lele's hug. The ache she felt at the child's touch took her unawares. Would she ever feel the embrace of a child who called her *Mommy*?

Lele looked over at David, then up at Natalie. "You get married now?" Between the dialect and Lele's slight lisp Natalie usually had to strain to understand her, but even if she didn't interpret exactly, she couldn't miss the girl's radiant smile.

"Yes! I *am* married. *We* are."

Lele's face fell. "But you can't be! We didn't come to your *casoriel.*"

Gabrielle approached, a sour expression marring her pretty face.

"Good morning, Gabrielle. So nice to see you!"

Lele's mother gave a perfunctory nod, tossed her hair over one shoulder, and grabbed Lele by the hand. "Quit bothering Miss Natalie, you silly girl."

"Oh, no... It's okay. I'm so happy to see you both." Natalie offered the young woman her best smile before kneeling in front of Lele. "I'm sorry you couldn't come to our wedding, sweetie..." She pointed in the general direction of the United States and struggled to put the Timoné words together. "But it happened far, far away. Where I grew up. Mr. David too."

"'Merica?"

Yes, America." An idea came and she smiled. "But we can still celebrate together. When school starts. Soon!"

"Mr. David will come to school?"

"Just for a little while. He has to work."

The small, brown face fell again.

"But we will have sweets! To celebrate."

"Promise?"

"I promise. You'll be there, for sure?"

She nodded vigorously. "I like school."

"I do too." Natalie rose, sensing Gabrielle's impatience and seeing Meena and Jamos waiting. "You'd better go with your mamá and your abuelos."

The girl reluctantly followed her mother and went to sit with her grandparents. Natalie was tempted to "tattle" to them that she'd spotted Lele wandering alone in the village, but seeing David head to the front with his Bible in hand, she found a seat on one of the long benches that served as pews and settled in for the sermon.

David cleared his throat loudly, signaling that he was ready to begin. The villagers began to take their seats and by the time David opened the service in prayer, Natalie counted twenty-seven people gathered, all people who'd attended services before. But a few, she was fairly certain, hadn't been here since their beloved Dr. Nate passed away. David would feel the pressure to say something that would convince them to return next Sunday morning.

But when he began speaking, she remembered why she'd fallen in love with this man. He read from the chapters of the book of John that he'd completed translating into the Timoné dialect. She loved the cadence of his words when he spoke the dialect, and she hoped these people could hear the compassion in his voice the way she did. David loved the Timoné people like family and felt a responsibility to them that sometimes over-whelmed and burdened him.

As Natalie had heard her father do on more than one occa-sion, she often had to remind David that God had called him only to love the Timoné and to share the Scriptures with them. He could not force them into faith. That part was in God's hands.

When David finished speaking, he asked the people to share their burdens. "So we can pray for you," he said, his smile warming Natalie.

But the people's silence went on long enough to make even patient David squirm. He looked pointedly at her, urging her, without words, to set an example and share her own prayer request. The only burden weighing heavily on her was her disagreement with David, and she didn't think he'd appreciate her bringing that up. She scoured her brain to think of some-thing appropriate to share, but finally just gave a tiny shake of her head and looked away.

Her silence would do nothing to mend the rift between them.

❧

DESPITE NATALIE'S ATTEMPTS TO DRAW HIM OUT, DAVID WAS silent on the walk home. The sun was warm on her shoulders, and while she'd looked forward to a quiet afternoon of reading and napping, now she felt like they needed to hash things out after last night's disagreement. She suspected David would rather pretend it never happened, but they'd agreed before their marriage that they would try not to let the sun go down on their anger. Never mind they'd done just that last night.

"Lele sure seemed happy to see me...*us*," she tried again, sneaking a look at him beside her.

"Uh-huh."

"And it was great that Gabrielle came, though I suspect she just wanted to find out if we really did get married."

"Uh-huh." He quickened his steps.

She lengthened her stride to keep up with him. "I thought Monni seemed really happy this morning. I can't believe how tall Miguel is getting."

No response.

Their *utta* came into view, and David turned to her. "So, was it that bad?"

She tilted her head. "Was *what* that bad?"

"The sermon. You've gone out of your way to avoid talking about it."

"What are you talking about? The sermon was good. Great, in fact."

"Then why didn't you say that?"

"What do you mean?"

"You've yakked about the weather, about Lele, what we're having for lunch, what you plan to read...but silence about the elephant in the room."

"David—"

"And it would have been really helpful if you could have set an example by mentioning a prayer request."

Help me hold my tongue, Lord. She took a deep breath. "I really did try to think of something, but you didn't say prayer requests, you said *burdens*. I didn't think you'd appreciate the only thing I could come up with, and it seemed even worse to offend God with a fabricated burden. Besides, David, your sermon is not the elephant in the room."

"What do you mean?"

"The elephant is our argument last night."

"What? I told you all was forgiven. I meant that."

"Yes, but *I* didn't say all was forgiven."

"Well, it is. You apologized and I forgave."

She was halfway up the steps to the *utta*, but she stopped and turned to glare at him. "You seem to think I'm the only one who owes an apology."

He cocked his head and looked at her as if still processing her words. Finally he bent his head briefly before looking back at her. "No, that's not true. An argument is never just one person's fault. I'm sorry, too. And I'm sorry if I didn't say it earlier. I guess...I thought I had."

"No, you didn't. And...what exactly is it that you're sorry for?"

"For...arguing with you. For raising my voice. For not speaking to you with the respect you deserve. Please forgive me."

She shook her head, her heart sinking. "You don't even know what I'm upset about, do you?"

He opened his mouth to speak, sputtered something unintelligible, then started again. "Please *tell* me. So we can put this behind us."

"You really *don't* know?" He couldn't possibly be as obtuse as he was pretending to be right now.

"I'm...not sure. I had a lot on my mind last night. Trying to get the sermon ready. I'm sorry. I wasn't as attentive as I should have been." He reached for her, then seemed to think better of it. "I really am sorry, Nat. Could we have some lunch first, and then I promise I'll give you my undivided attention and we'll hash it out."

It wasn't a dismissal. They'd talked before about how it wasn't good to have a difficult discussion when one of them was hungry or over-tired. She knew that was his intent, but it still rankled her that he was skirting the issue.

"I'll have lunch ready in twenty minutes."

"I can help."

"No, it's okay. You go change. It won't take me long." She turned and climbed the rest of the stairs.

He didn't try to stop her.

Home from church, David changed quickly into his usual jungle "uniform" of blue jeans and long-sleeved T-shirt. Even if at times it was too warm, the clothing had saved him more than once from being bitten by insects—or reptiles—or being burned to a char by the afternoon sun.

Back in the kitchen, Natalie was crisping two round fried flatbreads on the skillet. A bowl of leftover rice and a hunk of the summer sausage they'd brought back from Natalie's family sat ready on the small countertop.

"Want me to slice some veggies to go with this?"

"If you want to."

She didn't meet his gaze, but started slicing the sausage into circles, arranging everything on a wooden board.

"Making a charcuterie board, are you?"

Natalie's sister Nikki had served sausage and diced vegetables and crackers on a board one night while they were in the States. She told them it was the latest craze in the culinary world, and he and Natalie had cracked up, since a wooden disk with meat, cheese, and veggies was their everyday fare.

But the joke fell flat now, and Natalie's chuckle was more like a sneer.

He sighed. This wasn't going away without a fight, so he steeled himself for it. And he wasn't blameless here. It wasn't fair for him to pretend he didn't know why she was upset. He knew all right. He just didn't know what to say. How to appease her.

They finished preparing the food in silence, and David carried their wooden platter to the covered porch. He sat at the table and waited while Natalie brought in their water glasses. He blessed the food and let her eat a few bites before he ripped off the Band-Aid, so to speak.

"Okay, let's talk. What are you stewing about?"

She cocked her head and eyed him. "Do you really not know?"

He curbed a grin. "I think I do, but I don't want to give you any ideas in case I'm wrong."

"I doubt you're wrong, David."

"Fine. I'm guessing it's what I said about children. Not thinking we should have any?"

"Then you'd be right." She said it with a smile, but her countenance quickly changed to one of distress. "I think what bothers me the most, David... I was trying to remember our conversations about this in the past. We talked about it. I know we did! I distinctly remember asking you, not long after Dad's funeral, if you liked the name Nathan David. I said if we had a boy someday, I would like to name him after Dad and you. Do you remember that?"

"I do." He did recall the conversation, but mostly because of how it had brought all the trauma of what had happened with Lily crashing back. But it didn't seem fair to drag Natalie through that again now—even though the remorse still overwhelmed him whenever this topic came up. He stared at the uneaten food on his plate. "And do you remember what I told you?"

"You said it had a very nice ring to it."

"Yes, but I said something else."

She thought for a moment. "About Daddy, you mean?"

He nodded. When Natalie had first come to Colombia, it had taken David a while to figure out that "Dad" and "Daddy"—Natalie's birthfather and the man who'd raised her—were two different people.

"You worried that it might hurt Daddy's feelings if I didn't use his name. I loved that you thought of him. And I said we could call our son Nathan *Cole* David. And you said that was too many names and offered to 'give up' yours tacked on the end and —" She stopped and stared at him. "Was that because...you didn't *want* a son named after you?"

"No. I just hadn't...thought it all through yet."

"You weren't just playing along with something you had no intention of ever actually being part of...were you? And if that's the case, David, how am I supposed to know which things you've told me are actually true?"

His jaw tensed. "Natalie, I am a lot of things, but I am not a liar."

"I know. I'm sorry. I didn't mean that."

Genuine regret softened her tone and he held back a harsh reply. "I meant what I said. To be fair, maybe I was just humoring you, but I was still getting used to the idea that I was getting married! I truly hadn't thought about us having children. And now that I have... Well, can't you understand why I feel the way I do, love?" His gaze swept the village. "Timoné isn't any place to raise children."

She gave a little huff. "Tell that to Lele and Zari and Miguel and—"

"That's different, Natalie. This is all they know. And they have each other. They were born into this."

She wiped a bit of cheese from the corner of her mouth and licked her fingers. "But don't you see? It would be exactly the same for *our* children. This is all *they* would know. They, too, would be 'born into this' as you say."

"Maybe born into it, but they wouldn't fit in. They would be different. Suspect, the same way we are."

"Is it so terrible for us? We've made friends here. Made a life here. Yes, we might be seen as outsiders, and some still look at us with suspicion, but the longer we're here, the more we've won people over."

She was right about that. He only wished they'd won as many to Christ as they'd won to a tentative friendship. But he dared not say that now or she'd accuse him of changing the subject. He tried a different tack. "Let me ask you something. If we were starting our marriage in the States, say we were working with a translator there... Would we still be having this conversation?"

"Well, I assume not, because you wouldn't be worried about our kids fitting in if we were in the States."

"That's not exactly what I was getting at."

She waited expectantly, curiosity etching her fine features.

"What I mean is..." He risked teasing her. "I know it seems much longer, but we've only been married for three weeks, love. No matter where we lived, I'd like to enjoy at least a while of just getting to know my wife. Is that so terrible for me to want some time with you alone? Just the two of us, learning about each other? Doing life together, as your brother-in-law put it."

That made her smile. "No, that's not terrible. But last night you made it sound like you didn't *ever* want children."

He hesitated. In truth, he wasn't sure he did. Wasn't sure children were a part of the calling God had placed on his life. But it would be cruel to tell Natalie that now. Because the truth was, he couldn't know for sure. He hadn't thought a wife was part of God's calling either, and just look at the beauty sitting across from him now. He reached across the little table and took her hand. "We can't know what God has in store for us, love. If it's children, then I will accept that as from His hand. But I'd like a chance to get to know my wife first. Can you accept that?"

The trace of a smile she wore said she was warming. "As long as you don't shut out the idea altogether. And"—she squeezed his hand—"could you sometimes let me dream a little bit?"

"Dream?"

"About the day—some future day—when we will...when we *might* have a family," she amended quickly. "That's important to a woman, David."

"I guess I never thought about it that way."

"Isn't it important to you?"

He scrambled for an answer that wasn't untrue. "I guess there have been *more* important things on my mind—" He saw a protest rise up in her, even before he could change his wording. "I'm not saying children aren't important. Maybe *urgent* would have been a better word. It's just that God hasn't made that a priority in my mind. Because a year ago it had never crossed my mind that God would put *you* in my life."

"So, do you think it could be the same with a baby someday?"

"I think...with God, anything is possible."

She didn't exactly roll her eyes, but he could read her frustration. To her credit, she chuckled softly. "Yes, anything is possible. Some day, I might even begin to fathom the mind of the man God gave me."

"See there?" He leaned across the table for a kiss. "A miracle of hope is already unfolding. You'll have to document it in that prayer journal of yours."

That earned the laughter he'd been hoping for and he dared to change the subject, wishing to put this behind them. "Speaking of which, did you ever find your highlighters?"

She gave a little gasp. "No! But there's one other place I was going to look..." She pushed her chair back and ran into the house, returning a few seconds later, empty-handed. "Where on earth could I have put those?"

"I hope you haven't fallen victim to our thief."

"We would surely know if someone broke in."

He nodded. "They'd have to slice the screens if they didn't come in the front door."

"And why would they leave everything else of value but steal my markers?" Natalie's brow furrowed as she gathered up their lunch things and carried them to the kitchen.

David followed her with his water glass.

"I guess I'm going to have to start locking those pens in the safe. If I ever find them."

"That doesn't sound very convenient."

Very few in Timoné actually locked their doors—at least not with any kind of lock that would thwart a determined thief—but he did latch the door and place the telltale ribbon whenever they left for any length of time. And of course, their generator was secured in the shed with a padlock. And even the solar panels that powered it were chained to the rafters. David had also placed a small safe in the floor of their bedroom under one leg of the bed where they hid their passports, the small amount of cash they kept on hand, and their laptops, on the rare occasions they didn't carry the computers with them. The bed sat on a thick *mittah*, a grass mat like the ones many of the Timoné slept on. The rug hid the little door and made it a bit of an ordeal to access the safe.

"I could have sworn I put them in the desk drawer on the porch after I used them Friday morning. You don't think those stupid monkeys could have gotten them, do you?"

He shook his head and began putting leftovers away. "Not unless you left them outside."

Pygmy marmoset monkeys traversed the trees of the village in the cool of early morning and late afternoon. He'd grown accustomed to the clicks and shrill whistles of these creatures that sailed from tree to tree like flying squirrels. Natalie had fallen in love with the adorable infants—until she learned pygmy marmosets were the source of the stench that permeated the trees. "I'd rather have a skunk," she'd declared to David.

She'd made an uneasy peace with the little monkeys after David and Nate informed her that they ate insects and consumed the fruit and vegetable scraps with the efficiency of an American garbage disposal.

"But their tails aren't prehensile," he told her now with a chuckle. "And even if they did get in, I don't think they're smart enough to open drawers. Or choose highlighters over ballpoint pens."

"Oh. Good point." She made a face. "Well, I don't know where else to look. I'm starting to think we really do have a thief in the village."

"I'm afraid we do, but I hope we're both wrong."

"Me too, but maybe we should buy some decent locks for the doors next time we're in Conzalez."

He shook his head. "I don't want people to think we don't trust them. But maybe I could at least get some latches so we're a little more secure when we're home."

She shivered. "It just gives me the willies that someone might have walked in here and just taken stuff from us."

"Are you missing other things?"

"No. Not since the pencils and pens from last fall. Such a strange thing to take. It's not like whoever took them could use them without everyone knowing where they came from."

"Not to mention, who has paper to write on here?"

The Timoné weren't completely primitive, but neither was writing—or even drawing, for that matter—high on their list of priorities. After all, David had come here because they didn't have a written language.

He hoped the theft had been nothing more than an adolescent dare. But he worried that instead, it had been a dry run. A test to see what it took to breach their security, such as it was. As much as he didn't want to alienate their fellow villagers, he would do whatever it took to make sure Natalie was safe in their home.

He suppressed a smile, feeling guilty that his ploy to change the subject had worked. But this topic was only slightly less disturbing than the one that had started their discussion.

He loved this woman with all his heart. And though he'd considered her challenging when they were merely colleagues in mission work, seeing her now, as his wife, and living under the same roof with her, he realized their former difficulties were nothing compared to what was likely coming.

She came around behind him and wrapped her arms around his waist, burying her head between his shoulders. "Now, what about that Sunday afternoon nap you mentioned?" She cleared her throat suggestively. "You *sleepy* yet?"

He pushed the dishes containing their leftovers aside and turned to take her in his arms, the fresh scent of her shampoo reminding him that there *were* rewards that went along with the enigma that was Natalie Camfield Chambers.

"Ah, I do believe I feel a nap coming on, love. Meet you in the bedroom?"

"Mmm... Sounds heavenly." She kissed him, disentangled herself from his embrace and started back toward their room, but before disappearing around the corner, she turned with a knowing smile. "But don't think for a minute that I've forgotten about our argument."

His shoulders shook with silent laughter. He'd won a brief reprieve, but he wasn't foolish enough to think he was off the hook.

‍❀ 5 ❀

Natalie wrote in large letters on the chalk board in the open air school: *Hollio*.

"Who can tell me what this says?"

Despite her fervent efforts to teach her few students to raise their hands and wait to be called upon, half a dozen shouts went up. *"Hollio! Hollio!"*

They pronounced the word without the *H*, making it sound like *oleo*, what her grandmother used to call margarine.

"And in English?'

"Hello! Hello!"

"Good! And hello to you, too!" Natalie smiled and decided not to fight the battle today. At least they were in school. Fourteen of them today, which might be some kind of record. Of course, she'd have to dismiss them in time for lunch, knowing they were expected at home to help with chores, collect firewood, or babysit infant siblings while their parents tended the gardens or hunted game. Or to fetch water from the stream if they didn't have indoor plumbing—and few did.

She scratched another word on the board and turned with a questioning look.

"¡Egracita!"

"And English?"

"Thank you!" the children shouted.

"Good!" She was thankful they hadn't forgotten over the weeks she and David had been back in the States. But she entertained no delusions that any of these kids would grow up and go off to college. David often reminded her that their purpose in educating the village kids was so that there would be someone to read the Scriptures when the day came that the Timoné had the New Testament in their language. And perhaps someday one of her students would write a history of Timoné that would include the advent of the peoples' faith in Christ.

Tados, who'd become David's right-hand man in the translation work, taught the older children in the mission office—when their parents allowed. The modified alphabet David had worked so hard on the past two years was complete. But he'd learned that Tados had an advantage, since he spoke English passably, and before they'd developed the Timoné alphabet, Dad had taught Tados to read a bit of English. Now the true test had begun as they taught this alphabet to children who'd never read a word of *any* language. To make matters even more challenging, Natalie was learning right along with them.

She called the children to gather around the low table and they played a word game she'd developed. She wasn't sure how educational it actually was, but the kids loved it and if it kept them coming back to the little school, it was worth whatever time it took out of the school day.

Amidst a volley of laughter when little Zari accidentally spelled a word that was "potty language" in Timoné, Natalie looked up to see David striding toward them. She'd promised Lele a party to celebrate their wedding, complete with an appearance by the groom, but she wasn't expecting him for another hour. And it looked like he'd forgotten the cookies she'd baked last night and asked him to bring when he came.

She waved, but her breath caught when he didn't smile or wave back. Something was wrong.

Only when a couple of the children spotted him and called out his name did he finally smile and greet the children, but Natalie recognized his forced cheer and too-stern voice. She clapped her hands to get the children's attention. "Boys and girls, quiet please."

David hurried to her side and whispered low in English. "We need to get the kids to the *oficina misión* right now."

She struggled to keep her voice steady. "What's wrong?"

"We have *visitors* in the village." He held her gaze and practically hissed. "Pray!"

Visitors was code for drug gangs and their allies. Or the guerrilla soldiers that made an appearance in the village just often enough to keep them fearful and on edge. David told her that before he'd left for the States, there'd been rumors of children going missing from some of the larger villages upriver—likely kidnapped because of the price they could bring from human traffickers in Bogotá.

Natalie shuddered, but went into action, praying even as she herded the children into a circle. "Okay, children! Follow the leader." She said it in English.

David quickly translated, telling the children. *"¡Sigue al jefe!"*

The children jumped up, not seeming to notice anything amiss.

"Dosa por dosa, kapaku. Two by two, please!"

Each child found a partner, and seeing how quickly David was walking, Natalie lifted little Lele into her arms and took up the rear.

David broke into a jog, turning to scan the horizon behind them every few seconds. The *oficina misión*—the mission office he'd worked in before having his home office—sat in a small clearing at the top of a rise. From its vantage point one could see the peaked, thatched rooftops of stilted huts jutting through the forest canopy and traces of the narrow unpaved trails that snaked through the village.

The children had no trouble keeping up with them, but

Natalie was winded by the time they'd climbed the hill and entered the office.

"Everyone inside! Quickly!" David said it with a tight smile while his eyes continued to dart in every direction, surveying the trail below. "Miss Natalie will stay with you here."

"Where's Tados?" she whispered.

"He took the older children down the path behind the office."

Natalie knew that meant to act as guards—and soldiers, if need be. She shuddered at the thought. They'd never actually been attacked by the roving gangs or guerrillas. Usually the dissident soldiers were just passing through, making their presence known, sometimes looking for fresh water from the spring. But David and her dad had told her of two occasions when they'd been forced to hand over supplies and food.

When her father was still in Timoné, she'd witnessed first-hand as guerrillas raided the village, herding everyone into the commons pavilion and holding them at gunpoint before finally letting them go. God had taken care of them in a mighty way that day, but that didn't mean it hadn't been terrifying.

"*¡Fuera de aquí!*" Outside, Anazu, one of the village elders, shouted at the guerrillas, insisting they leave.

She thought the elder was speaking the Castilian Spanish the soldiers used. But she didn't understand the unfamiliar dialect of their replies.

"What are they saying?" she asked David. "Is it a gang?"

He held up a hand, listening. "I can't tell for sure, but it sounds like they're asking for drugs. Medications, I mean. But it's guerrillas, not the thugs."

She frowned. There was more to fear from the drug gangs, but saying the guerrillas weren't as dangerous was like saying pit vipers weren't as dangerous as anacondas. There was a fine line between the two and no one was ever sure who either of them worked for.

He backed toward the door, reaching for the knob. "Lock the door behind me."

"David!"

"Stay here with the children, and don't open the door to anyone until I give you the all-clear."

"Okay." She nodded, her hands trembling. She prayed none of the parents came looking for their children. She locked the door behind him and pulled the blinds on the two windows that had them. She'd never been so grateful for real windows with thick glass panes and a door with a sturdy lock.

Turning to the children, who now seemed to understand that something was afoot, she forced cheerfulness into her voice. "Everyone take a seat and get ready for a test."

They groaned in unison and Lele frowned. "But what about the *casoriel* party?"

"We'll talk about that later, Lele. For now you need to take a seat."

For once the little girl didn't argue.

Natalie waited for them to find places on the two long benches in the middle of the room. She scrambled to think of something that would take their minds off of what was happening outside, and fill whatever time they had to wait.

The soldiers voices had grown distant, telling Natalie that David and Anazu had been successful in leading them away from where she and the children were holed up. She prayed under her breath for David's safety and for the first time she understood how terrified her mother must have been when she thought Natalie's dad had been killed. And twenty-plus years ago, communication here had been even more primitive than now. At least she had the sat phone if she needed to get word to her parents or the mission. *Please, God, no.*

She realized the children were waiting for her. She gave two claps of her hands, the signal for quiet. Never mind that they were all sitting in utter silence. "Who would like to go first?"

No surprise, Lele's hand shot up.

"You always go first!" Zari complained.

"Would you like to volunteer, Zari?" Natalie motioned for her to come to the front.

The girl dropped her head, realizing she'd walked into that one. Zari was probably six or seven, but small for her age. But she scooted off the bench and made her way to the front of the small room.

Natalie somehow rustled up a random question from her imagination. "Zari, tell the class about your favorite animal. Describe that animal using many words."

But before the girl could open her mouth to answer, more shouts came from the trails below.

From their seats on the benches, the children craned their necks trying to look out the windows. If the guerrillas came up the trail, they'd be able to see in the windows as soon as they reached the hut. Thinking quickly, Natalie grabbed a stack of newspapers from a box in the corner and a box of thumbtacks from the ledge of a bulletin board. David always brought the daily newspapers from Bogotá whenever they traveled to Conzalez for supplies. He kept abreast of the news that way, but also scoured the papers for words and phrases that might help him with his translation work.

"You three taller ones, come here. Shh. Very quietly." Three older boys—twins Paku and Daric, and a boy called Voric—came forward, eager for a chance to peer out the windows. Natalie was grateful there was nothing for them to see. The trail was empty below, save for a donkey and two goats grazing at the path's edges, but shouting could still be heard in the distance. "Take these newspapers and cover the windows. Like this...you see? Let's keep...the sun out of here."

She unfolded a paper and tacked several layers to the window frame on three sides. The room immediately darkened.

The boys caught on quickly and set to work, holding down the papers while she tacked them up.

When they finished, she beckoned them to the corner farthest from the door. "All of you, come over here and sit."

She debated what to tell them, and finally decided not to tell the whole truth, but not to lie either. When they were all seated on the floor, she lowered her voice. "Let's pray for God to be with us and make us brave. And then, I'm going to tell you a story. But you must be very, very quiet and sit still no matter what happens, okay?"

They nodded solemnly and she bowed her head and whispered a simple prayer of protection, stumbling over the Timoné words and hoping she was making sense. Of course, God knew, but she didn't want to alarm the children any more than they already were.

After the amen, she looked up and waited until she had their full attention.

She didn't have to wait long. They stared at her with round eyes.

"This is a true story," she said, knowing exactly what story to tell and praying God would help her with the language. "It's kind of a scary story, but it's about how God, who created the heavens and the earth, watches over his children. You've heard me say this many times, right? Our God cares for us."

"Your God made me well when a bat bit me!" Zari said in a too-loud voice. "It hurt!"

Smiling, Natalie put a finger to her lips and dropped her own voice to a whisper. "Yes, I remember. But He is your God too, Zari. And your mamá's. You have both given your hearts to him, isn't that right?"

The girl nodded.

"Well, this is another story of our God's care. When Dr. Nate was in the vill—"

"Dr. Nate. He is your father," Lele offered in a stage whisper.

"That's right, he was." Again Natalie shushed them with a finger to her lips, but it touched her that even little Lele remembered Nathan Camfield. And Dr. Nate's connection to her.

"Many months ago, some bad men came to the village wishing to...*hurt* us." She used the same Timoné word Zari had used for how the bat's bite had hurt. She hoped it was the correct one.

"The bad men made us all go to the pavilion. They pointed their guns and shouted, "*¿Dónde están los Americanos?*" They were looking for Dr. Nate and Mr. David and me"—she pointed to herself—"the *Americanos.*"

She looked from face to face. Her story had accomplished its goal. The children were enthralled and completely silent. "I was standing right there in front of them!" She made a silly face. "Do you think they might guess that *I* was the *Americano?*"

That drew laughter. She shushed them and reminded them how important it was to remain quiet.

"You have the yellow hair," Paku snorted, using the English word for *yellow.*

"Not yellow...blond," his twin corrected him.

"But not Timoné, for certain." Paku bobbed his chin.

"And yet, the soldiers looked at me...looked straight into my eyes"—she paused for effect—"and then they walked away, taking their guns with them!"

The older boys shook their heads in disbelief.

"They must have been blind," Voric scoffed.

"Shhh." She waited again for them to still. "I think God hid us from their sight because we prayed for his protection. Whenever we ask—"

Heavy footfalls sounded outside and the scuff of boots on the stoop made them all jump. Someone pounded on the door. Natalie's heart pushed at her throat, but she forced a smile and willed her voice to remain steady. "Shhh! Not a sound."

The knocking came again, louder, and the door latch rattled.

A scuffling sound and something slammed against the door. Her heart raced as the thin wood quivered and the latch creaked.

$\mathcal{H}$ 6 $\mathcal{H}$

Trembling, Natalie shook her head at the children, who sat as still as a family of opossums caught in the headlights of her dad's pickup truck on a dark Kansas night.

Shouts came from the village path below. Then David's voice, also shouting. But he was too far away for her to understand his words. *Oh, Lord, protect him! Watch over us all...*

The heavy thud came against the door again, and then silence. Another shout and the footsteps retreated while an angry exchange drifted up from the village below them. She and the children sat, stock-still, looking from one to another for what felt like an eternity. Natalie tried to put confidence in her expression for the sake of the children, but her fingers trembled like leaves in a zephyr.

The voices in the village retreated then finally fell silent. Hoping no one was waiting outside the office, Natalie whispered, "Let's stay just a little longer. You all did so well! But just a little longer. And pray!"

They nodded their agreement, but Lele whimpered softly. Natalie pulled the little girl into her lap and held her until her eyelids closed and her breaths came in even puffs.

Twenty minutes later, at the crunch of approaching footsteps Lele's eyelids flew open and she sat upright in Natalie's lap. A knock caused the children to stir. They turned expectantly toward the door. But again, she motioned for quiet.

"Natalie? It's me."

David!

"You can open the door."

Relief flooded through her. She carefully set Lele down on the floor and jumped up to unlock the latch. Her legs felt like overcooked noodles and her stomach churned.

David entered and locked the door behind him, studying her as he did. "Is everyone okay? They didn't bother you?"

She kept her voice low. "They pounded on the door and tried to get in, but the lock held and they finally went away."

"Thank God." David's voice caught.

"Who was it? What happened?"

"Guerrillas. Same as last time. Just on a scouting mission, I think. They threw their weight around and made some idle threats but—"

"How do you know they're idle? They sounded pretty serious to me!" She hadn't meant it to come out sounding so harsh. She was aware David was downplaying the incident for her sake.

He gave her a look that caused her to remember the children. "I'm sorry." She put her arms around him briefly.

"I know. You're scared." He pulled her close and patted her back in a rare show of open affection.

A chorus of giggles and tittering came from behind them, and Natalie clung harder to David, smiling at the children over his shoulder. "Mr. David is big and strong, no?"

The laughter began hesitantly, but then the boys bellowed and the girls cheered and chattered together, giving her and David furtive looks. It was, no doubt, just what they needed to get their minds off the harrowing experience they'd just been through.

David made a goofy face at her and flexed a muscle for the

kids, but turning serious, he ran his hands down her arms as if checking for injuries. "You're sure you're okay?"

"I'm fine. Just shaken up. I thought sure they'd break down the door."

"They would have if they'd been determined." He replied to her English in kind, which made the children eye them with interest.

She threw them a quick smile before turning back to David and shaking her head in disgust. "Why can't they just leave us alone?"

"I think they will now. For a while anyway. They just like to keep us on our toes. Make us aware that they're watching."

She shivered. "Well, I'm aware. And I don't like it."

David chuckled. "I'll inform them of that next time they show up in the village."

"I wish you would!" She glanced toward the door he'd locked behind him. "You're sure they're gone?"

"Anazu trailed them and saw them get into boats at the Carra inlet. There were six of them, same as came through here."

"Why did you lock the door then?"

"Just playing it safe. On the kids' account."

She eyed him, trying to tell if he was only attempting to make her feel better.

"You can unlock it now, love. They're gone."

She glanced at the clock on the wall. "We should send the children home. Any of the parents who heard the commotion will be worried."

He tossed his head. "They would have been up here with machetes if they'd heard."

"Do you think it's safe to send them home? By themselves?"

"I do. But why don't you walk Lele home."

Natalie nodded. "I usually do. Even though they let her roam all over the village by herself. I'll never get used to that! She's not even four!"

When—*if* they had children she would never allow her

toddlers to roam unsupervised—especially not after today. But she didn't dare tell David that. She would not provide him with any more reasons why it wasn't a good idea for them to have a baby. Although today had come closer to convincing her than any of the feeble excuses he'd made.

"I'll see you at home?" He paused, his hand on the doorknob.

"Yes. I'm hungry."

"Me too. But I'm probably going to be eating at my desk tonight. I've got a lot of lost time to make up for. But I'll help you cook as soon as you get home."

"Mmm... I knew there was a reason I married you."

Shoulders shaking with silent laughter, he ducked beneath the doorframe and exited the office.

Natalie dismissed the students. "You all were wonderful today! I'm proud of you. Tomorrow we will celebrate with cookies! But—"

They erupted in cheers.

She held up a hand and waited for them to quiet. "Now, listen carefully. I want you to go directly home from school. No stopping at the spring to play. Understand?"

The children made feeble protests, but agreed.

"And I'll see you tomorrow back at the pavilion. With cookies!"

They filed down the stairs, chittering over one another in shrill voices. Natalie could only make out about half of their conversations, but from the words she could decipher, the talk was all about the day's excitement.

"Are you ready to go, Lele?" She knelt in front of the diminutive girl who still looked sleepy-eyed from her restless nap. Lele lifted her arms to be carried.

Normally, Natalie wouldn't have indulged her. After all, if she was grown up enough to go to school, she could go on her own power. But this had been an exceptional day. Natalie slung her bag across her shoulder and picked up the featherweight. "Let's get you home."

୬

LETTING STEAMING CUPS OF *CAZHO* WITH GOAT MILK WARM their hands, David and Natalie wove their way through the village trails, crossing the little footbridge over the stream, waving to the few villagers who were up before the sun. Anazu had told him the natives thought their morning walks a strange habit, but they'd apparently grown used to it and most ignored them.

For the first time since the guerrillas made their appearance in the village a few weeks ago, David felt at ease. They'd all been on edge in the days following the scare. And he all the more now. He had a wife to protect. Being married came with additional responsibilities, and loving someone else the same way you loved yourself came at high cost. One he'd struggled mightily with. But it only took one look at the woman beside him, her pale hair ruffling in the sultry breeze, to kindle a quick attitude adjustment. And even though she sometimes frustrated him, he loved the way she challenged him to look at things differently. More compassionately. And he loved having an intelligent, thoughtful, spiritual companion to bounce things off of.

Such a treasure Natalie was to him. Helpmate, supporter, friend. And lover. That part had taken him by delightful surprise and made him ever grateful for the redemption he'd found in Natalie's love.

They reached the narrow beach along the Rio Guaviare's tributary just as the sun peered over the horizon, painting the sky in sherbet shades. They stood gazing over the water, arm in arm, until the sun burned off the mist hovering over the river.

"When I talked to Mom yesterday, she said they got six inches of snow overnight."

"That seems weird, doesn't it?"

She nodded. "I never thought I'd miss February in Kansas."

He kissed the top of her head. "We'll go for a visit some

winter. Next Christmas maybe. Or Valentine's Day. You could celebrate your birthday there."

"Oh, that would be perfect. Valentine's Day is Mom and Daddy's anniversary too. That would make them happy. And me."

A short way up the shore, a fisherman dragged his boat into the water and paddled downstream.

David waved at the man, then slipped his arm around Natalie. "Ready to head back?"

She nodded. "I want to get the rest of the garden in this morning before I go to school."

They'd worked together over the past week to get a little garden planted behind the hut. Those tiny seedlings gave him a false sense of security. There was never a guarantee they'd harvest what they planted. Rain, pests, or thieves could undo their work at any juncture. Nevertheless, he enjoyed the pleasant routine of working together with their hands.

They returned to the *utta* and worked in the garden for an hour before going in for breakfast.

Natalie brewed *cazho* while he fixed plates of scrambled eggs and thick slices of guava and banana.

They ate in silence, and after a while, he slid his laptop in front of him and opened an article from a linguistics magazine. He was grateful to be able to download digital versions of books and magazines whenever they got to the library in Conzalez.

"Did you hear me?"

He looked up to see Natalie staring at him expectantly.

"I'm listening." He glanced back at the article he'd been reading, scrolling to mark his place.

"Um...a little back channeling would be nice. A phatic expression here and there, you know?"

He looked up again, laughing softly as her words computed. "Well played, love." He hadn't realized how much of his lingo she'd picked up while he talked things out with her, mulling over decisions of whether to add a diacritic to a new word or whether to make a compound word two. He closed his laptop and placed it on the table. "Okay. I'm fully here. All ears."

She opened her mouth to speak, then shook her head. "Now I forgot what I was going to say."

"I'm sorry. We were talking about the garden before…"

"Oh, yes. I was going to say that I desperately need a haircut." She pulled her ponytail around one shoulder and inspected the ends.

"And exactly how did you get from gardening to haircuts? Never mind. I'm not sure I want to know."

She laughed her musical laugh.

"But speaking of haircuts, I could use one myself." He tossed his head, purposely causing his hair to droop in front of his eyes.

She jumped up and came around behind him, running her fingers through his curls. "I'm kind of liking it longer. Especially with your beard. You look like a movie star."

"Um…which movie star?" He wasn't sure he liked the comparison.

"Well, not that I know any of the current crop of actors. I just mean you look handsome enough to star in a movie."

Reaching behind him he tipped his head to meet hers and pulled her down for a kiss. "I guess we'll both have to wait on those haircuts till next time we go to Conzalez for supplies."

"Ugh…" She yanked at her ponytail again. "I don't know if I can stand this mop that long."

"I'm willing to give it a shot if you trust me."

"You? Cut my hair?"

"I can *trim* it. It won't be anything fancy, but I used to do a pretty good job grooming our dog when I was in high school."

She gave him a playful shove. "I do not appreciate the comparison, buddy."

He pulled her down for another kiss. "You're way prettier than Patches, and I'm guessing you'll sit still better than she did."

Another shove. "Do you trust me to cut yours?"

"Maybe not if I keep making bad jokes. But hey, you're the one that'll have to look at me if you mess me up, so that's your call."

"Let's give it a go. How bad could it be?"

He laughed. "Famous last words. Are your scissors sharper than mine?"

"Probably." She went to the porch and returned with a pair of pink-handled scissors.

He scooted his chair away from the desk, stripped off his T-shirt, and headed for the deck in front of the house. He smiled at the sudden realization that he and Natalie hadn't had an argument in several weeks. It seemed his prayers had been answered.

He had his cheerful wife back. At least for now.

$\mathscr{H}$ 7 $\mathscr{H}$

Natalie awoke to a vivid image of one of the stinky monkeys picking her tomato plants clean. "No! Stop!"

She fought her way through the mosquito netting and rolled out of bed, ready to run and protect the tiny green tomatoes that were doing so well in their little garden, then laughed at herself when she came fully awake and realized she was panicking over a dream.

But her laughter was short-lived as her stomach began a dance that was becoming all too familiar. She hurried to the bucket in the corner that served as their nighttime toilet.

What on earth? This was the third morning in a row that she'd overslept and awakened feeling nauseated. The sensation had passed quickly enough on Saturday morning that she didn't even mention it to David. Then yesterday morning, she'd begged off going to church with him, convinced she was, indeed, coming down with some bug. She'd felt guilty when she started feeling better a short while after David left.

But again this morning? She retched, but to no avail. She listened for David, grateful when the silence told her he'd likely already gone over to the mission office. She stood over the wash basin for several minutes, wishing she could just throw up.

But her breath caught as a new possibility rolled over her. April was more than halfway over. Her period was at least two weeks overdue, maybe three now. Her cycle had been erratic since they'd returned from the States, but her period had never been more than a week late. What if…?

But surely this wasn't *that*. They'd been careful. Every time. David made sure of that.

Still, this was the strangest case of the flu she'd ever experienced. And it was too coincidental that she was only sick in the morning. Joy welled up inside her. Could it be true? *Was* she pregnant?

The bubble of joy quickly collapsed when she imagined David's reaction. It had taken them weeks to get over the friction their disagreement over having children had caused. He was adamant about not wanting to raise a child in Timoné. And given that he believed they had been called by God to Colombia —to this village—indefinitely, it appeared that unless she could change his mind, they would likely never have children.

She'd gone into mourning for a while at the prospect. Even after he promised her they'd revisit the question in a year or two. She suspected he'd only told her that to placate her. And now—if her suspicion was true—what should have been one of the happiest moments in her life was instead filled with anxiety and even a little fear. Not that she was actually afraid of her husband, but she feared his reaction would suck all the joy out of what should be a precious time. Something she'd waited a lifetime for.

If she *was* pregnant, would David blame her? That would hardly be fair, given that he was the one who'd taken responsibility for their birth control.

She retched again and waited for another wave of nausea to pass, then quickly brushed her teeth and dressed.

"Did you call me, Nat?"

David appeared in the doorway. She jumped and hid her warm cheeks with a hand towel, pretending to dry her face. "No. Just getting ready. Sorry I slept in."

"Are you okay?"

His scrutiny unnerved her. "I'm fine. Have you eaten? I can make some—" She stopped. The very thought of cooking repulsed her.

"It's okay. I already had toast. I'm going over to the office to use the printer." He grabbed an empty tote off a hook beside the closet.

She grabbed her hairbrush and bent at the waist, flipping her mane to comb out the night's tangles, grateful the position would give her an excuse for her flushed face.

She felt his eyes on her and finally stood upright, coiling her fine, flyaway hair into a knot atop her head. She tucked and pinned a loose strand into the bun and spoke over the row of hairpins she held between her teeth. "I'm leaving for school in a few minutes. But I should be back in time to make lunch."

Studying her, his brow furrowed. "You sure you're okay?"

"I'm fine. You'd better go before the rain starts."

His expression said he was unconvinced, but finally, he pecked her cheek and left the room without comment.

She finished pinning her hair and went to find something to eat that might settle her stomach. Even as the thought came, she realized the queazy feeling had abated.

It was probably just wishful thinking that she was pregnant. She'd read about the phenomenon of phantom pregnancies, women who wanted so desperately to have a baby that their bodies actually started mimicking the clinical symptoms of pregnancy. Not that she was desperate. At least not yet.

Pushing away the thoughts, she started water to boil for oatmeal. Outside their windows the clouds announced that the rainy season was upon them. Once the morning rains let up, she would walk to the village commons to teach whoever happened to show up. That would be Lele, who never failed to be waiting in the pavilion right on time. But now that the rainy season had begun, school had mostly come to a halt.

In preparation for the coming rains, Natalie had spent her

evenings sweeping the floors of their *utta*, beating the rush mats clean, and moving what little furniture they had toward the center of the rooms so it would't get wet in the torrential downpours of the long rainy season.

She'd never minded the daily rains. There was something rather cozy about being holed up in the *utta* with a pot of vegetable soup simmering and a good book to read. A bit like winter in Kansas, give or take sixty degrees.

She finished her oatmeal and tidied the tiny kitchen, then tossed her school bag over one shoulder. She latched the door behind her and walked through the village to the pavilion.

Lele was already there along with the twins. Paku and Daric's matching glum expressions said they were in attendance against their will. They'd rather be swimming or fishing in the river. She smiled and challenged herself to eliminate those frowns before the morning was over.

"Daric, would you get the crayons from my tote, *kopaku?*"

"Markers?" Lele said in English.

"Not today, Lele."

The little girl groaned. The children enjoyed crayons, but much preferred the "magic" markers, a name she'd quit using for the colorful pens after Voric tried to convince the younger children that the markers actually had magical powers. They had enough trouble combatting the occult practices and myths that flew in the face of the science lessons she and David taught, especially when it came to health issues. But many of those superstitions were in opposition to the faith they tried to impart as well.

She'd taken the markers from her school bag and had been using them for her Bible study in place of the highlighters that had gone missing. But they were a poor substitute, some of the colors bleeding through the page.

"Paku, would you help me hang the paper?" She took a heavy roll of kraft paper and helped him roll the paper the length of the movable wall they referred to as the "bulletin board," a sheet of warped plywood that also served at various times as dividing wall, art easel, and sometimes puppet stage.

Five more children straggled in and for the next hour, the nine of them worked together plotting out a map of the village on the long stretch of paper. While the boys worked on palm trees and hills, Lele and the other girls colored in the river at the bottom of the page with blue markers, even though the brown of the kraft paper was a more accurate color for the Guaviare.

The project turned out to be several lessons in one: art, geography, spelling—as much for Natalie as the children, since she used the Timoné words—and even math, when she attempted to draw the map to scale. She earned the smiles from the twins that she'd worked so hard for even before she dismissed class early and sent them home.

The afternoon rains held off until she reached the *utta*, and when she told David over lunch about having the kids measure the distances by pacing out the steps to various landmarks in the village, he complimented her ingenuity.

"Sounds like you managed to sneak a P.E. class in there too."

"That's right, I did!" She laughed and added that to the mental list she was keeping. "I'm calling that a successful day."

"And what are you going to do for an encore?"

"This afternoon?"

He nodded.

"Probably laundry. May as well take advantage of the rain."

"Do you need help?"

"No." She flashed a coy grin and scooted her chair away from the table. "Not unless you just *want* to help me."

"The day I want to help with laundry is the day you need to take my temperature and ferry me to the ER in Conzalez because I'm definitely sick."

She turned away, wondering if he was hinting about her being sick this morning, but reluctant to meet his gaze for fear her own eyes would give too much away. She rose, put a cauldron of water on to boil, and snatched two rumpled dishtowels from the counter. "If you want to add anything to the laundry, you've got until the water boils."

"Yes, ma'am." He pushed away from the table.

She gathered a pile of dirty clothes and the detergent they'd bought in Conzalez, and climbed down the stairs to the area underneath the porch where they'd set up a large galvanized tub and hung two rows of clothesline between the coconut palms. David had rigged a crude but very workable system of troughs that directed rainwater into barrels and could be routed into the laundry tub as well. Besides making laundry less of a chore than hauling it to the river, the system did a good job of keeping the space beneath the porch dry too. It almost felt like they'd gained a whole new room in the *utta*.

She doubted Dad would have approved and felt a small twinge of guilt, even as she was grateful that David had no problem innovating an easier way of life for them. He'd told her just last week that a couple of the men in the village had asked him if he would help them put a similar system underneath their *uttas*. She would have bet a basket of clean laundry that the men's wives had put them up to talking to David.

She sorted the whites from the colors, wondering if this time next year she'd be washing a third load—of diapers. She smiled at the thought, but her expression quickly turned to a frown as she realized that she felt perfectly fine, with none of the "morning sickness" symptoms she'd been experiencing. Disappointment overtook her until she thought of how she would have had to break the news to David, and then the emotion was replaced with relief.

An hour later, with clean clothes draped over the clotheslines to dry under cover of the porch floor, Natalie braved the afternoon rains and hurried back upstairs. She sometimes left their laundry on the lines to dry overnight, but in this humidity nothing ever really got dry. And she didn't trust the monkeys not to soil anything she left out. Someday when funds and time allowed, she would convince David to screen in the area under the porch. A screen might not keep the snakes from slithering underneath, but at least it would keep out the pesky monkeys and the larger flying insects.

She went through the house and out to the porch to watch the rain. A commotion in the dense foliage behind the *utta* made her stop, every muscle tensed. Ever since the guerrillas had stormed through the village six weeks ago, her senses had been on high alert. But her pulse slowed as a flash of pink darted in and out of the low, lush ferns below the porch. Natalie recognized the T-shirt Lele had worn to school this morning—*and* the high-pitched giggle that followed the T-shirt.

"Lele? What are you doing?" Natalie peered over the rail.

Silence.

"Lele?"

One more flicker of pink before the ferns undulated behind the girl as she slinked away without answering.

Natalie sighed and went back inside. It was unnerving to have someone, no matter how small and harmless, sneaking around the *utta*, watching from the shadows. But she didn't know what could be done about it. David wouldn't want to stir up trouble by tattling to Lele's grandparents, and it wasn't as if there were rules forbidding the child from wandering the village on her own.

Maybe if she appealed to the girl's grandparents, reminded them of the guerrillas' invasion, they would keep a closer watch on Lele.

The jungle was full of danger. She didn't think the Timoné people took the threats seriously enough, despite the deaths and near tragedies Dad had attended during his time here. It was part of the reason David was so reluctant to raise children here. But all it took was a more watchful eye.

Still, it wasn't David's only reason. She began a mental list of his arguments—and her rebuttals—and headed upstairs to type them out. Just in case she needed them sooner rather than later.

❧ 8 ❧

Ugh! Covering her mouth with her hand, Natalie slid beneath the mosquito netting and half-crawled to the bucket in the corner. This time her stomach easily gave up its contents and she waited for the relief that should follow.

Instead, she retched again. This made four mornings in a row. *What else could it be?*

Before she could pick herself up off the floor and wash her face in the basin, David's voice came from behind her.

"Nat— What on earth? Why are you cleaning at this time of morning?"

She rose awkwardly and splashed water from the basin on her face without answering or turning around.

"Natalie? What's going on?" His expression held curiosity… and something else.

She pivoted to face him, attempting a smile. Instead, a sob worked its way up her throat.

"Love? What is it? What's the matter?" He took her by the shoulders, then his gaze went from her to the toilet bucket and back. "Are you sick?"

She inhaled deeply. "I'm okay."

"You don't look okay. You're as pale as the sheets on our bed."

The genuine alarm in his eyes touched her.

"I'm fine, David. Something must not agree—"

"Something you ate? Or do you have a fever?" He felt her forehead with the back of his hand.

"I'll be fine, David." *In a few months.*

"Maybe we should try to reach Meghan. How long have you been feeling this way?"

"Not long. David, I..." She took a shuddered breath and shrugged out of his embrace. Walking hunched over, she went to sit on the edge of the mattress. "I haven't gotten my period for—"

"Oh...this is just that? Then you'll be okay in a few days? You're not usually nauseated with that though, are you?"

"I can't be sure, but... I don't think I'm going to get my period. Not for a few months anyway."

His brow knit and he eyed her. "What do you mean?"

"This is the fourth morning in a row I've been sick, David."

"Wait... What are you saying?" Suspicion laced his tone.

Still, she couldn't help the giggle that rose in her throat. "I think we can probably expect this to last about nine months."

"Nine month—" His eyes went wide. "Are you telling me what I think you're telling me?"

"I think I'm pregnant." It came out in a squeak. She repeated it, surprised by her rising emotion and by how much it mattered to her that he be happy about this news. "I can't be sure yet, but it's looking that way."

"No. That's not possible." It was definitely not happiness coloring his tone.

"Of course it's possible, David."

"But I told you—" He clipped off the sentence, his shoulders sagging. "Are you sure?"

"No, I'm not sure. How *could* I be? It's not like I can run to Walgreens for a pregnancy test."

"Then maybe you're not. Please, God..." Those last words were muttered under his breath, surely not intended for her, but the desperation in his eyes crushed her.

She swallowed hard and looked away.

"Why would you tell me something like that if you're not sure?"

"David." Anger overtook her disappointment. "I clearly said I *can't* be sure. But you asked me why I'm puking my guts out every morning. And I told you what I suspect. Did you want me to lie to you?"

"No, of course not." His tone softened. "But you didn't need to scare me to death jumping to the worst case scenario either."

"Worst case?" She glared at him. "Well, excuse me if the possibility of God blessing us with a child terrifies you. Funny it didn't seem to scare you when we were making love." Her voice caught on a sob.

"Natalie, I—" He pulled out the chair that sat by the door and slumped into it, putting his head in his hands, elbows resting on his thighs.

It felt like an eternity before he looked up again. "You should go back to bed. Here..." He rose and pulled back the covers on her side of the bed.

Not knowing what else to do, she lay back on the bed and let him draw the sheet and blanket over her.

She waited for him to sit on the bed beside her, apologize for his harsh words, tell her everything would be all right.

Instead, he tucked his hands in the pockets of his jeans and backed toward the door. "I'll be back in a little while."

"Where are you going?"

"I—I don't know. I just need some time. I'm sorry."

"David—"

But he was already through the doorway. She heard him walk across the living room to the front door. A moment later, the door closed and his footsteps quickened down the stairs.

She closed her eyes. And when another bout of nausea came,

she knew it wasn't caused by pregnancy, but what felt like a betrayal by the man she'd given her life to, trusted her life with.

Reeling, she sat up and pulled the mosquito netting over her as if it could protect her from the assault of David's reaction. Then she curled into a fetal position in the middle of the bed and prayed for sleep to come, despite the fact that she'd only been awake for twenty minutes.

DAVID PLUNGED DEEPER INTO THE VERDUROUS RAIN FOREST, navigating a path he sometimes took when he wanted to be alone. He'd purposely left the trail rugged, not beating down the vegetation too severely and varying his route week by week, lest it be discovered by the village children.

He tried in vain to pray as he ran. How could this have happened? They'd been so careful. *He'd* been so careful. It was like everything with Lily was happening all over again. He shook his head, pushing a thick stand of banana leaves out of the way.

But this wasn't the same. Not at all. Natalie was his wife. Before God and before man, legally. Then why did he feel every bit as guilty, ashamed even, as he had when Lily told him she was pregnant?

Because it wasn't responsible to have a child here. Even if a baby wouldn't interfere with their work here in Timoné—and it most certainly *would*—how could they deal with the logistics? Even getting to a hospital in time for the birth presented all kinds of problems. And he wasn't about to let the local midwives deliver this child. Or God forbid, deliver it himself. He'd helped Nate with a delivery once. The baby had been born with the umbilical cord wrapped around his neck. He would never forget the terror of that bright blue baby he'd thought sure was dead.

Monni, the mother, and her little boy, Miguel, had both survived and now thrived. But births didn't always have happy endings here in the jungle. And if not for Nate's presence, Monni would likely have buried her son. He shuddered.

No, without a doctor in Timoné, they'd have to go to Conzalez or Bogotá. Or return to the States. That would be the safest choice. But for how long? He'd felt like a fish out of water when they went to Kansas before their wedding. What would he do there? *This* was his calling. His translation work. This was what God had called him to. What he'd assured their supporters he *was* doing.

His breaths came hard now and he forced himself to slow down, get his bearings. This trail was treacherous when the rains came, and he'd lost track of time, though it had been early in the day when he'd found Natalie bent over the bucket. The memory made him gag. And not just from a reflex. But what the memory represented.

He went to his knees, feeling lightheaded. "Lord, please don't let it be true. Don't make me go through this."

Even as the words came, he recognized they were utterly selfish, completely unwarranted, and yet he couldn't help but beg God to relieve him from the heavy burden of Natalie's news.

Still, there was hope. By her own admission, she wasn't *sure*. Maybe this was merely some kind of test. Even as he preached the glorious Gospel to the Timoné people, he still struggled sometimes to believe in his own forgiveness. Maybe God wanted him to settle that once and for all.

But God knew his heart. And what else could he do to prove himself? In His gracious love, God had allowed him the comfort and joy of a wife. But he'd always known after Lily's abortion that, despite being forgiven, he would not have children. Not only because of his sin. The things he'd told Natalie were true. Timoné was no place to raise a child, and besides, he was thirty-four years old. Nine months from now, he would be thirty-five. Even if that weren't the case, he had a calling on his life that did not leave time for...whatever a child involved. And that was just it: He didn't know the first thing about being a dad. His own father had been a workaholic, never home, never involved. Natalie's dad had been more like a father to him than his own.

But even if those salient reasons weren't enough, a far greater one loomed over him. Even all these years later, the truth of it strangled the breath out of him: He had taken the life of his own child. The child that would have been his firstborn. In no way would he ever deserve another chance. Not when there were couples all over the world who longed for a baby like the one whose life he'd allowed to be snuffed out.

The fusty scent of the afternoon rains moved in, and he gathered himself and carefully picked his way back to the village, sliding down the trail now slick with mud, letting the pelting rain mingle with his tears.

Once back on the winding village streets, he hurried to their *utta*. He'd been gone longer than he intended and Natalie would be worried. It was cruel to have walked out on her like he did. This wasn't her fault alone.

Maybe it's a false alarm.

He let the thought comfort him as he continued down the streets. A short distance from home, he spotted Lele in front of her grandparents' *utta* gleefully catching rain on her tongue. Her feet and legs were sheathed in mud up to her thighs.

"Did you fall in mud pit?" He forced a smile he didn't feel.

Lele laughed as if his joke was the funniest she'd ever heard, and his smile turned genuine. She waved and hammed it up, stomping in the puddles in front of the hut.

But as he started to pass by, she told him matter-of-factly, "Mamá ran away."

"What's that? *Your* mamá?" He went to the front little stairway and knelt in the rain beside her.

Lele nodded. "Abbé is sad. No—" She scrunched up her little nose. "She is angry. Mamá is in so much trouble."

David didn't feel he should pry, yet he wondered where on earth a young woman could "run away" to. The nearest village was several hours away on foot, and Conzalez was half a day on the river.

David mumbled a generic condolence and started to turn away and continue toward home, but the sound of his name made him stop and turn back.

Meena, Lele's grandmother, stood in the doorway to their hut. "Lele! You clean up that mud!"

She called David's name again and waved him inside.

Reluctantly, he climbed the stairs to the *utta's* stoop. "I'm soaked," he told her. "I don't want to get everything wet."

She shook her head and pulled him in. It was only then that he noticed the worry lines furrowing her forehead.

"Is everything okay, Meena?"

"It's Gabrielle. She's gone." Meena uttered a mild Timoné curse, very out of character for the affable woman, especially since she'd started coming to church with Jamos.

"Gone?" David looked past her to a space that was tidy except for a basket of rocks and shells arranged on a floor mat and a tiny stray shoe on the table—signs that Lele had recently been playing in the room. He saw no sign of Meena's husband. "Where has she gone? I don't understand."

"Jamos is looking for her, but she won't come back. She's run off with that *brihacho*." She spat the word—idiot—as if it were bitter in her mouth. "Probably thinks he's going to give her a fancy *casoriel*."

"She's getting married? To whom? Where?"

"That wet-nosed guerrilla *brihacho*. He cast a spell over her that day they breached the village. She's been meeting him at the river, planning her escape." Her words tumbled out so fast, David had to listen carefully to catch them all. "She took everything. Everything except her daughter."

"Are you sure, Meena? Did she tell you she was leaving?" Given Gabrielle's tryst with Lele's father, David didn't doubt she was capable of running off with a soldier, but he wanted to make sure he hadn't misunderstood. "Are you sure she left…of her own accord?"

Meena made a spitting sound over her shoulder. "She went of her own accord. Jamos had words with her, but her head is stubborn like a donkey. She says she is in love." She spat again. "She left in the middle of the night. She had no intention of obeying her papá."

He shuddered to think what that young guerrilla had in mind for Gabrielle. Maybe she thought she was in love but a soldier had no use for a woman, unless it was for his own convenience and purposes. Or if he could make a tidy profit selling her to sex traffickers.

"She told Jamos she was going to stay with her uncle, Jamos's brother in Conzalez. That is where he was headed."

"He took the boat? When did he leave?"

"Yesterday, the minute we knew that she was really gone." She wrung her hands. "But he should be back by now."

"Maybe he is staying for a while? With his brother?"

"I don't know. He said he would overtake them before they reached Conzalez. He should be back by now," she said again.

"We will pray, Meena. And if he's not back by tomorrow, we'll send someone to search for him." If Gabrielle had truly run off with one of the guerrilla soldiers, Jamos could be in great danger if he tried to bring his daughter back against their will.

Worse, this whole situation might bring trouble to the village if the soldier—or the whole guerrilla contingent—followed him back.

🕱   9   🕱

"I just don't even know what to do, Mom. I just brought up the *possibility* that I might be pregnant and he stormed out like I got pregnant on purpose. All by myself." Natalie felt guilty "tattling" on David—and using up minutes on the sat phone without talking to him about it first. But if this didn't constitute an emergency, she didn't know what did.

She had to talk to someone, and she was grateful Kansas was only an hour behind Timoné. Her dad had just left for work and Mom was having her second cup of coffee, a luxury Natalie had forgone this morning, just in case she needed to limit caffeine.

"Nattie, you don't even know for sure if you *are* pregnant. Do you have access to a pregnancy test."

"No. I'll have to get one from Conzalez next time we meet Hank and Meg for supplies."

"I'm surprised your father didn't have pregnancy tests in his medical supplies. Didn't he leave some supplies there?"

She hadn't thought of that. "There are some supplies, but I don't remember seeing anything like that. Of course I wasn't looking for that the last time I was in the clinic. I'll have to check later."

"Honey, just don't let this turn into a huge deal between you and David before you even know for sure. Give him some time to—"

"But if I *am* pregnant and he won't accept it, what do I do then?" She maneuvered into the hammock chair that hung in one corner of the living room.

"What choice will he have? Besides, he'll accept it. It might take a while, but I have no doubt he'll come around. He's a good man. This would be a big responsibility and I'm sure it's over-whelming to him to consider it—especially when he wasn't expecting this."

"Neither of us were."

"And again, it may not even be the case. I know my cycles were sometimes wonky, especially when we'd been traveling."

Almost without thinking about it, Natalie put a hand over her mid-section. "I just have a feeling I am. Something seems... different."

"Well, you know that nothing would make Daddy and me happier. Whatever God's timing turns out to be."

"Do you think I should come home to have the baby? If there *is* a baby...?"

Her mother's thin sigh came across the miles. "Let's cross that bridge when you come to it, Nattie. See what David thinks. There's plenty of time to make those kind of decisions."

"I know you're right. I just..." She swung one leg over the edge and gave a little push with her bare foot to set the hammock swaying. "I want to know everything. Right now."

Mom laughed. "Nobody can fault you for that. I want to know too! A grandbaby in Timoné. I can hardly believe it."

"Well, we don't even know for sure it's true yet." She mimicked her Mom's tone from moments before.

Daria laughed. "Okay, okay. You're right. But you'll let me know the minute you find out?"

"I wish I'd thought to bring a pregnancy test. But we weren't planning on this. Not so soon anyway." She couldn't bring herself to reveal that David didn't want children. It would crush her to have her parents angry with him. And it would have felt like a breach of David's privacy to tell them without his permission.

"Is everything okay otherwise?" A hint of worry—and suspicion?—had edged into Mom's voice.

"It's fine. This has kind of overshadowed everything else, but things were going well until now." She hadn't mentioned the unwanted visit by the guerrillas either. Even though Mom had experienced that when she lived here, and knew it was just part of life in this part of the world. Still, she didn't want to give her anything to worry about unnecessarily.

Footfalls outside the hut made her jump. "Oh. I think David is home, Mom. I'd better hang up and talk to him."

"Of course. Give him our love. And be easy with him, Natalie. I know David. He'll come around," she said again.

David walked in the door, and Natalie gave him a little wave, twisting in the hammock to sit up. She put both feet on the floor. "'Bye, Mom. I love you. Give Daddy my love."

"I will, sweetheart. We pray for you and David every day."

"Don't stop." The lump in her throat kept her from saying more. She turned off the sat phone and faced David. "I called my mom. I hope you don't mind. She sends her love."

"You told her? What you suspect?" David's tone was impossible to read.

She nodded. "I'm sorry, but I had to talk to someone."

The look he leveled at her said he hadn't missed her unspoken barb: *...since my own husband won't talk to me.*

With effort, she softened her tone. "We didn't talk long. And Mom said they'd buy us more minutes if we need them."

He waved off the idea. "I understand."

"You're not mad?" But she almost hoped he *was* angry. This needed to come to a head.

"No. And— I'm sorry, but I need to talk to you about something...unrelated. I promise we'll get back to this."

A frisson of alarm shivered up her spine. "What's wrong?"

"Gabrielle ran off with one of the soldiers."

"The guerrillas?"

He nodded. "Meena said Jamos went after her yesterday. This guy has been meeting Gabrielle at the river and Meena said he talked her into running off with him."

"How on earth did she get mixed up with him?"

"They apparently connected that day the guerrillas came through."

"Oh, no." She gave a little gasp. "She didn't take Lele with her, did she?"

"No. I just saw her with Meena. She's fine. She seems completely unaffected, even though she's the one who told me her mamá ran away."

"That poor little girl. It just makes me sick to my stomach."

He looked at her with a funny expression.

When she realized what he was thinking, she smiled. "Just a figure of speech. I'm not going to throw up or anything."

His dry laugh somehow made her feel like they were one again, and as curious as she was about his willingness to talk now, she wouldn't push him. She'd learned that her husband needed time to process things and it always went better if she waited until he was ready. For now, she'd stick to the subject at hand. "Do you think Jamos will bring her back?"

"I'm sure he'll try." David blew out a sigh. "I think his and Meena's lives would be easier if he left her there. And probably ours too."

She frowned. "What do you mean?"

"If Jamos does manage to talk her into coming back with him, I wouldn't put it past Gabrielle's soldier to bring his buddies and come after her again. As a matter of honor."

Natalie shuddered, thinking of that day with the kids, locked inside the mission office with a guerrilla trying to kick the door in. She wanted to wring Gabrielle's neck. The girl had put the entire village at risk! And left her own precious child behind.

How Lele kept her eternally cheery disposition, Natalie didn't know.

David worried his bottom lip between his teeth. "I'm more concerned about Jamos. Meena thought he would be back by now. He intended to overtake them on the road to Conzalez."

"You don't think they'd hurt him, do you?"

"It's hard to say. But they aren't somebody you want to cross."

"I'll be praying," she assured him. "Maybe we could take supper to Meena and Lele?"

"That would be nice. I'm glad you thought of it. What would you think about having them come eat with us?"

"It's fine with me, but I'm sure Meena won't want to leave the *utta*...in case Jamos comes home."

"Of course." He leaned over the hammock to kiss her forehead. "Why don't I ever think of these things?"

"Because you're not a woman. And thank the Lord for that."

He smiled. "Amen. I wouldn't make a very good one. Do you need help with supper?"

"Not until it's time to carry everything over. I thought I'd make *ajiaco*." The chicken stew was a favorite of his, made with potatoes and corn still on the cob and served with avocado.

"Mmm... I hope you're making enough for us too."

"Of course. But are you hungry now?"

"No. I had a couple of bananas on the trail. How about you? Have you been able to keep anything down?"

She shook her head. "I haven't tried yet. But I am kind of hungry now. Do you want some oatmeal?"

He thought for a minute. "I'd eat a small bowl. We can talk then?" He made it a question.

"Yes. Please." She reached for a hand and he helped her rise from the awkward hammock seat.

"I'll go change into dry clothes and meet you in the kitchen."

With a much lighter heart, she took a pan out to the rain barrel and filled it half full of water. Back inside, she flipped the switch to ignite the gas burner on the *fogoriomo* and waited for the water to boil.

The oats were thickening under Natalie's spoon when David appeared, his hair and beard freshly combed. He wore the yellow plaid shirt—her favorite of his—that brought out the gold flecks in his dark eyes.

"Do you want some fruit?" he asked.

She started to decline, then thought of the baby she might be carrying. "Just a banana, please."

"How are your parents?"

"They're good. My dad was already at work, but Mom and I had a good talk. We didn't talk long. And I'm sorry, David. I should have waited for you to talk to them with me. I know it's expensive, but... I just kind of needed to talk to my mom."

"Natalie, you don't need my permission to call your mom. And don't worry about how much it costs." David dropped his head briefly. "I'm sorry, *mi carru*. We'll get through this. Maybe it's all just a big mistake and—"

Natalie flinched and held up a hand. "David... Please stop. If I *am* pregnant, I don't want our child to ever know that you saw him—or her—as a mistake."

He looked stricken. "No, of course not. You're right. I shouldn't have said that. I'm sorry." But he didn't sound convinced that anything good could come of this.

"You said we could talk about this?" She placed her palm over her still flat belly.

He nodded.

"Could we have Meg send a pregnancy test with Hank next time he brings supplies?"

David rubbed the space between his eyebrows. "That's the only way you'd know for sure?"

"Well, I guess we'd know in a few months if I start showing, and if I still don't get my period. I'd just like to know for sure before that happens. If I am pregnant, I probably shouldn't drink so much *cazho*. And it would be good to start taking some prenatal vitamins. We could have Hank bring those too…just in case."

He blew out a long, heavy breath.

"We can wait," she whispered. "I'll just behave as if I am, just in case, and act accord—"

"No. It's fine. We can have Hank bring those things. No harm in that. It'll probably be at least another week before he makes it down here though."

"I'll e-mail Meg so you don't have to talk to Hank about it." She knew that was probably bothering him worse than anything else.

"That would probably be best. I wouldn't even know what to ask for. Get anything else you think you would need…within reason, I mean. If it turns out you don't need it, then one of the women here can use it."

"David, I know you don't want it to be true, but I think you need to prepare yourself that it might be." She poured thick cream skimmed from goat's milk into the pot and sweetened the oatmeal with brown sugar. She carried the bowls to the little dining table and they sat down across from each other.

They ate in silence for a long minute, their spoons clunking against the colorful pottery bowls.

Natalie thought David was ignoring her comment, but after a while he set his spoon in the bowl and looked at her. His words were gentle even if the sentiment wasn't. "If it's true—if you are pregnant—there will be plenty of time to prepare. Right now, it's all I can do not to freak out, so you go ahead and do whatever you need to do to prepare. But if it's all the same to you, I'd prefer to wait until I know something for sure." His jaw tensed and she could tell he was struggling to keep his voice steady.

"Of course." As if she had any choice.

"Now—" He put a hand over hers and squeezed gently. "I really need to get to work, love. Do you mind if I take my oatmeal to my desk?"

He was already halfway out of his seat.

"Oh...okay."

"Let me know if you need help with supper. I'll help you carry it over to Meena later on."

She nodded, the too-familiar disappointment washing over her like a rainy-season torrent.

So much for his promise that they would talk this out. She was apparently on her own where this subject was concerned.

Remembering her mom's suggestion that there might be a pregnancy kit in the medical supplies her father had left behind, she told David she was going for a walk. She quietly retrieved the keys to the clinic and the supply cabinets within.

Outside, the afternoon breeze whipped the fern fronds at the edges of the trail into a frenzy. The birds of the rain forest sang a cheery vesper as if welcoming her back down the mossy path that led to the tiny clinic. The trail was overgrown and she realized that she'd only been inside the clinic once since they'd returned from the States. The little building was mostly used for storage now.

She opened the door and waited for her eyes to adjust to the dimmer light. This place held so many memories of her father. She inhaled deeply, surprised by the emotion that overtook her. But wasn't being overly emotional another indication that she was pregnant? She smiled to herself. David would say she'd been overly emotional since the day he met her. Maybe it was true. She resolved to try to temper emotions. Well, at least her outward ones.

She crossed the small room and after moving a pile of empty cardboard boxes, she unlocked the largest of the cabinets where Dad had stored first aid supplies. She opened the door to find dozens of bottles and boxes, but the dates on some of the ibuprofen and acetaminophen were well past their expiration. She made a mental note to spend a couple of hours sorting through the supplies and disposing of anything that might be dangerous past its expiration date. She was surprised the clinic hadn't been targeted by the soldiers who'd come through the village last month. Maybe they thought since the doctor was no longer in the village, there would be no medications. It would have been different if it had been the rogue gangs or the drug cartel who'd come, despite the fact that the shelves had almost exclusively held over-the-counter drugs even when Dad was here.

She sent up a prayer that God might send a doctor or nurse to Timoné soon. They'd been lucky not to have any true medical emergencies since Dad had passed away. But it chilled her to think what they would do if they did. And all the supplies in the world meant nothing if there wasn't somebody who knew how to prescribe and administer them.

Not finding what she was looking for, she closed and locked the cabinet and used the same key to unlock the smaller one. There, on the bottom shelf beside a package of bandages with cartoon characters printed on them, was a lone box with a logo familiar from ads she'd seen online. She inspected the box for an expiration date and found one embossed on a flap of the lid. The test was expired, though only by a few months and expiration dates usually erred on the side of caution. It wasn't like pregnancy tests were ingested, so what could be the harm in trying this one?

She searched for a small bag to conceal the test on the walk home, even though she doubted any of the villagers would know what she was carrying. Glancing up at the far corner of the ceiling, her eyes landed on an oval metal track and the now dingy privacy curtain it held. Her dad's primitive exam room.

She tugged the curtain aside to reveal an old toilet chair like the one they had in their *utta*. A plastic seat over a five-gallon bucket. She could do the test right here and throw the evidence in the trash to carry home.

She went to the window where a ray of sun landed on the countertop. She read the step-by-step instructions in the package twice. She only had one chance to do it right. Plenty of days had passed since her last period for the test to detect the pregnancy hormones.

She checked to be sure the clinic doors were locked and pulled the curtain around the toilet chair.

Ten minutes later she was staring at a single line that, no matter how she read the instructions, meant *negative*. She should have felt relief. The negative result should have been a reset button—one that put her and David back where they'd been when they arrived in Timoné after their wedding. Happy, madly in love, with having babies the furthest thing from their minds.

Instead she felt like someone had died—which was completely silly. The only thing that had died was an assumption. A wish. And although it made her feel like a traitor to her husband, she couldn't help but hope the pregnancy test was wrong.

❧ 10 ❧

Natalie sat on the screened porch with a cup of weak tea, watching the rain fall in sheets outside. Thunder rumbled in the distance while the rain played a rhythmic tune on the thatched roof. Below her, the streets of the tiny village flowed like the Guaviare, dark brown sludge collecting around the pilings of each *utta* and matting the grasses flat against the earth. The paths to the commons were rivers, and the pavilion would be flooded. There would be no church this morning. And for that, she was grateful.

She took a sip of the fragrant green tea she'd bought in the airport in Bogotá and thought of her mom's love for this particular variety. Back in the States today, they would be celebrating Mother's Day in every sanctuary. She would call home and wish Mom a happy day this afternoon. But she had no news to tell.

It had been more than three weeks since she'd used the expired pregnancy test, and she wished now that she'd never found it. Because even though the results had been negative, her symptoms continued, and she couldn't shake the feeling that she would be celebrating Mother's Day in a whole new way by this time next year. All the signs were still there—the morning sickness, tender breasts, fatigue to the point of exhaustion.

But the rains had kept David from making a trip to Conzalez, so she still hadn't been able to get a new pregnancy test kit or any of the other supplies she'd requested of Hank and Meghan. And David still showed no interest in discussing any of it.

She forced her mind to happier thoughts and smiled, remembering Meg's joyous reply to her e-mail: *Seriously, girl? Oh, that would be the Best. News. Ever! I bet that husband of yours is over the moon!*

If only her friend knew the truth. Natalie had made sure to leave her laptop open where David would see Meghan's message. So he would know what a husband's reaction was *supposed* to be. But if he'd seen it, he hadn't commented. In fact, there had been almost a solid month with no comment from him. At least on that subject.

They were cordial to each other, and at times it almost seemed as if everything was back to normal between them. But how could it be, when they couldn't even speak about the one thing uppermost on her mind?

"Do you want some mango?" David appeared in the doorway holding up a small bowl.

"Maybe just a couple of bites. I had toast earlier." Dry toast was the one thing she'd discovered that seemed to settle her stomach.

"Could you be ready for church in a few minutes?"

"Church? You don't think anyone would show up in this downpour, do you? How would we even get there?" She glanced out through the porch screen.

"I just meant home church. You and me."

His shy smile reminded her of the early days when they'd first begun falling in love. It made her sad for what they'd lost.

"I'm ready whenever you are."

He nodded. "For a few weeks anyway, it'll probably be a rare Sunday that we can use the pavilion."

"I remember Daddy would hold house church if we got

snowed in." A wave of homesickness came strong with the memory.

"I just don't want to get out of the habit of keeping Sundays special. And having that day of rest, too. Okay if I come out here with you?"

"If you don't mind the competition." She smiled and cupped an ear pointedly toward the cacophony of rain on the roof, palm fronds whispering in the breeze, the high-pitched trill of the tiny monkeys, and the melodic warble of the wood wrens. Chaotic as it was, the song of the rain forest had become the sound of home for her. As much as she missed her parents, now Timoné, this *utta*, and David were home for her.

"I think God can hear us just fine over the noise." He brought his Bible out to the porch and settled into the matching low chair beside hers.

"I feel bad we couldn't open the pavilion today. I know Jamos and Meena could have used the support." Jamos had returned two nights after he'd gone looking for Gabrielle, but he'd returned alone, in defeat, and they still hadn't heard a peep from their daughter. Meena wore her grief as anger, and Jamos walked through the village as if he were carrying a bull ox on his shoulders.

"We'll pray for them. And Gabrielle." Reaching for her hand, David bowed his head. "God, your Word says that wherever two or more gather, you are right there among them. It's just the two of us today, Lord, but Natalie and I praise you for this day that you have made. And we pray for our friends, Jamos and Meena. Comfort them Lord..."

No matter how irked she might be at David, hearing him pray always warmed her heart toward him.

Giving her a sideways glance, David opened his Bible and read a passage from the book of Ephesians. "*In the same way, husbands ought to love their wives as their own bodies. He who loves his wife loves himself. Indeed, no one ever hated his own body, but he nour-*

ishes and cherishes it, just as Christ does the church. For we are members of His body."

He stopped and closed the cover of his Bible, clearing his throat, his head still bowed. "I wanted—*chose*—to read this today, Lord, because I haven't done a very good job of loving my wife recently."

He reached for her hand and closed his eyes again. When he looked up, she could tell that he was struggling to keep his emotions in check. She wanted to ask him what was wrong, but somehow sensed she should wait.

After a long minute, he opened his eyes and squeezed her hand again, but didn't quite meet her gaze. "Will you forgive me, Natalie. I know I've...put you off, shut myself off from you. Because of the pregnancy. The baby. God has been working on me about that. I won't lie to you... I'm not there yet. But I'm trying. And if God chooses to give us a baby, I'm sure He'll help us work out the details."

Her heart soared. "Thank you, David. *Egracita.*"

He smiled at her purposeful use of the Timoné. "I want to be excited. For your sake. I feel bad that I haven't been willing to talk about it. And I have been praying for you. And the baby too...if there is one. I should have told you that a long time ago. I'm sorry."

"Of course I forgive you." Forgiveness came easier than she'd expected. David was sincerely doing the best he knew how at being a husband. At being a good man. He hadn't had very good examples of either in his own father, and she reminded herself to give him grace for that. She was still learning how to be a wife too.

"Still, I should have told you before now."

She squeezed his hand before letting loose, overwhelmed with love for him...even as she longed for the closeness that they seemed to have lost. "It's okay, David."

He shook his head. "No, it's really not okay. I'm scared, love.

Terrified, to be honest." He gave her a sheepish grin. "But that's no excuse for the way I've been acting."

"Why are you so scared, babe? I mean, what are you scared of?"

He let loose of her hand and pretended to look at a watch he wasn't wearing. "How long do you have?"

"I'm not going anywhere. Is it just the whole thing about raising a child here in Timoné?"

"That's part of it, but there's so much more."

"Like?"

"Like what if I have to deliver the baby?"

"You won't have to, David. If I don't go home for the birth, Meena or Delita are both good midwives. I'd love for you to be there, maybe cut the cord, but you don't have to do the actual delivery. Maybe Mom could even come."

"That helps. A little."

"What else?" She truly couldn't imagine what he found so terrifying about such a natural process. "I guess growing up on the farm with a veterinarian for a dad, I saw hundreds of animals being born. Mom and Daddy were always so matter-of-fact about stuff like that, I've never given it a second thought. So, what else?" she asked again.

He hesitated. "I don't want to scare *you*," he said finally. "But what if something goes wrong. What if you need a cesarean, or you lose too much blood? Or something is wrong with the baby."

"I've thought about all those things, and I'm truly not afraid, David. Whatever happens is in God's hands."

He nodded slowly. "I know you're right. I'm still terrified."

She patted his leg. "It'll be okay, babe. Everything will work out. And you'll be a great father and—"

"And that's the other thing. One of them. I don't have the first clue how to be a good father."

"You're a good man, David. You'll learn. We'll both learn how to do this. We'll help each other." She offered a soft smile. "You said 'that's one of them.' What else has you so worried?"

"I— If you are pregnant, Natalie, you deserve to enjoy this pregnancy. Every moment of it. And I'm sorry I've already robbed you of the first few weeks of celebrating everything. But I *don't* deserve it."

"Because of Lily?"

"Lily. And what happened...what I *let* happen to my first child. How can I ever—"

"David Chambers." She slid from her chair and knelt before him, gripping his arms. "How can you not remember all the things you told me when I was trying to figure out how to redeem my own life?"

He blew out a breath as deep as the Guaviare's fathoms. "Could you...remind me? I don't seem to be doing very well reminding myself."

"Of course. Of course I will." She took his face in her hands and leaned into his broad chest, taking comfort in the steady rhythm of his heartbeat. And finding herself soothed all over again by the difficult but precious memory, she recounted how—*after* she had asked God to forgive her—she had clung tightly to her self-reproach, waiting until she could finally, somehow forgive herself. But of course, she never could.

David had chided her, saying, "The God of the universe, in his great mercy and unfailing love, already forgave you. But you're not satisfied with that. That wasn't good enough for you. You're still holding out, trying to obtain forgiveness from one last source."

"Oh, David, don't you remember what you told me?" She affected a serious tone, quoting him. "I'm sure glad *my* salvation doesn't depend on forgiveness from the great and mighty Natalie Camfield."

He gave a low chuckle.

She burrowed deeper into him now, memories flooding her. "You were so angry with me. But... Something broke inside of me when you said that. And I knew it was true. Finally, I knew that whether I felt it or not, I *was* forgiven. How foolish that I thought I could forgive myself. Jesus *died* so I could let go of my condemnation. And I did. Finally, that day I did," she breathed. "Now, will you let go of your guilt, David Chambers? And give it to Him?"

She felt his chest quake beneath her hand and looked up to see tears beaded on his dark eyelashes.

When he opened his eyes, a soft smile came and he bowed his head over hers. "Now that was church," he whispered. "*That was church.*"

❧

DAVID STOOD IN THE DOORWAY TO HIS OFFICE, GRATEFUL FOR a Monday morning that had offered a short window of sunshine after a stormy weekend. Stormy in more ways than one, and yet, he would have given up that sun in a heartbeat in exchange for the peace that had taken up residence in his soul since his heart-to-heart with Natalie yesterday.

His large desk was cluttered with maps and charts and open reference books stacked one upon another like a collapsed Jenga tower. The cork surface of his bulletin board was lost under index cards, word lists, and cryptic notes written on scraps of paper. He really needed to take a day to tidy things up, but he knew where everything was. He felt most productive with all his tools and references spread around him and seeing his office this way felt like an invitation. He was so close to finishing the translation of the book of Galatians, and he couldn't wait to get back to work.

He reached for a stained mug with a used teabag glued to the inside. One of several in similar condition. It was a miracle his neatnik wife hadn't confiscated them. But she'd learned the hard way, before they were married, not to disturb his desk. He was well aware that it took all the willpower she had to refrain from tidying up his space. The least he could do was get rid of the dirty dishes that had collected on his desk over the past week.

He gathered an impressive stack of plates and cups and carried them out to the kitchen. Seeing that the dishpan was empty and the kitchen already tidied, he started the kettle to boil.

Natalie came in from the porch where she'd been working on their newsletter to supporters. "Another cup of tea? You're going to float away."

He shook his head, not turning around. "No tea. Just doing up my dirty dishes."

"I already did the dishes."

"I cleaned off my desk."

"About time!" She ducked under his arm and nudged between him and the sink. "But get out of here. I'll do those. You get to work. I know you were on a roll."

"That wouldn't be very nice when you already had the kitchen cleaned up. Besides, you're working too."

"I don't mind. I've got an hour before I need to leave for school. I was drawing a blank on what to write anyway."

"Quit being so nice. I'm trying to turn over a new leaf here," he argued. But he stepped aside.

She tiptoed to give him a quick kiss. "And I love you for it. But seriously, go to work. It will take me two minutes to finish up here."

He hugged her from behind, kissing the top of her head. "I don't deserve you."

She reached around to swat him on the rear end. "I know. Now get moving."

"Okay, okay." He started for his office, then turned back. "And hey, just so you know, I'm calling Hank later this morning to figure out when we can get those supplies. It's time we found out for sure. About whether there's a baby coming."

"Thank you, babe." Her voice trembled ever so slightly and her soft smile was his reward.

He mentally berated himself for being such a jerk for so long.

Back in his office, he dove in to the final read-through of Galatians, making notes in the margins of a copy Tados would review. The Timoné native had been a godsend. The modified alphabet Tados and he had created was second-nature for both of them now. Through the process, Tados had become ever more fluent in English since Nate had taught him the English alphabet the Timoné script was based on, and he'd proven to be extremely conscientious in the translation work, especially where culturally sensitive content was concerned. The lexis was ever-expanding and David felt confident they'd achieved what they hoped in localizing the dialect.

He uncapped his pen and scratched out another note for Tados, filling the entire margin of the page. Needing further explanation, he opened his desk drawer to retrieve a pad of sticky notes. Strange. He'd brought a whole new package of colorful pads with him from the States. He was certain he'd put them in the top drawer. He rifled through the jumble of office supplies and made a note to clean out his desk next weekend. The sticky notes weren't in the second drawer either.

Frustrated at getting bogged down by such a petty inconvenience, he went to find Natalie. She was in the bedroom, working her hair into a thick braid.

"Sorry to bother you, love, but did you happen to borrow the sticky notes I brought back with us?"

"Sticky notes? No, I haven't seen them."

"You didn't take them from my office?"

Her fingers stilled and she aimed a nonplussed look at his reflection in the mirror. "Do you think I didn't learn my lesson?"

He chuckled. "Just this morning, I was thinking about that infamous scouring you gave my desk."

She shot him a rueful smile. "That just about ended our relationship before it even started, as I recall."

He winked. "I'll keep looking."

But a thorough search of his desk drawers and file cabinet only unearthed the fact that a box of large paper clips was also missing.

He returned to the bedroom, growing more frustrated by the

minute. "I'm not accusing you, but just reporting that I'm also missing that package of big colorful paper clips I brought back. I know we got here with them because I've got a couple of them marking pages in a book."

"Well, I promise I haven't touched them."

"Like I said, *not* making accusations."

"Do you want me to help you search?"

He sighed and waved her off. "No, you go on. I'll use the old ones, but I was hoping to color-code this manuscript for Tados."

She blew out a little huff. "I'd offer to loan you my pretty markers, but they're still missing too. I'm seriously beginning to think those stupid monkeys have figured out a way to get inside this house."

He laughed at the image that came of the tiny monkeys unlatching the front door, making off with office supplies, then replacing the security ribbon in the door just so and re-latching it before making their getaway. "They're probably setting up office in the trees right under our noses."

"They'd better *not* be!" Natalie shook her head in disgust. "But seriously, David, where is all this stuff going? Could it be the parrots? I've heard they're attracted to shiny things. It seems like everything that's gone missing is shiny or colorful."

He waved off her suggestion. "And just how would a parrot get inside this house?"

"I have no idea, but surely you and I aren't so scatterbrained that we're misplacing all these things. Somebody—or some*thing* —is stealing from us."

"It does seem that way, but why would they leave our computers and food and your jewelry, and take office supplies, of all things?"

She tilted her head with that faraway look she got when concentrating. "When was the last time you saw those sticky notes or the clips?"

He shrugged. "I'm not sure. Maybe a month ago? Six weeks?

If you're thinking the soldiers took them, I doubt they're big on office supplies."

Slipping into her sandals, she frowned. "No. Not them. I hate to even suggest this, but...you don't think Gabrielle took them, do you? Before she ran off."

"Why would she do that?"

"I don't know. Maybe she thought she could sell them."

"If she was looking for something to sell, she would have taken the computers. Or your jewelry."

"My jewelry isn't worth anything. She's seen me wear it. She'd know that. And good luck trying to take my wedding ring." She raised her left hand and wriggled her ring finger that claimed the tattoo matching his.

Natalie owned a few "friendship bracelets" her little niece had made for her and a puka shell necklace Cole Hunter had brought back from a trip to Hawaii with Daria. Her other "jewelry" was trinkets the school children had given her, seeds and pods strung onto knotted reeds. Not that his wife valued them any less than she would have precious gemstones. And she was right: the Timoné might be a remote and primitive people, but Gabrielle would have known that Natalie's jewelry wasn't worth anything.

David returned to his manuscript, convinced now that the missing items had been stolen. He was grateful the losses were petty, but who was to say it would stay that way? It hurt to think a villager was stealing from them. But the thief had to be found.

11

Natalie pulled the knit shirt over her head and smoothed the hem around her hips. Even if the pregnancy test Meghan had sent from Conzalez hadn't confirmed it, there was no doubt now that she was pregnant. Not only did she have a little belly, but her hips had widened and she had cleavage she'd never enjoyed before. David had noticed—and appreciated—the changes, even if he couldn't yet fully appreciate the growing baby that caused them. Would he still be so enamored with her full figure when she couldn't tie her own shoes over a basketball belly?

But at least he'd acknowledged his own certainty that this all meant she was, indeed, carrying a baby. "I guess there's no going back now," he'd said with a ghost of a smile last night, placing a palm tenderly on her rounded belly. But she'd detected a hint of resignation in his tone, too.

He'd reached for her in bed, initiating their sweetly familiar ritual of lovemaking. But just as things grew heated, he pulled away. "Is...is this okay, love? It won't hurt the baby?"

She pulled him back to her, wanting him desperately. "It's perfectly fine," she whispered. "I read it in the books Meg gave me. We can make love almost right up until the baby comes."

He tensed and stilled. "And...after the baby comes?"

"I might need a little time to heal." She stroked his hair away from his forehead. "But only a little. Maybe a couple of weeks."

He let go of a long-held breath and she felt the tension leave him. "I can probably survive that."

She laughed. "Don't worry, sweetheart. From everything I can gather, this"—she kissed him deeply, her voice turning breathy—*"this* goes on as long as we both shall live." She rose to her knees on the bed and leaned over him, convincing him with her kisses.

Reliving the memory, she finished dressing and went to find David in the kitchen.

He held a slice of bread between tongs over the open flame of the *fogoriomo* burner, their poor man's toaster, as he called it. "Want some toast?"

"It smells good. But I can make it. And coffee."

"You're having *cazho*? Is that okay?" He motioned toward her belly.

He was coming around. Ever so slowly, but he was coming around. She curbed a smile. "I can have a cup a day."

"Ouch," he teased. "That's really going to mess with your mojo, isn't it?"

"It'll be worth it." She gave him a smile, knowing he knew what she meant.

But he merely shrugged. "I would have made you a cup when I brewed mine but I figured you couldn't have caffeine."

"It's okay in moderation, and like I said, it'll be worth it." She didn't want to push him, but she also didn't want to go through her entire pregnancy tiptoeing on eggshells.

She opened her mouth to press further, to force some kind of response from him, but a childish voice and little feet coming up the stairs stopped her. "Miss Natalie!"

David winked. "Looks like you've got company."

She could have sworn his expression said *saved by the bell.*

She sighed and went to open the front door. But one look at Lele's face and alarms went off.

Tears streaked the child's cheeks and her eyes flashed with panic. "Miss Natalie! *Kopaku!*"

Natalie hollered for David, worried she wouldn't be able to interpret the little girl's jumbled words.

She knelt and drew her inside. "Lele? What's wrong?"

She felt David behind her.

"Abbé is throwing up." The girl made a comical retching sound.

"Oh, dear." Natalie brushed the hair from Lele's eyes. "She's sick? Is your abuelo home?"

Lele shook her head somberly and pointed in the direction of the river. "He went down the river. In a boat."

Natalie threw David a look over her shoulder before turning back to Lele. "To find your mamá?"

Her bronze eyebrows knit together. "Yes. And to kill that *brihacho.*"

"Lele..."

The child was likely only repeating something Jamos had said. But she also hated hearing a word like that—loosely translated *idiot*—spew from the child's mouth. A sudden thought stopped her, and she asked David in English for confirmation. "She means kill the soldier, right? Not Gabrielle?"

He nodded, looking amused. "Yes, she used the masculine form."

Lele looked back and forth between them, obviously curious, and no doubt aware they were talking about her.

Natalie kept to English. "David, maybe I should go make sure Meena is okay."

"I'll come with you. We might need to bring this one"—he tipped his head toward Lele—"back with us. If Meena's really sick and not just angry."

"Lele said she was throwing up."

"Then she's either *really* mad or she's sick." He touched her shoulder. "Can you handle that?"

"A little vomit?" She rolled her eyes at him. "I'm an expert by now."

He chuckled and lifted Lele into his arms. "Let's go check on your Abbé."

Natalie grabbed clean rags from the kitchen along with a loaf of bread she'd baked yesterday and a jar of broth cubes. She tucked the things into a basket, and steeling herself, followed them.

Once down the stairs, David lifted Lele high and placed her high on his broad shoulders, much to the girl's delight.

"Be careful you don't smack her into a tree," Natalie warned, laughing.

In reply, he veered off the path, headed directly for a lower branch, but ducked out of range at the last minute. Lele trilled with glee.

Natalie's heart swelled. Whether he'd admit it or not, David was going to be a wonderful father.

When they arrived on Jamos and Meena's stoop, Lele climbed the rickety stairs and burst in the door, holding it open wide for them and hollering, "Abbé? Abbé?"

David motioned for Natalie to precede him. "Meena? It's David Chambers. May we come in?"

Natalie stopped, noting a musty odor in the house. She waited for her eyes to adjust to the darkness. She'd been inside the *utta* once before when she made school visits throughout the village. As she remembered, Jamos and Meena had shared the one small bedroom in the corner, and Gabrielle and Lele slept in an open loft over the living area. She looked toward the ceiling but couldn't see into the loft. "Meena? Are you okay?"

"Here!" Lele pointed to the doorway of the bedroom and pushed aside the grass matting that served as a door. "Abbé? Are you still sick?"

Natalie made a knocking motion on the doorjamb, which was nothing more than a few bamboo poles tied together with reeds. She pushed the grass curtain aside. "Meena? May I come in?"

When there was no answer, she stepped tentatively into the bedroom. Immediately, the sour stench of vomit assaulted her nostrils. "Meena?"

The woman was lying on the floor mat, curled into a fetal position. Natalie spoke her name again and went to stoop beside the mat, careful what she touched. The thin blankets were damp and soiled. Meena was breathing but her inhalations were shallow and came with effort.

"David?" Natalie called softly.

He ducked under the doorway. "Is she okay?"

"Can you run home and get me some clean sheets and blankets? The ones folded under our mattress." They only had one extra set of sheets, but she doubted Meena and Jamos had any extras. She would wash the soiled sheets and trade them out later. "Also, can you fill a bowl from the rain barrel and bring it to me?"

"Do you want the kettle?"

"Not now. She's hot. Cool water will feel good. But we'll need it later for broth."

He nodded. "I'll take Lele with me."

"Yes. Good."

A minute later he returned with a wooden bowl sloshing with rainwater. Natalie soaked a clean rag and smoothed Meena's matted hair away from her face and gently bathed her thin body. Much thinner than Natalie remembered. Meena opened her eyes briefly and attempted a wan smile.

Natalie leaned closer. "Meena, how long have you been sick?"

The woman closed her eyes and shook her head almost imperceptibly. Natalie had never wished harder that her father was still here, offering his medical skills to the people, assessing how serious each illness or injury was. And knowing exactly what to do about each.

By the time she finished the sponge bath, David returned

with the fresh bedding. He helped her remake the bed, using the soiled sheets to turn Meena from side to side while they tucked in the clean ones. Every few seconds Natalie stopped and checked to make sure Meena was still breathing.

With the bedding clean and Meena sleeping deeply, Natalie went to pile the soiled sheets and rags on the stoop, then went back to spot clean the floors around the mat. She pushed aside the curtains that covered the room's single window and a gust of fresh air entered the room, along with a thin ray of sun.

David built a fire in the pit outside the *utta* and put a kettle of water on to heat for broth. From inside, Natalie overheard David engaging Lele in a silly conversation about talking monkeys. The little girl's carefree laughter testified to his success at distracting her.

No—Natalie smiled to herself—not good father material at all.

That afternoon, with the house tidied and Lele napping in the loft, David helped her prop Meena up enough that Natalie could ply some broth between her lips. The older woman drank half a cup and kept it down, but even so, Natalie didn't feel comfortable leaving her alone in such a weakened condition.

"I think I should stay here until Jamos is home. If he doesn't come home tonight, I'll stay and you can go sleep at home and check on us in the morning."

David shook his head. "Not with everything going on with Gabrielle. I'll stay here too."

"Where would you sleep, babe? I can sleep in the loft on Gabrielle's bed, but there's not room up there for three of us. I'll be fine."

But he was adamant. "If Jamos comes home in the middle of the night, in his state of mind, he won't know who you are. He's likely to think you're an intruder, beat you to a pulp, and ask questions later. I'll bring our blankets over later, and the cushions off our futon."

"And the mosquito nets?"

"Oh. I hadn't thought of that." Though they'd grown accustomed to the mosquitoes and other bugs that thrived in the muggy climate, they owed most of their acclimation to the mosquito nets they slept beneath. "I wonder if there's still an extra net from when you and your dad's sister came to visit that first time. Where do you think he might have put those?"

"Oh, that's right. Aunt Betsy left hers behind so she could take some of the souvenirs she collected on our trip. If Dad didn't give it away, it's probably in storage in the clinic. Or maybe with the stuff from his office that we moved to the *oficina misión*. You might check that first."

"I'll see what I can find and bring bedding from home. Should I bring something to eat?"

She realized with a start that it was past their usual supper hour. She'd seen Lele with an empty banana peel earlier, but wondered when she'd last eaten a decent meal. Lele hadn't complained, but then that wasn't her nature.

"I'm not that hungry," she told him, "but Lele needs to eat. I saw some fruit in the kitchen, and I brought bread, but you might want to grab something more substantial. There's goat cheese in the cooler and nuts in the cupboard."

"You need to eat something too, love. Whether you feel hungry or not."

She patted his cheek. "I will. Don't worry."

His brow furrowed. "I hope you don't get sick. I never should have let you be exposed to whatever Meena has."

"I'm fine. I'm strong and healthy. My body was made to handle this."

He started to kiss her, then drew back. "Maybe I should refrain—until we know what we're dealing with. One of us needs to stay well."

"Good point. Although Lele seems fine. And I feel fine too." She glanced over her shoulder making sure Lele wasn't listening. "I'm a little worried that Meena may have been sick for a while. Did you notice how thin she is?"

He nodded, looking somber. "I wish your dad was here."

"Me too," she whispered. "I don't want Jamos to be tempted to bring in Sanadori." Unfortunately, the local medicine man was not sought after for his medical skills—and certainly not for his track record—but more because of the bizarre incantations he pronounced over his patients. *Victims* was more like it.

Sanadori had appeared in the village one day about a year before Nathan Camfield's death, announcing that he had been sent to "doctor" them. Dr. Nate had dared not challenge the man, since his own motives would have instantly been suspect. Never mind that Nate had never charged for his services. But after the medicine man's magic supposedly healed a young boy who'd been lame since a fishing accident, Natalie's father had struggled to convince the villagers that Sanadori's chaotic gyrations and magic spells were not worth the price he commanded.

David's sigh now told her he was having the same thoughts.

"No. I'd like to keep him out of it." David looked at the floor before meeting her gaze "And I'll tell you another thing... This just confirms it for me. You are not having our baby in Timoné."

His declaration surprised her. And warmed her heart. It was the first time he'd referred to the child in her womb as "our baby."

"We'll talk about that later," she said. "For now, you need to go find those mosquito nets before it gets dark."

Again, he leaned down for a kiss, but pulled away with a feigned gasp. "Germs!" With a comical grin, he wiped his mouth on the back of his hand.

"Funny," she deadpanned.

He gently brushed a strand of hair from her eyes. "Guess I just can't help myself."

Giggling, she turned to see Lele eyeing them with a curious expression, as if she'd never seen a tender exchange, but also, as if it she liked what she saw. A memory came, from her teenage years, when she'd caught Mom and Daddy in a passionate kiss. When they saw her, she made a gagging noise and told them to "get a room," but even now, it warmed her to remember how loved and secure it had made her feel. That was the kind of marriage she wanted with David. The kind of example she wanted their child to see.

As closely as Lele always scrutinized David and her, Natalie was surprised at how indifferent she'd seemed to her mother's disappearance and even to Meena's illness, now that she and David were here to help.

Lele had endured the stigma of not having a papá, the recent loss of her mamá, and now Jamos was gone and Meena was seriously ill. Yet Lele seemed to trip through life happy and carefree. Was she just adept at hiding her worries? Of course, at not even four years old, Lele wouldn't understand the ramifications of any of those traumas. They were all she'd known in her few years.

"I'm going to see if I can get Lele to eat something and then put her to bed in the loft before I look in on Meena again."

David nodded. "I'll be back in a few minutes. I need to check on the chickens."

"Gather the eggs, too, would you?"

"Sure."

"Watch out for snakes in the straw."

"Don't worry."

"And come in quietly when you get back." She put a finger to her lips, then pointed. "This little one is exhausted."

He followed her gaze to where Lele sat on the floor of the *utta*, hugging her knees and lolling against the wall. Her tawny head bobbled and her eyes rested at half-mast.

12

Natalie awoke with a start and sat up in the low-ceilinged loft, the corn husk mattress crinkling underneath her. It took her a minute to remember where she was. Beside her, Lele's whiffling breaths mingled with the night sounds of the jungle. She'd just been dozing off when David came in and tossed the mosquito netting up to her. She'd tried to put it over Lele too, but the girl quickly freed herself of the unfamiliar encumbrance. A prickly reminder of how spoiled she and David were, and of how much they still clung to their Americanized lives.

She'd begun to struggle with what that would mean for their child here in Timoné. She might have to learn to live without some of the luxuries they'd allowed themselves in order not to raise a child who would seem pampered and entitled compared to his peers.

David had looked in on Meena before he bedded down on the floor below them. According to him, Meena had taken a few sips of water and thanked David by name, surely a good sign. Natalie wasn't sure how long ago that was, but she wouldn't feel right not checking again. Besides, her bladder was complaining. Again.

She was tempted to go back to their *utta* and use the bucket, but the thought of walking even that short distance in the dark was every bit as daunting as braving the *poucochet* behind Jamos and Meena's *utta*. She found the small flashlight she'd taken to the loft and climbed down the ladder, then stepped over the snoring lump on the floor that was her husband.

Once outside, she made enough noise to scare away any animals that might cross her path. She'd just have to take her chances with the spiders and nocturnal snakes. She took comfort in remembering how often she'd seen Meena sweeping out the *poucochet* with a stiff sedge broom.

A few shivering minutes later, she returned to the *utta* and checked on Meena. The woman slept soundly and didn't feel overly warm, but her emaciated frame alarmed Natalie—and made her feel sure that Meena had been suffering for some time. Whether she just hadn't been able to keep food down, or if there was some cancer eating away at her, Natalie couldn't be sure. Dad would have known, and she would have given almost anything to have his medical knowledge for a brief moment.

Meena didn't stir when Natalie adjusted her pillow and pulled the thin blanket over her. She knelt at the woman's bedside and listened for a long minute, counting the shallow breaths. "God, be with Meena," she whispered. "Heal her and give us wisdom to know how to treat her." Her words seemed so insignificant in light of how ill the woman was, and yet when she uttered an *amen*, peace came with it. They'd done all they knew to do.

❧

MEENA FADED BEFORE THEIR EYES AND EXACTLY ONE WEEK after little Lele had alerted them, Meena took her final breath with Jamos by her side. It was almost more than David could bear to watch as Lele sat on her abuelo's lap and leaned in to pat her precious Abbé's cold cheek. She seemed to understand that her grandmother was gone. But it would have been easier to see her wail or throw a tantrum than this stoic demeanor.

David glanced at the date on his watch. July 7. Beside him, Natalie wept silently, and he pulled her close as they observed, set apart, yet feeling deeply privileged to witness this unfolding scene. Heartbreaking as it was, he was in awe of the utter peace that filled the room and painted Meena's countenance in death.

When Jamos returned three nights ago, he hadn't seemed shocked by Meena's condition. Which gave further credence to Natalie's suspicion that Meena had known she was dying. Jamos had insisted on taking the night shift with his wife while Lele slept on the screened porch in David and Natalie's *utta*. Natalie had declared the porch most like the airy loft Lele was accustomed to.

David watched with pride as Natalie tirelessly served the little family, making sure they were well-fed and encouraged and that Lele got the sleep she needed. That she did it all while depriving herself of comfort and sustenance humbled him. He vowed to do better.

He was proud too, that Jamos held fast to his faith in Christ as they ushered Meena home to the heaven she'd only believed in for a short time. But no doubt, her husband's fortitude would be tested greatly in the days ahead. Jamos was on a mission to bring Gabrielle home and now, with his wife gone, it was clear the man was only biding his time until he would return to the hunt for his daughter.

David had offered, after clearing it with Natalie, for Lele to stay with them as long as needed, but selfishly, he hoped Jamos would soon be home—with Gabrielle in tow to take over the care of her daughter. Maybe being forced to take responsibility would finally make Gabrielle grow up.

Though he'd grown to love Lele as much as Natalie had over the past days, the girl *had* turned their lives upside down and tested his patience to the breaking point.

While Lele added energy and hilarity to their little *utta*, she also cramped their style—at least *his*—in ways he'd never imagined. How was he supposed to make love to his wife when a little one might peek around the corner at any moment seeking a drink of water. If this went on much longer, he might have to build a locking door for their bedroom.

And how could he get any work done when those bright eyes peeked over his desk and a tiny, curious voice asked, *"Qué topi? What's this? What's that?"*

Whether she'd admit it or not, Natalie had struggled with the adjustment too. It was one thing to have Lele roaming the village at all hours when she was in someone else's care, but Natalie insisted that if they were responsible for the child, Lele would not go outside their *utta* without supervision. And she chafed at the restrictions like a cornered pit viper, which meant Natalie spent most of her time trying to entertain the girl and distract her from exploring.

As touched—and surprised—as David was by the joy Lele brought to their home, he fought against the image of their own child wreaking similar havoc. Lele was a temporary visitor with a time limit. The baby Natalie carried wasn't a temporary babysitting job. There would be no one coming to relieve them of that child's care. At least not for about eighteen years. And the thought terrified him.

As if she sensed his thoughts, Natalie ducked out from under his arm and went in to Meena's kitchen. He thought to follow her, then realized she needed the time alone. This week had taken a heavy toll on her. From a dim corner of the *utta*, he watched as she methodically sliced two pitaya fruits in half, scooped out the fruit, diced it into cubes, and mixed in a variety of berries that Lele had foraged in the jungle two mornings ago. Natalie placed the resulting fruit salad back into the bowls formed by the pitaya peel the way she'd seen the Timoné women do.

Lele looked up and brightened seeing the fruit bowls. David motioned for her to come and eat. And while Natalie ministered to the little girl, David rose and went in to the bedroom to help his friend and neighbor prepare his wife's body for burial.

&

"LELE! LELE!" NATALIE SLIPPED INTO A PAIR OF FLIP-FLOPS AND hurried down the steps of the *utta*. Somehow the little scamp had escaped again, and heaven only knew where she might have wandered off to this time. Keeping track of the little roamer was like trying to corral mosquitoes.

David had gone to the clinic to make copies on the printer. She thought she heard the low drone of the generator in the distance, powering the old copy machine someone had donated long before she arrived in Timoné.

She wouldn't enlist David's help yet. He would only tell her that it was impossible to tame a wild animal. He didn't mean it as an insult, only a metaphor, but she happened to disagree with him. She was determined to train Lele to stay near the *utta* and get permission before she ventured off their property.

She scoffed at the word. No one really owned "property" in Timoné—at least not where the land itself was concerned. One might claim the hut he built and the belongings he collected inside, but unless you put up a fence, which few did, another family's yard—even the space beneath their house—was common property where children might play or teenagers gather. Some had built enclosures under their *uttas* to house livestock or chickens, or like her and David, a place to hang laundry.

She passed a group of women coming from the river with laundry baskets on their shoulders. As soon as they saw her, they began to whisper among themselves. Natalie didn't have to guess what they were saying. She understood enough to know that they made fun of her because she tried to tame a little girl who'd been given the run of the village her entire life. They thought her foolish to even try to reform Lele.

For the first time, she wondered how she would be judged for the way she chose to raise her own child, for some of her and David's methods would surely be different than the manner in which Timoné children were brought up.

Hearing the women giggle and talk among themselves, an overwhelming sense of loneliness engulfed her. Though she was older, Meena had been the closest thing Natalie had to a friend here, and now she was gone. Mom and her sisters were thousands of miles and an ocean away, and she didn't know when she'd next get to see Meghan—probably not until the baby came. If then.

She called Lele's name again, but it came out in a sob. Unbidden tears coursed down her cheeks.

"Hey! Are you looking for Lele?"

David's voice behind her made her stop and turn. She brushed away the tears, pretending to smooth her hair behind her ears. "Yes." It came out wobbly and she worked to steady her voice. "Have you seen her?"

"Not since I left the house. She'll be fine, Nattie." He rarely used her childhood nickname and somehow today, the way he said it, broke her.

He came closer and studied her, looking alarmed. "Are you... crying? What's wrong, *mi carru?*"

She attempted a smile. "I'm fine. Probably just hormones."

He put an arm around her shoulder and walked on with her. "So, let me get this straight. You were just out here walking, searching for Lele and out of nowhere the waterworks start? Is that how these hormones work?"

He was teasing, trying to cheer her up, but his words had the opposite effect, and she burst into sobs, crumpling against him.

"Love?" He stopped in the middle of the trail and turned her toward him, tipping her chin up, forcing her to meet his gaze. "What's wrong?"

"Everything!" she wailed. "I can't find Lele, I miss Meena, I miss my mom and my sisters. The women in the village make fun of me, I don't have *any* friends, and—"

"Hey, hey... Am I not your friend?"

"You don't count."

"Well, *ouch*."

"You know what I mean."

"You mean because you can't talk about recipes and decorating and girlie things with me?"

"Kind of." She had to admit, already feeling a bit better. "I'm sorry, David. I'm just being a baby."

"You're just *having* a baby." He pulled her into his arms.

"I'm just a little lonely." She buried her face in his strong chest and tears threatened again. "And I'm starting to wonder if our baby will be shunned the way I am. And Lele too. I don't know if it's because of Gabrielle or if it's the way she looks."

"It's something we'll have to consider. Maybe our baby can be friends with Lele."

"The Island of Misfit Toys?"

He ruffled her hair. "Something like that."

"David, don't you find it odd that people welcomed my dad—and you—with open arms, yet Gabrielle and Lele are almost outcasts. And yet people loved Jamos and Meena."

"They did until Gabrielle shamed them by having an out-of-wedlock child. It didn't help matters when they gave their hearts to Jesus. Suspicion crept in after that. And the reason people accepted your dad is because he came as a doctor. And he did try to fit in—at least to live as simply—but he also didn't pretend to be one of them."

"Yes, but you haven't done that and still they love you."

"They love you, too, Natalie. They just have you...set apart in their minds. You're the teacher. My wife. That makes you different. Once you get better with the language, and once we start up school again, you'll make friends. Maybe we can be more intentional about having some of the younger families over to share meals? Get to know people more one-on-one—or two-on-four, or whatever it might be?"

She shrugged. "Maybe. I kind of have my hands full with Lele right now. And speaking of which..." She spun a three-sixty, searching the path each direction. "Where is that girl?"

"Hey..." He pulled her close again, his tone gentle. "Let her be for today. She knows this village like the back of her hand. She'll come back when she gets hungry."

She blew out a weighted breath. "What are we going to do, David?"

"About Lele?"

She nodded. "Jamos will go looking for Gabrielle again, and I won't let him take Lele with him! It's too dangerous."

"You don't have a say in that, love. I'm sorry, but she's not ours." He cleared his throat. "Maybe it's time she went back to Jamos."

"No!" It came out too harshly. "Not if he's going to traipse all over the jungle looking for Gabrielle. Please, David, would you tell Jamos to leave Lele with us if he goes?"

He sighed. "I don't think it's good for her to go back and forth between us. He needs to step up and take responsibility."

"But don't you see that's what he's doing with Gabrielle? You can't blame him for making his own daughter his first priority. For wanting to find her and bring her back."

"I guess you have a point there. I wish she was more worthy of his dedication."

Natalie conceded with a nod. They couldn't be sure, but given that nothing else had disappeared since Gabrielle ran off, they both agreed that she likely was the thief who'd stolen from their *utta*, the *oficina misión*, and even from her own parents. Had Jamos and Meena suspected that their daughter was the village thief?

Whether Gabrielle was selling the items, pilfering them for the soldiers, or just found them pretty and wanted them for her own purposes, they'd likely never know. But at least the thievery had stopped. It was one less thing to worry about.

He shook his head and sighed again. "I don't know what the answer is."

"If Jamos does go after Gabrielle, it would be less traumatic for Lele to stay with us rather than him trying to take her with him into dangerous territory." She waited for David's response, feeling like she was on the verge of winning him over, yet not sure she wanted to. As much as she loved Lele, she was a handful.

Natalie sighed. She wasn't looking at things clearly, exhausted as she was with her pregnancy and all they'd been through nursing Meena to the end.

"We'll pray about it," David said finally. "Now come home, and let's fix something to eat so it'll be ready when Lele decides to come back."

$ 13 $

"Lele! Get in the house this minute!"

David's voice boomed from above her and Natalie smiled, remembering how six weeks ago he'd been the one saying, "She'll come back when she's hungry."

Now he worried about the little girl almost as much as she did.

For once, she was thankful to be up to her elbows in soapy water in the space under the screened porch that she'd started calling the "laundry room."

Through a thick clump of ferns, she spotted Lele trudging up the trail, muttering to herself. At least she was obeying David, even if she was in no hurry to do so.

Jamos had been gone almost four weeks now, determined to find his daughter and bring her home. Natalie was beginning to fear something might have happened to him. Lele had stayed with them nearly every night since Meena's death almost two months ago. Even when Jamos was here, Lele had started sleeping on David and Natalie's screened porch on the little pallet of quilts they'd set up for her.

It had been a difficult few weeks, but finally they'd found their rhythm, and Lele had adjusted to life under far more constraints than she'd been accustomed to in her short life. Even if she did still chafe at her loss of freedom.

Lele climbed the stairs to the *utta*, still muttering, and Natalie hid from sight behind the trunk of a coconut palm. She hadn't realized how quickly the child was growing until she'd gone to get clothes for Lele from Jamos's house and found that even her loose, shapeless tunics were tight and much too short on the growing girl.

She'd asked Jamos for Meena's clothes and had cut them down and fashioned several cotton tunics for Lele like those most of the Timoné women and girls wore. Some of the villagers had begun to adopt more Western ways of dressing and were especially fond of T-shirts. Unfortunately, those purchased in souvenir kiosks in Conzalez often bore inappropriate sayings. Of course, most were written in English the Timoné couldn't read, so she and David tried to ignore the "billboards."

With one exception. David had reluctantly informed Tados about a particularly vulgar slogan on his assistant's shirt. "I figured since he works with words and is learning a little English, it might save him some embarrassment," David had told her. "Especially since he claims the name of Christ too."

Although the two T-shirts Lele owned didn't have any writing on them, Natalie had thought to relegate them to the rag bag. But they were so faded, torn, and stained that she ultimately put them on the burn heap. Probably just as well since, knowing Lele, she might have tried to retrieve them from the rag bag.

When she heard the *utta* door latch and Lele moving around inside, Natalie finished wringing out two of the little tunics and hung them on the line to dry. She'd wanted so badly to sew colorful feminine dresses with buttons and collars, but that would only have set Lele further apart from her peers than she already was. As Natalie's own wardrobe likely did for her.

She tugged at her own khaki-colored cotton shirt and realized she would need to get herself some new clothes as well. Or maybe take to wearing David's T-shirts. For the first time, she wondered if this baby would grow up in baggy cotton tunics, running barefoot through the winding village streets. She couldn't quite name her own feelings when she pictured such a thing, but she understood David's reservations better now.

"Did you understand what I said, Lele?" David's patient voice carried down through the floor of the *utta*.

"*Sí*, Mr. David. *Mi pakuko.*"

An apology? That was new. Maybe they were finally getting through. Smiling, Natalie took her time finishing the laundry, relishing the conversation overhead and her husband's tender, yet firm way with Lele.

"You are forgiven. Lesson learned?"

Natalie could just picture the solemn nod. Lele wanted to please.

"Now, come outside. I have something to show you."

Lele's little bare feet followed David down the steps. Natalie watched from her hiding place as David took Lele's hand and scuffed the ground with the toe of his tennis shoe.

"Ah, here we go." He bent and picked up a fallen branch. Breaking off two pieces the length of his hand, he handed one to her and kept the other. "Has Miss Natalie showed you how to play Pooh Sticks?"

Natalie's heart swelled, remembering. She'd been so surprised to learn that David had gone his whole childhood never playing Pooh Sticks. He'd found her playing the game with Manuel and Chago and some of the other children on the little footbridge that spanned the stream. They were constantly having to repair the rustic bridge, mostly because the rain washed it out, but in no small part because the children had turned it into a playground.

That day, she'd teased him about not knowing what Pooh Sticks were, and David had confided, "I didn't grow up like you did, Natalie. My parents were too busy with work and their social clubs to play games with me." Much later in their relationship, he'd told her he thought that was the day he'd begun to fall in love with her.

Still smiling, she watched as he knelt in front of Lele explaining that the twigs were like little boats. Racing boats.

"Look closely at your boat so you would recognize it if you lost it."

Lele complied, turning the twig over and over in her chubby palm.

"Okay, now give it to me."

She handed the twig to him and David took it in his right hand, then hid them both behind his back. From her vantage point, Natalie could see him switch Lele's stick to the other hand.

He held them both out to her again. "Now, do you know which one is yours?"

Without hesitating, she nabbed the stick from his left hand.

"Good girl! That's it."

"Okay, come with me to the footbridge and I'll show you how it's played. Don't forget which one is yours."

"I *know* which one is mine, Mr. David!"

"Good girl." He tousled her hair.

She ducked from under his hand and ran ahead of him, their playful exchange fading with the distance.

Natalie smiled, her heart full. He was going to be the best father.

Instinctively, she cradled her growing belly with her right hand. Assuming she had her dates right, she was now more than halfway through her pregnancy. The morning sickness was mostly gone and her energy had returned. She rather liked being pregnant, though no doubt she'd feel differently once the growing baby caused her to waddle like a goose.

"*Hollio!*"

She started at the masculine greeting, trying to place it, knowing it was familiar.

Not until she heard Lele's joyful cry and hurried footsteps

and then David's greeting in return, did she recognize it as Jamos's voice.

She peered out from her hiding place, looking past Jamos, expecting to see Gabrielle come up the trail behind him. But Jamos was alone, his hunched shoulders hinting at how his search had gone.

Lele ran to him. "Abuelo!"

He lifted her into his arms. "*Hollio*, little one. Have you behaved?"

"She's—"

"I obey." Lele interrupted David. "Most of the time."

The two men embraced, laughing softly.

"That sounds true," Jamos said, still chuckling.

Natalie was beginning to feel like an eavesdropper, so she picked up the empty laundry basket and came out from beneath the *utta* and walked toward them. "Hollio, Jamos."

He gave a nod of his chin.

"How was your...journey?" David asked.

Jamos shook his head, frowning. "Not successful. I must go back."

"How will you ever find...what you're looking for? It's a big country, my friend. How do you even know where to search?" David spoke ambiguously for Lele's sake.

Lele hugged her abuelo tighter and shot a look in Natalie's direction. Defiance?

The poor girl. She couldn't possibly understand why so many people vied for her obedience, and the ones who *should* have commanded it hadn't. Or were gone. Still, she couldn't blame Jamos. The deep creases in his forehead spoke to the profound grief he still carried. For Meena, but also for Gabrielle.

"I need to speak with you, David." Jamos slid Lele to the ground beside him. "Alone."

David caught her eye and she read his thoughts. "Lele and I will go fix some supper. Come whenever you're ready. Jamos, please share the meal with us?"

"I will. *Egracita*."

Lele wrapped her arms around Jamos's leg and clung to him.

He pulled her arms away. "You go with Miss Natalie. I will sit by you at supper."

That seemed to pacify her and she followed Natalie back to the *utta*.

Natalie strained to hear the men's conversation, but Jamos kept his voice low and soon the sounds of the jungle drowned their conversation out altogether.

ॐ

"I MET A MAN WHO TOLD ME WHERE TO FIND HER," JAMOS said without preamble, as soon as Natalie and Lele were out of earshot.

"How did he know?" David tried to keep skepticism from his voice, but the defensiveness in Jamos's expression said he'd been unsuccessful.

"I've put out word that I am desperate to find her. At any cost, one father will help another find his daughter."

"Do you believe Gabrielle wants to be found?"

The man's jaw tensed and he steeled his gaze. "It doesn't matter what she wants."

"Jamos... These are dangerous men you are dealing with and—"

"*I* am a dangerous man when they have my daughter," he shouted. He looked past David as if aware his voice might have carried to Lele, but she and Natalie were already inside the *utta*, their high voices carried on the evening breeze.

He tried another tack. "They have weapons and there are many of them. They help each other. You won't stand against their might, friend."

"They are not the only ones who can command an army."

He shook his head. "I don't understand."

"A reward speaks louder than an army."

"You have means to offer a reward?" Jamos and Meena had never lacked for food or clothing, but like most of the Timoné, they lived simply. A few dozen chicken eggs held no bargaining power and he couldn't imagine what else the man might have to offer as reward—or how he would get the word out.

"Not all of value is material."

David cocked his head, not following. "I understand you want your daughter back, but friend, if she doesn't *want* to come back, a reward of any size is worthless. I wish I could help, but—"

"You can help. That is why I am here. To ask your help. But I must leave tonight. It's not safe for me here."

"What do you mean?"

"The *brihacho* my daughter ran off with knows I am looking for her. He is determined to keep me from finding her."

David shook his head. "What have you done? This could put the entire village at risk, my friend."

Jamos stared up at him, his expression enigmatic.

David forced his voice down a notch. "I know you love your daughter, Jamos. I commend you for that. But she is a grown woman. She left of her own accord. She has a husband now."

"*If* he married her, he is a poor excuse for a husband. I don't think for a minute that he did." Jamos stood with his feet apart, arms akimbo.

"Even so, if you insist on continuing to search for her, you must not involve the village. If you're going to challenge an entire army, then take your fight elsewhere. And be sure they know that you are *not* to be found here." His own bravado surprised him. Who did he think he was, challenging this native man? He had no authority in Timoné, even though some seemed to afford him that very thing. But he would use it now because he was right: Jamos was putting the village in danger, putting Natalie and the baby, and especially his granddaughter at risk with his misguided intentions.

Jamos stared him down for a long minute, then his expression hardened, as if he'd suddenly found a new resolve.

What he saw in Jamos's countenance made him wonder what had happened to his gentle friend.

A long minute passed before the man spoke again. "I will leave, as I said. But you must promise to be a papá to Lele. She respects you. And your wife is good to her. Miss Natalie was a true friend to my Meena. Please say you will take Lele. Until I bring Gabrielle back. Then we will see."

"We will take her." He spoke the words without hesitation. Though he had a sense he was making a commitment with profound import. Truth was, they'd practically adopted Lele already. At least it seemed that way. And as difficult and cantankerous as the little girl could be, he all of a sudden knew he couldn't have loved her any more if she were his flesh and blood.

Jamos raised his right hand to his forehead in a salute. The gesture was not one familiar to the Timoné, except what they may have witnessed when the guerrilla soldiers invaded the village. What had his friend gotten mixed up in?

David responded with a hand over his heart, the Timoné equivalent of a handshake. He fully understood what he had just, in essence, sworn to: responsibility for Lele until he gave her to another man in marriage.

He supposed he should have at least discussed it with Natalie. And yet he was so sure of her response that there had been no need, no hesitation.

Even so, he knew that their lives—and Lele's too—had just shifted irrevocably.

With a curt nod, Jamos took a step back. "I will go now. If I find her, I will bring her back. If I do not return, you will know that I am still looking. Or I have lost my life in the hunt."

"I will pray."

"If I have not returned in one moon, my *utta* belongs to you. The chickens are still laying?"

"Yes, we've enjoyed the eggs."

"They are yours as long as they come and the chickens too. And one day it will all belong to Lele." It sounded too final. As if Jamos did not believe he would return.

"I will pray," David said again, a lump rising in his throat. "That God will help you find your daughter and that he will give you both wisdom. Be safe, my friend."

Jamos shook his head. "If it was safety I sought, there would be no use in me going."

David knew him well enough to know that was true, and it said much about the man. "Then may God go with you."

"Pray that our God will walk beside me when I step into trouble. And when the time is right, tell Lele that if she was lost, I would come after her with my very life as well." With a final nod, Jamos turned and strode toward the river.

David stood watching until he disappeared from sight. His friend's sobering words moved him, and slowly, the realization came: Jamos had left a little "lamb" behind to go and find the one that was lost. At the same time, Timoné had lost another of its believers, and the village had few to spare.

"Use him, Lord. Guide him and keep him faithful. Keep him from danger."

He only hoped danger hadn't already followed Jamos to Timoné.

 ❦   14   ❦

Natalie hoisted her backpack onto one shoulder and nudged Lele in the direction of Jamos's *utta*. The village streets were quiet this October morning, and even though the skies were clear for now, something seemed off. As if a storm was approaching. She couldn't quite put her finger on it.

Probably just her own emotions. Their baby would be here in a few short weeks—maybe sooner—and she wasn't prepared. Not for the birth and not for this trip to Conzalez where she and Lele would stay until the baby arrived.

David would stay at Hank and Meghan's with them for a few days until she could see a doctor and hopefully get a better idea of her actual due date. But unless the doctor thought the birth was imminent, he would return to Timoné to work until she called to tell him she was in labor. She couldn't even let herself think about what she would do if she couldn't reach him on the sat phone.

As it was, by the time he could make the day-long journey again, there was a chance he would miss his baby's birth. Natalie frowned. Those concerns were probably what made her feel so unsettled. That and the fact that she'd waited until the last minute to pack for Lele, only to discover that the girl had only one set of clothes that was suitable for the more "civilized" lifestyle in Conzalez. Yes, they could shop for new clothing after they arrived, but she didn't want to feel pressured to do that the minute they arrived.

She'd intended to get the rest of Lele's belongings from Jamos's *utta* long before now, but it wasn't until she started packing this morning that she realized they only had one pair of flimsy flip-flops that fit this child who went barefoot ninety percent of the time.

Integrating Lele into their family had taken every last ounce of energy she had, and while she loved the little girl with everything in her and was so grateful David had said yes to Jamos, she also withheld a tiny piece of her heart from Lele. Because it was still possible that Jamos might return to Timoné—with or without Gabrielle—and then Lele would leave their *utta* and go back to the home she'd been born into. But without Meena to guide her into womanhood.

Natalie thought she understood now how Hank and Meghan must feel about the children they had fostered in Conzalez— loving them wholeheartedly even while they were forced to hold them with an open hand. The Middletons had recently sent two brothers back to live with their birthparents, so didn't currently have children in their home—the reason it worked for her and Lele to stay with them until the baby came.

"It'll be good to have your little family here, Natalie," Meg had told her when they'd confirmed arrangements on the phone last night. "Something fun to take our minds off of how much we miss Teo and Matthias."

She'd heard the tremor in Meg's voice and was eager to talk to her about the boys and all the emotions her and David's tenuous "adoption" of Lele had brought to the fore.

If all went well, they'd be in Conzalez before darkness fell. Though they'd be travel-weary and there likely wouldn't be time tonight for more than greetings and a light supper before they put Lele to bed and slept themselves.

But she and Lele would be in Conzalez for a month, maybe more, depending on how accurate her dates were so there would be plenty of time to catch up.

After wavering between going back to the States or going to Bogotá for the baby's birth, she and David had finally compromised on staying with the Middletons. Meghan knew and recommended the obstetrician who worked in the tiny hospital there, and she and Hank had volunteered to care for Lele while Natalie was in the hospital.

As much as she longed to settle in with their baby in their own *utta* here in Timoné, she was grateful she'd have a friend to confide in and a professional nurse to help her adjust to the baby after they came home from the hospital.

Mom and Daddy had been disappointed they weren't coming back to Kansas, but they admitted it was probably the best plan, given the complications Lele added to the equation. "I guess we'll just have to come to Timoné to meet our new grandbaby— both of them," Mom had declared when they called to break the news.

And while it warmed her heart to hear Mom claim Lele as family, it was just one more reason she dared not let her heart grow too attached.

She quickened her steps, but when they neared Jamos's *utta*, Lele stopped in the middle of the trail and looked up at Natalie, her tiny brow furrowed. "Who will gather the eggs while we are gone?"

"Don't worry, Tados has promised to take good care of your chickens. Come now, we need to make this quick. Mr. David wants to beat the afternoon rains."

They reached the *utta* a minute later and she hurried up the steps with Lele trailing her. Though they went by Jamos and Meena's *utta* every day on the way to school to care for the chickens and gather the eggs, Lele had only gone inside once since Meena's death. Natalie hesitated to bring her this morning, but she needed Lele's help finding sturdier shoes, and something to serve as a jacket. It could get chilly on the water.

Waiting for her eyes to adjust to the dim light of the *utta*, she let the backpack slide from her shoulder and knelt to speak to Lele. "We need shoes and a jacket—something warm. Do you remember where they would be?"

Lele shook her head, but her gaze was trained on the doorway to the bedroom where Meena had spent her last days. "Do you want to go see?"

Lele nodded and ran eagerly to the room as if she expected to see Meena in the bed.

What had she been thinking? Natalie closed her eyes, bracing for Lele's reaction.

But when she entered the room, Lele was smiling broadly. "Abbé was so happy that day!"

"What day, sweetie?"

"The day Jesus came to get her."

"She *was* happy, wasn't she? She knew she was going to heaven."

Lele nodded solemnly. "We weren't ready to let her go, but she wasn't happy when she was sick. So we had to let her go because she was ready to be with God."

"Who told you that, Lele?" While they'd told her that Abbé was in heaven, they'd never worded it that Jesus came for her, for fear Lele would fear someone might 'come to get' *her* or her abuelo."

"Abuelo. After Jesus came to get Abbé, there was still a smile left on her body."

"I remember." Natalie smiled, picturing Meena's peaceful countenance in death, and grateful all over again that they'd allowed Lele to be with her till the end. What peace it had given her.

"We can come back again sometime if you like. But for now,

Mr. David is waiting and we need to find your things and get home to finish packing for our trip."

"My other shoes are in the kitchen but I don't like them. They hurt my feet."

"I know, but you might need them if we have to walk on rocks."

"But I—"

"Don't argue with me, Lele. Go get the shoes. I'll see if I can find a *jacket*." She used the English word, forgetting the Timoné word for a seldom-worn item.

Lele made a goofy face. "I don't have a *jacket*."

Natalie ran a hand up and down her own arm and made the motion of putting on a jacket. "Something to keep you warm."

"*Mantal?*"

"A *mantal?*" But a blanket might have to do. "Do you have a *mantal* you *wear?* With sleeves? Jacket?" She made the motion again.

Lele looked confused.

Natalie laughed. "Okay. You go get your shoes. I'll see what I can find in the loft."

Natalie climbed to the tiny loft where she'd slept with Lele during those days Meena was ill. It seemed like such a long time ago. The wooden crate where Lele's clothes had been was empty except for a wrinkled, much-too-small tunic. The homemade cornhusk mattress crinkled under her knees and she pulled up one corner thinking some clothing might have been forgotten underneath the mattress. The seam was torn open on one end of the mattress and a few strips of cornhusk poked out the opening. She stuffed them back in and made a note to bring a needle and thread when they got back from Conzalez.

She started to climb down, but something caught a glint of sunlight. Natalie lifted the mattress further. She stopped, not certain what she was seeing...

And then it all became clear.

She lifted a three-foot-long chain made of paper clips—the large, colored metallic kind David used to mark his word lists. The kind he'd accused her of "borrowing" since his were nearly gone.

Woven between the wire of each paper clip were colorful strips of folded paper—sticky notes. Strung through each sticky note "bead" was a strip of dried corn husk, each decorated with a geometric pattern made with colored markers. The chain mimicked a bright Hawaiian lei. The end of the chain was attached to a familiar and long-missing emery board that bore a design similar to the pattern drawn on the corn husks.

Natalie stared at the creation, her mind reeling. It was a work of art, no question about that. Nor about where the materials to create it had come from.

She lifted the mattress with both hands and shook it, but the floor beneath was empty except for dust bunnies and a few shriveled corn husks. "Lele? Come here, *kopaku*."

Footsteps pattered beneath the loft. "I found my shoes, but they hurt my toes!"

Natalie peeked over the edge.

Lele held up a pair of plastic, closed-toe sandals.

Ignoring the offending shoes, Natalie lifted the chain and dangled it over the side of the loft. "Lele?"

Her eyes went wide. "You found it! No! You weren't supposed to see."

"Did your mamá make this?"

"No! Not Mamá. *I* made it!" Indignation painted her tone. "I made it for you. But it's not done yet. You were not supposed to see it. It was a *sorpressia*. For you!" Her face crumpled and tears sprang to her hazel eyes.

"*You* made this? Lele?"

Her tawny head bobbed up and down and her chest puffed out.

"Did Gabrielle—your mamá—help you?" She could hardly believe Lele capable of this work of art, yet the little girl's obvious pride said otherwise.

Lele's tears turned to anger. "No! I made it all by myself. Nobody helped me!"

"Where did you get the things you used to make it?"

Lele hung her head. "It...it was long ago. When I was a baby."

"Lele, look at me." She held up the chain. "Did you take these things from Mr. David's office?"

She nodded somberly. "And yours. But I was just little. I didn't know any better."

"Lele..."

"I wanted to make it for you. To hang in the wind. To make music."

"Ah...wind chimes." She made a tinkling motion with her fingers.

Lele nodded, then her mouth drooped in a frown. "But it didn't work. No music."

A thought came. "Did Mr. David know you were making it?" Maybe he was in on the surprise.

"No. It was a *sorpressia* for him too."

She frowned. "We'll have to talk about this...*surprise* later, Lele. With Mr. David." She coiled the colorful chain and placed it on the mattress. There were too many more urgent things on David's mind today. This would have to wait.

Maneuvering her awkward body over the edge of the loft, she started to climb down.

"No! Don't leave it. It's for you. I made it for you!"

She climbed back up one rung and retrieved the "wind chime." How on earth should they handle this? The sweet girl was so pleased with herself and so excited about the *sorpressia*...

But they couldn't let her get away with stealing. How had the little squirt gotten into their house anyway? And presumably, into the mission office as well? Of course, Lele shadowed them every chance she got. She probably hadn't broken into anything. She'd simply followed them inside and explored the house while they were otherwise occupied.

Retrieving her backpack from beside the door, she opened it for Lele to drop the shoes into, then she carefully placed the coiled chain of paper clips and corn husks into an outside pocket.

"Hurry up, sweet girl. Mr. David will be wondering where we are."

Horologium:
The Clock

15

"How much longer?" Natalie shouted over the barrage of rain pelting the tattered Bimini top of the eighteen-foot pontoon boat.

"Less than an hour now," David shouted from the helm.

She pulled Lele close to her on the bench seat, but the flimsy canvas canopy over their heads offered little protection from the sideways rain. They'd been on the river for almost three hours now and only an hour into the trip, an angry wall of clouds had moved in, veiling the sun. The waters of the Rio Guaviare roiled against its banks and even though the heavy rains were normal for early October, being on the water made the storm feel treacherous.

Every time she and David got on the river, she remembered taking this same trip to Conzalez when she was twenty-two and Dad had forced her to return home to Kansas, fearing for her safety after a band of guerrilla soldiers raided the village and stole computers and other supplies.

David had been the one to go with her in the boat to Conzalez, and the trip had been a turning point in her life—not only because it was when she first knew for certain that she'd been called by God to serve in Timoné, but also because it was when she first knew beyond doubt that she'd been forgiven for the accident that killed Sara. She could never change what happened with her precious friend, but David had helped her see that, like Sara's family, God had forgiven her and given her purpose in life and a reason to live.

She hadn't known it at the time, but she'd had malaria—probably even before she left Timoné. She'd nearly died, but by the time she recovered in Conzalez, she also knew for certain that she was in love with David Chambers.

She regarded him now, piloting the pontoon through waters as dark as the jungle on either side, his senses on alert to any dangers. The responsibility he bore for her and Lele—and even for the borrowed boat—lay heavy on his shoulders and the tension in his jaw showed it.

Twenty minutes later, the rain stopped, and without warning, David throttled down and turned the craft toward shore. Natalie pulled the thin blanket over a napping Lele's shoulders and slid toward the bow, closer to David.

"Is something wrong?"

"I think we're going to wait out the weather for a few minutes." He cut the engine and let the vessel drift under the overhanging trees into a murky inlet.

"But the rain stopped." She peered over the side of the boat, then into the branches overhead. "And this looks like a good place for crocodiles and snakes to me."

"Hand me the sat phone, will you, love?"

"David? Is everything okay?"

He studied her as if deciding whether to answer. "I thought I saw some...activity on the opposite bank. It's probably nothing, but thought it might be best not to draw any unwanted attention. Just in case."

She took in a shallow breath and squinted, looking across to the other side. A mist hung over the water and across the river, the barest breeze rustled the vegetation. In the undulating movements, her imagination conjured every possible danger—

snakes, spiders, guerrilla soldiers, drug gangs, even a jaguar slinked along the water's edge. She shivered. "I'll get the phone."

"Try not to wake her up." David nodded toward Lele.

Now *her* senses were on high alert. She climbed back to where Lele slept on the bench seat and ferreted the sat phone bag from a storage compartment under the seat. Staying low, she crept back to David.

He took the phone from her and eased into the captain's seat. "I'm going to let Hank know we might be a little later than expected."

She nodded, fastening her eyes on the opposite bank.

David kept his voice low, but she could sense the relief in his demeanor when Hank answered. "Hey, friend. We're about thirty-five minutes out but laying low in an inlet for a few minutes. It may not be anything, but I thought maybe I saw...a small group single-file on the west bank. You don't have any intel, do you?"

He listened for a minute, but his face showed no emotion and Natalie couldn't make out Hank's end of the conversation.

Finally, David started nodding. "Okay... Yes, that sounds like a plan... No problem. We can do that. See you in a little while."

Natalie released a breath she hadn't realized she'd been holding. "What'd he say?"

"He didn't know of any issues, but he's having us dock about a mile from the compound and walk in." He gave a hint of a smile and eyed her belly. "You up for that?"

"I am. I'm not sure about Lele."

"She can sit on my backpack. Hank's going to meet us with the Jeep so it won't be more than a mile. We'll come back for anything we can't carry in the morning."

"If it's still here."

"It's a chance we'll have to take. There's nothing we can't replace in Conzalez."

"Yeah, except the boat." She finger-combed her hair. "I wish I didn't look like a drowned rat."

He waved her off. "You look fine. Maybe we'll come across a beauty salon on the trail."

"Haha. Very funny."

"Hank told me a better place to moor, but we're going to go in slow." He started the engine and waited, letting it idle for a few minutes before expertly steering back into the river's current.

He motioned toward the stern. "In about ten minutes you can wake up Sleeping Beauty and get her shoes on. If we walk about a mile, Hank can get the Jeep in to pick us up."

She nodded and unzipped Lele's stuffed tote bag. They'd ended up cutting out the toes of the little plastic shoes in order to make them fit. But the soles were sturdy and would protect little feet from thorns and critters on the trail.

David's gaze roved from shore to shore and back again as they trolled close to the nearest bank. The sun peeked through thick cumulus clouds at intervals, but the air remained thick and muggy. Thankfully, the mosquitoes mostly left them alone.

"I think this is it," he finally said, aiming the nose of the pontoon into the inlet. "Get Lele ready. Do you have on good walking shoes?"

She held up a sneakered foot in reply.

"We'll carry everything we comfortably can, but leave anything you don't need tonight. It'll be safer in the boat than having to abandon it on the trail." He pointed to the locked storage under one seat. "Secure everything we can fit under here. I'll tie up."

"Be careful, babe."

"Believe me, I'm not looking to have a run-in with a croc today."

After rousing Lele, Natalie gathered her backpack and the girl's tote and stuffed them with everything she could fit inside and still get the zippers closed. "Hurry up, sweetie. We're almost there. You need to get your shoes on."

She held out the little shoes, but Lele batted them away. "I can go barefoot."

"No. You need shoes here. There might be thorns or scorpions on the trail."

"I don't care. I can't walk good in th—"

"Lele!"

The harshness in David's voice told Natalie he was more worried than he let on.

"Come on now," she whispered to Lele. "Do as Mr. David says." She splayed a hand on top of Lele's head. Heat radiated from her scalp beneath the tangled mop of damp sun-streaked hair.

With a sigh, Lele slid from the cracked vinyl seat and knelt on one knee to wiggle the first shoe onto her pudgy foot.

"Need help?"

"No." She rolled her eyes like a teenager. "Stupid shoes."

Natalie let it go. No use getting her worked up when they had a mile to walk still. She wasn't quite awake. She'd cheer up once there was something to explore.

David pocketed the boat keys, then they rolled up the Bimini top and replaced the cover. "Okay, ready?"

Natalie nodded and hitched her backpack higher on her shoulder. She collected the sat phone bag and Lele's tote bag. The baby turned a slow somersault within her. He'd been especially active today. *He.* She'd begun to think of the baby as a "he" though she would be every bit as thrilled if this turned out to be a little girl. Especially since Lele had become such a big part of their lives. Their baby would have a built in "sister" to play with. And maybe that would help David's adjustment to the idea.

"Here, I'll carry those." David took the phone bag and tote from her. "Lele, you carry this for a little bit, okay? Miss Natalie has enough heavy things to haul." He looked pointedly at her mid-section and placed the handles of the tote over Lele's arms and onto her shoulders like a backpack.

She took the bag without complaint, looking from David's backpack to Natalie's, obviously pleased to be "matching."

Though it was only about one p.m. and the sun was shining on the water, the shadows the trees cast near the banks of the Guaviare made it seem like dusk.

"Stay here, Lele. I'll be right back for you." David helped Natalie from the boat and through the tepid shallows to shore, then returned for Lele, carrying her through the water and up the bank to an overgrown trail that looked like it hadn't been traversed in a long time.

"You doing okay, Nat?" David eyed her with concern.

"I'm fine." She stretched, rubbing the small of her back. "The baby just decided this would be a good time for gymnastics practice."

He grinned. "Let me know if you need to stop and rest."

"I'm *fine*." She held out an open hand. "I can carry the phone if you want me to."

"That's okay. I've got it."

"Hey, Lele?" He called softly to where she'd skipped a few feet ahead in chase of a *colibrí*—a hummingbird—stopping to examine every leaf and stone on the path, singing all the while. He beckoned her closer. "Your song is beautiful, but we need to be very quiet while we walk, okay? Sing to yourself. And stay close to us, okay?"

She sighed, but nodded agreement and went back to skipping.

They followed the narrow, unmarked trail parallel to the river for ten minutes before the path widened into a rough road. David stopped and held his phone over his head, looking up at the screen. He shook his head. "I was hoping we'd have phone service by now."

"Let me check mine." They'd learned that even though they had the same international carrier, sometimes one of them had a better signal than the other. She sighed. "No bars either. Do you want to use the sat phone?"

He shook his head. "Hank said when the trail starts to widen, we're almost to the road...kind of a back way in. Let's try again when we get closer. He knows we're coming."

"Good, because I really have to pee." She grinned. "That's one thing I will not miss about being pregnant."

They walked for a few minutes and the road ended in a wide Y. "According to Hank we turn right here. But we have another fifteen or twenty minutes of walking before we're in civilization. Can you wait that long?"

"No way."

"Well, go ahead then. We'll wait. But stay close to the road. You don't want to meet that crocodile."

"You've got that right. Lele, do you need to go potty?"

The girl shook her head and hiked up her backpack on her shoulder, imitating David.

"Okay. Then you stay right beside Mr. David. I'll be back in a minute."

Lele wrinkled her nose. "You have to go *again?*"

"Cut it out!" Natalie gave her a playful swat.

Laughing, David hoisted Lele onto his shoulders—her favorite mode of transportation. "Now, you keep your head down. You don't want to smack it on a tree."

Natalie smiled as he galloped in a circle. Lele shrieked with glee, but David stopped the "horse" with a low *whoa* and shushed her.

Picking her way through the spongy forest floor, she found a wide tree to hide behind. She quickly took care of her needs, then gathered her backpack again and went to where David was waiting with Lele still astride his shoulders.

They walked on, the jungle's birds and frogs droning monotonously. Suddenly feeling incredibly alone in the vastness of the rainforest, she moved closer to David, falling in stride with him. The road wound through the trees and every time they came to a bend, she prayed Hank would be there waiting.

David seemed less concerned now that they'd gotten off the

water, yet he still warned them several times to keep quiet along the trail. She gave him a sidewise glance, trying to read his demeanor. She felt sure he hadn't told her everything Hank said on the phone, but there had to be a good reason their friend suggested they leave the boat and walk in to Conzalez. She'd be relieved when they were safely at Hank and Meghan's.

The frogs' screeching quieted and for a minute she thought she caught the distant rumble of a motor. She stopped to listen.

After a few steps, David did the same.

"Do you hear that?"

He listened. "I do." They'd only been walking for ten minutes. Maybe Hank's pickup spot was closer than David thought.

He quickened his steps and she hurried to keep up, but struggled on the rocky, rutted surface. Though this road was wider and less canopied than the trail, it was uneven and ever more winding.

They rounded another curve and the unmistakable sound of a truck engine came from their right, getting closer. She blew out a sigh of relief. "Finally. There's Hank."

David set Lele down beside him and shaded his eyes, watching in the direction of the sound.

"I see my *colibrí*!" Without warning, Lele darted across the road after a hummingbird like the one she'd chased earlier on the trail. "Lele! Get back here this minute!"

Natalie started after her, but David shed his backpack on the edge of the rocky surface and waved for her to stay. "I'll get her."

He sprinted across and grabbed Lele by the arm. Squatting beside her, he chided her quietly.

Natalie could barely hear his words over the growing noise of the approaching truck. She still couldn't see anything, but there was a sharp bend in the road to her left.

David rose with Lele in his arms. He looked both directions, renewed concern etching his forehead. He started to cross to where Natalie stood but stepped back quickly at the unmistakable revving of an engine.

The jungle fell silent, the roar of the engine the only sound. A black truck rounded the bend, coming fast. Straight toward her. He must not see them. She waved her arms and called Hank's name.

"No, Natalie! No! It's not Hank! Get off the road!" David motioned wildly, but there was a steep drop-off on her side, and there wasn't time to cross to the other side.

Brakes screeched and the back end of the truck fishtailed, creating a tornado of dust.

With Lele still in his arms, David raced across in front of the truck, his long legs pumping. He called her name loud, panic in his voice.

She moved as close to the edge as she safely could, but the truck was almost upon her. The roar of the motor and tires crunching gravel drowned out David's voice. The cloud of dust was so thick now, she couldn't see David or Lele. She started to run, pictured herself diving and rolling down into the ravine. But with her vision obscured, she reeled and stopped, struggling to keep her balance, afraid she was already too close to the edge.

Sand and dirt pelted her, stinging like the bites of a swarm of black flies. She sucked in dirt and coughed, gasping for air.

"*¡Entra! ¡Ahora!*" a man shouted roughly.

Get in? What did they want?

"David!" She didn't have time to run, even if she could have seen her hand in front of her face. The dust morphed into a jumble of camouflage and muddy boots on the ground in front of her. She struggled for breath.

What was happening?

But she knew. She knew exactly what was happening.

Gunshots split the air in quick succession and men's voices shouted in rapid-fire Spanish, but the only word she understood was *¡Vamos! Hurry.*

"David!" She spewed out his name again in a fit of coughing.

A strong arm came around her neck and she felt herself being dragged, then lifted high by the straps of her backpack by a tangle of arms. Instinctively, she grabbed her belly and tried to curl into a ball, cradling the baby tightly as a heavy cloth fell over her face.

She flailed, scrabbling to get free, desperate to draw a breath so she could scream.

"Help! David! God, please!" The words were a mere squeak, and she clawed for air through a fog of confusion.

Then everything faded to black.

16

"Natalie!" David ran toward the truck, dodging deep ruts in the road, Lele heavy in his arms. But he couldn't risk putting her down.

A thick cloud of dust made it nearly impossible to see, so he kept running in the direction of Natalie's screams, praying with every step, yet unable to form those prayers into actual words. Gunfire sounded again and the engine revved louder, tires spinning on the rutted road, spraying them with a barrage of rocky shrapnel. For a minute he thought he'd been shot, and he spun away from the assault, protecting Lele with his body.

Mud plastered the windshield and he couldn't see inside the vehicle, but earlier, he'd spotted at least three men hunched down in the truck bed, their camouflage marking them as guerrilla soldiers—or a drug gang who'd bartered for uniforms. His blood ran cold.

The truck fishtailed again and headed directly toward him. He couldn't tell if the awful sound was the brakes screeching or Natalie's screams. He hoped to God the latter because at least that would mean she was alive.

The vehicle backed up to a wider spot in the trail, spun a tight circle, and roared off in the direction it had come. His breath came with effort and his mind reeled. Had they recognized that Natalie was pregnant? Did they think they could hold her for ransom? And why hadn't they taken Lele too? She was a more likely target for human trafficking. He pulled the little girl closer.

His thoughts ricocheted off of each other. Should he go back and get the boat? Try to cut them off at the next inlet? But with Lele in tow, he would lose too much precious time. And they were likely headed inland anyway, to Bogotá or to some secret compound farther north. "Oh, God, what do I do?"

Every instinct made him want to run after the truck, but there was no way he could catch them. And he'd be taking Lele into certain danger.

The dust settled around them and he gagged on a deep breath. He spit in the dirt and checked his cell phone again. Still no signal. *Please, God!*

He ran another twenty yards and checked again, then knelt in the road and set Lele down beside him. She whimpered pitifully and clung to him, tears leaving muddy trails on her cheeks. "Shhh... It'll be okay. Lele, it'll be okay." *Liar!*

He retrieved his backpack from the side of the road, dug out the sat phone, and dialed Hank. The call went straight to voicemail.

Time seemed interminable while he waited for the beep. "Hank, they took Natalie!" His voice broke and he swallowed hard, his heart pounding in his chest. "She's been...abducted. Guerrillas, I'm pretty sure. Four of them. Maybe five in...a Silverado. I think a late model. I'm not sure."

He forced himself to relive the attack. Details were crucial if they were to find her. "I think the truck was black, but maybe navy. But hard to say. It was caked with mud. The tags too. But there was so much dust..."

He picked up Lele again and rose, forcing himself to relive the horror of Natalie's screams. He *had* to remember. Her screams had been muffled after they carried her off. But he didn't think it was as if they'd put a gag in her mouth. More like she was on the floor of the truck bed. Or maybe inside the vehicle with the windows down?

"I couldn't see everything, but I think they threw her in the back of the truck. It had one of those extended cabs. But maybe they put her inside. It all happened so fast...and I couldn't see," he said again, frustration and fear colliding. "They headed north on the road you told us about. We're maybe half a mile from our rendezvous point. Please, Hank, if you get this, call the local authorities and alert them." His hopes circled the drain. Because in this part of the country, the guerrillas and paramilitary *were* the "local authorities."

His breaths came hard and he was starting to feel light-headed. "I have Lele and we'll get to the crossroads as fast as we can. I know the road is bad, but if you can get farther in and pick us up quicker... Please!"

No telling who might be listening so he was being purposely ambiguous about where they were and where they were headed. Hank would know what he meant.

He shifted Lele to his shoulders. It took everything in his power to run in the opposite direction from the truck, but he ran, pushed to the limits of his endurance, trying to comfort the little girl he carried while he thought of what to do next.

If they'd been looking for valuables, they would have stopped him too. Natalie had nothing of value on her, except her cell phone. That thought gave him a sliver of hope, but if they kept heading north with her, the chances of cell service diminished by the mile. He remembered how she'd offered to carry the sat phone when they got off the boat, and he mentally beat himself up for not allowing her to take it.

He had to get to Conzalez. Meet up with Hank and find the authorities there. He fought the temptation to turn around and go after the truck. But even if by some miracle, he could have caught up with them on foot, he had no money to speak of, nothing to bargain with, and no weapons. And they had them and weren't afraid to use them. He would not take Lele into that kind of danger.

But Natalie... *Oh, Nattie.* Why would they want her? Surely the minute they realized she was pregnant, about to give birth any day, they'd let her go. These men wouldn't want to be saddled with an imminent birth. A newborn. *His baby.*

"Oh, Lord, please," he whispered. "Be with her. With *them.*"

Why had he robbed Natalie of the joy of looking forward to this child? He was a fool—and now she was gone. If they'd kidnapped her thinking they could collect a ransom...

His heart sank. Gospel Linguists didn't pay ransom. It was policy. As difficult a decision as that was, paying even once would put every missionary and humanitarian worker in the country at risk—and their organization in particular.

Most mission organizations had the same policy. The guerrillas knew that, so why had Natalie been targeted? *If* indeed she had been targeted. But did they even know she was a missionary or had they mistaken her and David for some crazy overlanders traveling the jungle for a notch in their belt, a sticker on their map?

It had been made clear to him—and Natalie, given that she was the more vulnerable target—that kidnapping was a risk they faced when they'd answered the call to missions. They'd both accepted it as a risk they were willing to take. While kidnappings of missionaries were relatively rare, they did happen. In the past, some families had paid a ransom privately, which meant, unfortunately, that even missionaries could prove valuable to the gangs and factions that roamed Colombia.

But Natalie's pregnancy changed everything. They weren't sure of her exact due date, but Natalie believed it could be as soon as two or three weeks. They'd allowed for the possibility of being off on her dates or the baby coming early. He'd heard hushed rumors of women in some factions being forced to abort if they became pregnant. Surely that only went for women who were soldiers. Where did they go for that...procedure? Or would a baby be an asset? Chattel to sell to some millionaire who could buy a child as if it were a fancy car? His brain spun with possibilities, each more horrific than the last.

He ran on, praying desperately, keeping his eyes peeled for Hank's Jeep, his senses alert in case the soldiers came back for him and Lele.

He'd stopped long enough to adjust his backpack lower so Lele could ride on his back, using the pack for a seat. He didn't know what had happened to Lele's tote bag, but it was gone. She'd quieted, whether from sheer exhaustion or shock, he wasn't sure. But how much longer could he run with the weight he carried? He felt at the end of his endurance.

Right now he would have paid ransom for a bottle of water. They'd finished what they'd carried with them before Natalie was abducted. Was she thirsty now? It seemed she was always thirsty since she'd gotten pregnant. *Oh, Lord, be with her!*

He set out again, his muscles screaming for relief, sweat drenching his back where Lele pressed tight against him. A cloud of dust ahead of him—like the one the Silverado had kicked up—sent his heart into his throat. He carried Lele to the side of the road and slid down a shallow embankment, crouching in the shadow of a giant palm until he recognized Hank's Jeep. Relief flooded him and he scrambled up the embankment, willing himself not to collapse before he reached the truck.

Natalie sucked in a jagged breath, telling herself she was breathing for her baby. The putrid odor of the cloth over her head made her gag. Had she thrown up before she passed out? She couldn't see anything except tiny pinpricks of light through the tight weave of fabric.

How long she'd been unconscious, she wasn't sure, but every muscle ached in the contorted fetal position she'd been forced into on the gritty floor of the truck bed. Every bump in the road felt like a beating. "Please...please, help," she squeaked out.

But she couldn't seem to make them hear her over the roar of the engine. The deep voices above her on all sides blended into one. She tried desperately to isolate one voice, to get a clue of who they were and where they were taking her. They spoke the Castilian Spanish of most of Colombia. David would have understood them, been able to communicate with them, but she could only catch bits and pieces. Strangely, it sounded like they were talking about a farm and animals. It seemed to have nothing to do with her.

A rough hand came around her neck and she stilled, remembering the game of "playing possum" from her childhood. Whenever they'd come home late at night from a visit with Grandma and Grandpa Camfield in Kansas City, if she played possum, Daddy would carry her in from the car and tuck her in bed.

She felt them ransacking her backpack and prayed they wouldn't find her phone. Her heart pounded double time in her chest. This couldn't be good for her baby. Especially the abuse her body was taking from riding in the bed of the truck. Why wasn't the baby reacting to the violent ride? Shouldn't he be putting up a protest? Rolling away from the constant bumping motion? She willed her baby to move, to let her know he was okay.

"*Ella está viva*," a masculine voice above her declared.

She is alive. Had they thought she was dead before? Oh, that she could convince them she *was* dead. Then maybe they'd toss her by the side of the road. But if they'd nabbed her for the reasons she suspected, they obviously had need of keeping her alive.

Trembling, she reached up and grasped the hand on her throat. "Please... Help me."

The man laughed and said something about *dinámica*.

Dynamite? A dynamo? They couldn't be talking about her. She felt half dead. Her breath caught. They didn't have Lele, did they? No! Lele was still with David. She was sure of it. But the soldiers had guns and she'd heard gunshots fired. She wracked her brain to remember if she'd heard either of their voices after the shots were fired.

Her heart sank. She couldn't remember anything after the screech of brakes and being lifted into the truck's bed and shoved onto the floor.

She faded into possum mode again. Until the vehicle revved and bounced, then hit bottom hard. She groaned in pain. *God, please help me. Be with my baby. Please, Father, prompt them to let me go. Please, Jesus...*

Her thoughts muddled, she wasn't sure if she was praying aloud or crying out to God in her spirit, but she stormed heaven, begging God to have mercy on her. And most of all, on her baby.

17

The tinted window of the Jeep rolled down and Hank's concerned face appeared. "Get in! Get in!" He indicated the back driver's side door. "It's unlocked."

David opened the door and pushed Lele to the far side of the bench seat, then climbed in behind her, pulling the door shut hard. Once they were in, Hank took off as if they were being chased.

"What happened?" he asked, catching David's eye in the rearview mirror.

"You got my message?"

"Yes. They have Natalie? Did you see who it was?"

"Uniforms...guerrillas, I assume. Especially judging by the vehicle. Not sure who else could afford wheels like that."

"How many?"

"I don't know." He raked a hand through hair damp with sweat. "Maybe five, six? It all happened so fast."

"Okay. Okay, man. We'll find her."

Hank sounded as helpless as David felt.

"How? What do we do now? We've got to get her back!"

"Here..." Keeping his eyes on the twisting road, Hank handed back water bottles. "Is the little one okay?"

David opened a lukewarm bottle of water and gave it to Lele. She drank deeply, looking into his eyes the whole time.

He patted her knees. "She's traumatized—and thirsty—but she's not hurt."

"I'm so sorry, David." Hank's shoulders slumped and he hung over the steering wheel, looking like he might be sick. "It looks like I steered you straight into harm's way."

"You couldn't have known, man."

"No, but I feel responsible. In recent weeks, we've heard rumors about activity on the water. Warnings that something might be afoot. But nothing concrete. It seemed best for you not to come in on the water. I thought the road would be safer."

"You made a judgment call. You couldn't have known," he repeated. "Who have you told? About Natalie?"

"I alerted mission headquarters in the States, and local police I trust. But we've got to be careful who we talk to. As you know…"

He nodded. "So, what do we do now?"

Hank eyed David in the rearview mirror. "If they targeted Natalie, there'll be a ransom demand soon."

"And we don't pay ransom. I know that." David dropped his head in his hands. He'd never felt so helpless in his life. "I can't just sit around and do nothing, Hank."

"I know. I know… That's not going to happen." They'd entered the outskirts of Conzalez and Hank slowed the vehicle. "Meg's at home, waiting, in case a call comes in there. But if it is a…targeted abduction…it's more likely to be headquarters—in the States—that gets the call."

They were both tiptoeing around the word *kidnapping*. But in some ways—despite knowing that their sending organization would not—*could* not—pay ransom, kidnapping was the lesser of evils. If they'd abducted Natalie for trafficking, there would be no ransom demands.

"How was she feeling…before? No contractions yet?"

Hank's question jarred him. He shook his head. "No, but

what if the trauma makes her go into labor? I don't know how that all works..." And once Natalie's abductors discovered a baby was imminent, there would be a price on their baby's head. A healthy infant might be sold on the black market and—

His blood turned to ice. Had Natalie realized that possibility? She'd certainly pondered the prospect of kidnapping—it was an ever-present danger to any foreigners living in Colombia, but especially for Americans. And they'd talked about it during their missions training...

But he couldn't let his thoughts take him there. He had to think about what to do.

"She's strong, David." Hank's voice calmed his raging thoughts. "And God is with her. Don't forget that."

They drove in silence for a few minutes before the mission compound came into sight. David leaned forward from the back seat and took in the lay of the land. The windows to the house and office glowed from within, even though there were still a couple hours of daylight left, but the doors to the small Quonset hangar at the end of the small airstrip were closed and padlocked.

"Is there a plane here now?"

Hank frowned. "We're short on pilots right now, and the Cessna that was out there last time you were here is in the States for maintenance. Not sure when the next one might be coming in. We can put in a request. What are you thinking?"

His hopes sank. "I don't know. I thought maybe we could find the truck if we could get in the air."

But he knew better. Having flown over the area in a small Cessna 172, he was well aware the thick canopy of the rain forest was almost impossible to penetrate with binoculars, and there were few places to land even if they could, by chance, spy the truck that had been used in Natalie's abduction.

Hank shook his head and again eyed him in the mirror. "By the time we got a plane here, they'd be long gone. There's a protocol, David. We're doing everything that can be done."

"Well, I can't just sit here and wait! I have to *do* something!" His words exploded in the truck's cab, and Lele cowered in the corner of the seat, whimpering.

David pulled her close, forcing a calm he didn't feel. He spoke to her in the Timoné dialect. The poor girl likely couldn't understand half of what he and Hank were saying, and she no doubt imagined the worst. She must be terrified. "It's okay, Lele. I'm sorry. Everything is going to be all right. We're going to help Miss Natalie. I promise."

THE TRUCK SLOWED AND NATALIE FELT THEM TURNING TO THE left. She felt like she would throw up, even though she had nothing in her stomach to relinquish. She prayed the truck would stop.

Almost immediately, her prayer was answered. A hard brake and the engine cut out. She lifted her head, trying to see where they were, but only a few pinpoints of light penetrated the shroud. She tried to sit up, but crumpled back to the floor. "Please? I don't feel well. I'm going to be sick. Please!"

Rough hands yanked her upright and she cried out in pain.

The soldier gripping her shoulders shouted something she couldn't interpret.

From a distance, another man barked a reply in English with a thick accent. "Lift the hood. We've gone far enough."

At first, she thought they were talking about the hood of the truck, but when they uncovered her face and she saw the black hood in his hands, she realized he was talking about her. And that they'd gone far enough she wouldn't know how to get back. They were right about that. Nothing looked familiar and the sky was too hazy to tell which way the sun was setting.

She took in deep gulps of the humid air and blinked, trying to memorize faces and make out her surroundings in the dim light beneath the jungle canopy. "Please, I need to use the bathroom."

Two of the men leered at her and exchanged derisive laughter. "Why of course, we have a full-service spa just ahead."

They spoke Spanish. She understood the gist of their sarcastic ridicule but pretended not to. It made her remember David teasing her about finding a beauty salon in the jungle. Had these men somehow overheard that conversation? The thought chilled her.

The man guarding her now pulled her to her feet and led her in halting steps to the end of the truck bed. Two others on the ground put the tailgate down. Her guard gave her a push.

She felt herself falling and screamed, clutching her abdomen, bracing for the impact, but strong arms caught her mid-air and set her safely on the narrow trail.

"*¡Vamos!*" Her guard pointed to the dense forest on the other side of the truck, then splayed his fingers. "*Cinco minutos.*"

Five minutes. She nodded and started down the trail.

Immediately someone yanked her back by the straps of her backpack. "Leave this here."

She'd almost forgotten she carried the pack. "No, please. I need this. Tissues..." She feigned embarrassment. "And...a change of clothes."

They laughed, but let her keep the pack. "Don't run off," her guard warned in English.

Instantly incensed at how they'd violated her freedom, she matched their sarcasm from earlier. "Where would I go?"

They laughed again, and she scrambled into the jungle, her mind racing.

When she'd gone far enough that the foliage concealed her, she relieved herself. Then, staying low to the ground, she unzipped her backpack and rummaged through it, taking inventory. Her phone was gone, as she'd known it would be, along with her sunglasses and the money she'd hidden in a pair of rolled up socks. If they'd found that, there would be nothing of value they hadn't taken.

She'd apparently passed out for some length of time, and she wasn't even sure which side of Conzalez she and David had come in on or how far from the compound they'd been when she was abducted.

But even if she had the phone—or a thousand dollars—what good would either do her in the dense jungle? She had no idea how far they'd traveled.

The rain forest extended for hundreds of miles, much of the dense landscape inhabited only by poisonous snakes and spiders, wild cats, and other dangerous creatures. Without a phone or even a compass, she might escape her captors, but she could be walking into a worse fate, never to be found alive *or* dead. She couldn't risk that for this baby's sake. And she would not leave David and Lele and her family back in Kansas wondering forever what had happened to her. Mom had already gotten a taste of that with Dad's ordeal.

No, her chances were better if she stayed with her captors, at least for now. *Show me what to do, Lord. Please, be a lamp to my feet...*

She unzipped the largest outside compartment. She felt for her pocket-sized New Testament but it, too, was missing. Instead, her fingers fished out the little wind chime Lele had created from the office supplies she'd stolen. Natalie crumpled into tears.

She'd intended to leave the wind chime at home. But in their rush to get on the river this morning, she'd completely forgotten about tucking it into her backpack. She hadn't even told David about it yet—that the mystery had been solved.

Now gratitude overwhelmed her. Somehow this cobbled-together wind chime—that didn't even work, according to Lele —filled her with comfort. And hope.

"*Señora?* Miss?" A different voice shouted. "Come on! Time's up!"

She quickly stuffed everything back into her pack, but as she started to coil Lele's chain of paper clips and colorful sticky notes to return it to its compartment, an idea formed. She carefully tucked the chain inside the waist of her skirt, hiding it with her baggy T-shirt. She hoisted the backpack onto one shoulder, then rose and started walking. She took two steps and her baby somersaulted inside her.

"It's okay, little one," she whispered. "Everything is going to be okay." *Oh, God, please!*

She placed a hand over the mound of her womb and felt the baby's undeniable movements beneath her fingers. There was a sense of relief that he still had life, but along with that relief, the ante had been raised.

For the sake of this precious child, she had to escape. She *had* to.

18

David dialed Natalie's phone for at least the tenth time. It went immediately to voicemail, but he listened to the message again, taking comfort in the cadence of the voice he loved.

He stared at the clock above Hank's desk, not sure whether to will the hands to move forward or backward. Mostly he wanted to do something constructive with his own hands. Yet, short of pounding the roads beyond the compound, he'd already done all he knew to do. But he absolutely would have pounded those roads if he thought it would do any good.

It was much more complicated than that. And even though Hank reassured him that both the local police and the mission authorities in the States were working with U.S. authorities to "resolve the issue as soon as possible," the only acceptable resolution was for him to have Natalie back in his arms unharmed and their baby still safe in her womb.

Meghan slipped from a guest bedroom and quietly closed the door behind her. "She's asleep."

"Oh, good. Thank you," he said softly, grateful for Meghan's presence.

When she'd learned that Lele's little tote bag had been lost, she rounded up a few outfits from the generic clothes they kept on hand for foster children. Lele had taken an immediate liking to "Miss Meg," and it lifted a huge load from his shoulders not to have to worry about the little scamp while there were so many important tasks related to finding Natalie.

"Thanks, sweetheart." Hank reached for his wife's hand and gave it a squeeze before turning back to his computer's screen. He'd pulled up a topographic map and they were trying to trace the path David and Natalie had taken after mooring the boat in the inlet. He tapped a spot on the computer screen. "You're certain it was here that they took her?"

David bent over Hank's shoulder and tried to orient himself. "If we used the inlet you told us about. Here." He pointed back at a cove on the map. "They'll be able to see where the truck braked and fishtailed on the road."

"We'll find out for sure in the morning when we retrieve your boat."

"If it's still there." He glanced out the window. "I wish we'd had another hour of daylight."

Hank shook his head. "That would just mean they'd have taken her farther into the jungle. They won't travel far in unfamiliar territory after dark. Too dangerous."

The officer Hank trusted from the National Police, Alejandro Moreno, had come by the house about an hour after Hank and David arrived in Conzalez. The man assured them they would do everything in their power to locate Natalie, but a light sprinkle had turned into a downpour a few minutes ago, and it would be foolish to try to traverse that unpaved road until morning. Of course, by morning, the rains might have washed away any trace of the truck's route.

Hank had suggested tracking dogs, but according to Moreno, by the time they could get dogs in from Bogotá, the heavy rains would have destroyed the scent trail.

Meghan touched his shoulder. "Are you sure I can't make you something to eat, David?"

He offered a wan smile. "Thank you, but I have no appetite."

"Maybe some *cazho?*"

"Yes, please. That would be good." He likely wouldn't sleep anyway, and he knew Hank's wife wanted to help. "Thank you, Meg. Natalie was so looking forward to seeing you."

"Oh, me too. I've missed her so much. Had she been feeling okay...with her pregnancy?"

"She was...*is* radiant with it." He would not go there until forced to. "She made it seem like the most natural thing in the world." His voice wavered. He hated that he hadn't given Natalie the compliment in person.

Meghan worked in the little kitchen adjacent to the small combination living room/office. She brought him a steaming mug. "You still take it black?"

"Black is fine."

"David, I don't mean to alarm you, but..." Meghan didn't quite meet his gaze. "Is there any chance Natalie was targeted *because* she was pregnant?"

He met her eyes, trying to discern if there was something they hadn't told him. "I don't know. I had the same thought. I'm not sure when they first got a bead on us, but if they saw us from across the river, I doubt they could have determined she was pregnant. She was wearing a loose skirt and a baggie T-shirt."

"Let me get that information down." He poised his fingers over the keyboard. "I know we already gave them some information, but they'll likely ask for more detailed description of what she was wearing, everything she had on her person."

David closed his eyes and tried to conjure up a clear image of Natalie. "It was a kind of blue-green T-shirt. One of mine. Hers didn't fit any more."

Hank grinned and typed hunt-and-peck style.

"A patterned skirt with that same color." He remembered how well she blended in with the rainforest on the trail. "Her clothes were almost like camouflage out there. All the greens and blues..."

"That could be to her advantage if she has a chance to escape. What else? Jewelry? Did she wear a wedding ring?" Hank typed, then looked up, waiting.

He held up his left hand, showing his tattooed ring finger that matched Natalie's. "She has a Celtic knot like mine, only a little narrower—" A storm of emotion hit him and he took in a halting breath.

Hank gave him the courtesy of pretending not to notice. He typed again. "Okay. What else?"

"Tennis shoes...sneakers. Sunglasses. But—I think she took those off once we got on the trail. It was pretty dark under the canopy." He scoured his memories, trying to remember. It took everything he had to hold it together. "Her hair was in a ponytail..."

"Take your time, man."

He nodded his thanks. "She had...her backpack. Was wearing it."

"What was in it?"

He gave Hank a questioning look.

"So we know what supplies she has," Hank explained. "Or...if she dropped it or they tossed it, they'll need to know how to identify it as hers."

"Of course." He wasn't thinking clearly. "It was just an ordinary gray backpack. Dark gray. Didn't show the dirt as bad, she said. It was mostly full of clothes. Her face cream, hairbrush and stuff... Probably a little New Testament. She had some money. A couple hundred dollars worth of pesos, I think. Her phone..."

"Okay, good. I've got it." Hank tapped the computer screen.

"Like I said, I don't think we were followed. Not on the river and not after we started up the trail. It seemed more opportunistic." He closed his eyes, remembering the attack. "We heard the engine, but the truck didn't speed up until they were right on us. And then they braked hard and that's when they took her."

He repeated the events he'd told Hank in the car, but couldn't add anything new to what he'd already told him.

"But you said you thought you saw someone on the opposite bank earlier, right? Soldiers?"

"I couldn't tell who. It was at a wider point in the river and the vegetation is thick. It could have been my imagination. You know how that is… Once you imagine seeing something, it looks more real every time you look. But it was just movement. Seemed like maybe people walking single file? I didn't hear anything. Just saw the movement. And I couldn't be sure it was anything. At all."

He groaned. It was because of what he *thought* he saw that Hank had advised them to get off the river and come in on a backroad. Hank blamed himself, but maybe *he* was the one who'd unwittingly led them straight into the path of the captors.

He looked up at the clock again. It was dark outside now. Seven twenty. The same time it was in Kansas. They'd gained an hour on the river, but time was running out for one task he dreaded with everything in him. He needed to call Natalie's parents.

BLISTERS ROSE ON THE HEELS OF HER FEET AND HER BACK ached with the weight of the baby. Natalie didn't know how long they'd been walking—climbing—but she guessed it had been more than an hour since the sun had set. Where they were taking her, she had no idea.

The soldiers—five of them, not counting a sixth who'd stayed behind with the truck—laughed and joked among themselves as they hiked the rugged trail, keeping her in the middle of the irregular procession. The few snippets of their conversation she could understand didn't seem to have anything to do with her. But it did seem the soldiers knew where they were going since they never hesitated when the beams of their flashlights illuminated a curve or a fork in the road.

They hadn't made any concessions for her but neither had

they been cruel. They'd treated her as they might treat a dog they picked up along the way.

The overgrown road—if you could call it that—curved again and Natalie reached under her T-shirt and tried to unclasp a section of paper clips from Lele's chain. When she finally got two links apart, she realized that the paper had come out of one.

"Hurry up!" a soldier behind her shouted, causing the two in front of her to turn and look.

"I'm going as fast as I can." Pulse throbbing, she prayed they hadn't detected her actions.

"This isn't supposed to be a stroll in the park," he barked. "Come on!"

When he turned his back again, she quickly slid the paper into the clip and let it fall in the road beneath her. The "crumbs" she left in her wake were nothing more than shiny paper clips with folded strips of sticky note woven through. Each link was no more than six or seven inches long, counting the strands of corn husk that fluttered from the colorful folded sticky note. She'd left two of the links attached in the road where the soldiers hid the trucks in the undergrowth. They'd gone on foot from there, plowed through the jungle, and at each turn on the narrow pathway, she'd dropped another link of Lele's chain.

She'd gotten more adept at separating the links without looking, but she was running out of links to drop. And with each one she left behind, she felt the distance from David and Lele grow exponentially. She wasn't sure she'd be able to let loose of the final link...her last connection to them.

She'd savored glimpses of the night sky, trying to discern a constellation, but they never stopped in one place long enough to see more than a sliver of sky. At times it felt like they were walking in circles and she wondered if they were just trying to confuse her.

After what seemed like another hour, she stopped in the road, exhausted. She stood there for a few seconds before her captors noticed that she'd lagged behind. If she hadn't been so utterly bone-weary, she might have been able to run away right then, to follow her own trail of the pieces of Lele's wind chime she'd dropped in the road, and if not find her way to Conzalez, at least elude these men.

But she couldn't make her feet move. Soon, the leader looked back and hollered roughly, in English this time. "Hey, you! Keep up!"

"I'm tired. Please... When can we stop?" She was still trying not to let on that she understood more than rudimentary Spanish...which was mostly true. The Castilian Spanish was similar to Timoné in the form David had written it, but the accents made the two dialects sound very different.

The leader, a man about her dad's age, made his way to the back of the line and walked backward for a few seconds, observing her as she plodded forward. He regarded her kindly. "Not much farther. You can rest soon."

She nodded and kept putting one foot in front of the other, despite the pain her blisters caused.

"What's that in your hand?" He pointed.

She followed his line of vision and sucked in a breath when she realized she was holding the last two links of Lele's chain. She opted for the truth. Just not the whole truth. "My young friend made it for me."

"What is it?"

"Just...something pretty to look at. A little craft project."

He scoffed. "If you say so. We'll be there soon." He turned then and ran to the head of the line.

She wanted to ask where "there" was. But she wouldn't get a straight answer. She knew that much. She was just grateful that they were almost ready to stop for the night. And that she still had two little paper clips linked together from Lele's wind chime. She clutched them as though they were a lifeline.

❧ 19 ❧

David woke with a start and looked at the clock on the bedside table. Just after two a.m. He'd slept for almost two hours and now it was a new day. Friday, October 12.

He sat straight up in bed. How could he sleep at all when his beloved wife was in danger? But after talking to Natalie's parents last night, they'd waited another four hours for a ransom call that never came.

Hank promised to wait up a few more hours, and of course David had slept with his phone in hand in case the call came directly to him.

Hank thought the call would come in to the mission headquarters—and they were standing by in the States—but usually, even if it was the family who was called, those calls were to be rerouted to the main mission. David had been informed by Gospel Linguists' mission headquarters that the Federal Bureau of Investigation would be part of a coordinated U.S. government effort to find Natalie and get her to safety. But due to FBI "operational considerations," all communications would come through headquarters and as of now, they had no further information for him.

Knowing the FBI already had boots on the ground in Bogotá gave him a small measure of comfort. The bureau in the capital had spoken with an envoy at the American embassy who assured them the bureau would "reach out" to the usual suspects in similar kidnappings. Which, sadly, were happening more and more frequently.

There were too many unknowns. The first being, would there be a ransom call and who would claim responsibility? And then, most importantly, where had they taken her?

Was Natalie able to sleep? Was she warm and fed wherever she was? He couldn't let himself doubt she was alive. He would know if she wasn't. They were one. He would know if she was gone from this earth. Wouldn't he?

He threw back the covers and eased his legs over the side of the bed. He had to find something to keep him busy before the terrifying thoughts began to encroach.

His phone call with Natalie's parents had gone about as he'd expected. Cole and Daria Hunter's faith was strong, but this was their beloved daughter and they'd entrusted her to him. Though they'd expressed shock and despair, they'd never uttered a word that laid the blame on him. Still, he felt responsible.

He trusted Hank's intel. Had no reason not to. But ultimately, the information had caused him to take a different route to Conzalez than they'd originally planned, and because of that, they'd walked right into danger. Yet, as Daria had said on the phone, the same thing could have happened no matter the route they chose.

And knowing that, he had to believe God had a purpose in what was happening. Cole Hunter had said the same thing.

Daria and Cole had offered to fly to Bogotá as soon as possible, but at Hank's urging, David had persuaded them to wait. "We might need you in the States to deal with things from that end."

And of course, they'd promised him their constant prayers. It was hard enough for him, being in the same vicinity as Natalie.

He couldn't imagine how hard it must be for them, thousands of miles away and—

His phone trilled and Natalie's photo appeared. Heart in his throat, he tapped Accept. "Natalie? Love? Are you okay?"

Distant voices speaking Spanish ensued. At least three different people carried on a conversation in the background. Natalie wasn't one of them. He strained to make out what they were saying, but it was soon apparent that they weren't aware they'd dialed him. Sounded like they were trying to figure out how to wipe the phone. Before he could think of the ramifications, he flipped on the overhead light and shouted into the phone in Spanish. "¡Hola! Let me speak to Natalie. Let me speak to my wife!"

More conversation on the other end. It didn't appear they could hear him. He hollered into the phone again, louder.

A knock sounded on the door to his bedroom.

"David?" Hank cracked the door open. "Everything okay?"

"Come in... Hank!" He held up his phone. "They're messing with her phone. They must have accidentally called me. I can't get them to respond, but they're talking about wiping the phone."

"Natalie's phone?" Hank strained to hear the muffled voices. "That must mean they've already called with their demands."

David's heart raced. "Or they aren't going to call. Why else would they be wiping her phone?" He tapped the volume up and tried clicking the mute button, thinking maybe he'd muted his phone accidentally. But that wasn't it.

He and Hank listened for a few more seconds before a thought struck him. "Isn't there a way to record a phone conversation?"

"Probably, but I don't know what it is."

He thrust the phone at Hank. "Hang on. Let me check..."

He googled how to record the phone's screen activity and within a few seconds had set the phone to Record. He motioned for Hank to be silent.

The voices were jumbled and increasingly loud as the men argued about how to wipe the phone. From the snippets David could pick out, it sounded like this phone wasn't working the way they expected. But maybe the authorities would be able to trace where the call had come from or at least get some clues from the voices and the conversation.

Was Natalie there with the men, watching them try to destroy her only way to contact him? Her only way to summon help? He tugged at his beard.

...from whence cometh my help. My help cometh from the Lord, which made heaven and earth.

The verse from the Psalms played again in his mind. Yes. Yes, of course. *The Lord* was where their help came from. *God, please, be her help.*

Hank held up a hand, his eyes widening, his focus on the phone. David listened.

"I *said* go ask her." A raised voice spoke clearly in Spanish. "And don't let her play dumb. She knows the code."

Go ask her. If it was Natalie they were talking about—and it had to be—she was alive!

"Thank you, God," Hank whispered.

"Yes..." His voice broke, but he quickly composed himself. They couldn't miss anything here. "I don't think Natalie ever locked her phone." He remembered picking it up in the kitchen of the *utta* the morning they'd left on this trip to check if Natalie had charged her phone. It had sprung to life, never asking for a code. "No. Unless she locked it *during* the trip. And how could they have dialed me if the phone is locked?"

"Maybe she had a chance to lock it after she was abducted?"

"I don't know. I seriously doubt she would have locked it. Maybe they're trying to get a code to something else? A password?" He scoffed. "If it's our bank account they're trying to break into, they're in for a rude awakening."

He checked to be sure the phone was still recording.

"You're getting all this?" Hank asked.

David nodded, then shuddered. "I just hope she cooperates. They won't take no for an answer."

"She's smart." Hank clasped his shoulder. "She'll do the right thing."

David nodded, but he knew how his wife could be. Under less stressful circumstances, she was as likely to shake a finger in their faces and give them a piece of her mind as she was to obey without question. But these men were not her students. They were trained killers and patience was not their virtue. She knew that. And she had the baby to think about.

A commotion came over the phone, shouting and angry voices. David held his breath, trying in vain to understand what they were saying.

And without warning, the phone went silent.

NATALIE STIRRED AND WRINKLED HER NOSE. THE KHAKI green sleeping bag they'd given her smelled of cigar smoke and sweat, and the ground beneath her was like concrete covered in sand, with an occasional jagged stone thrown in for good measure. And yet, she'd slept. For at least a few hours she thought, though time was nearly impossible to measure in the darkest hours of night.

There was some type of barrier overhead because there were no silhouettes of foliage and not a star in sight. A cave maybe? Or a heavy tent? She was afraid to move, in case there was anyone else sleeping nearby. But the room was pitch black and she couldn't see her hand in front of her face.

She was just drifting back to sleep when something... someone nudged her and a bright light all but blinded her.

"Wake up!" A man's harsh voice.

She gave a little cry but sat up, shielding her eyes, feeling muddled.

A phone—her phone—was thrust in her face.

"Password!" the man demanded in heavily accented English.

Natalie pretended not to understand what he was asking.

But then he shoved her phone closer and she saw the website of their American bank.

Funds from supporters wouldn't land in the account until the end of the month and she doubted they had more than a few hundred dollars in the account. Nowhere near enough to appease kidnappers who were likely asking for thousands.

"Enter the password!" He spoke as if talking to an imbecile.

She couldn't feign ignorance anymore and typed it in.

The page for their joint account opened. The soldier took one look and spat a word that was the same as a Timoné curse word. Had he seriously thought they had the means to pay a hefty ransom from their personal bank account? And did the fact that he was even considering their account mean they'd already gotten the anticipated *no* from Gospel Linguists on a ransom demand?

It wasn't the end of the world if they took a few hundred dollars from their bank account. And maybe if she accessed their bank account, it would alert David and give anyone who was looking for her some clues. A jolt of excitement shot through her. They had cell service. They couldn't be too far from civilization. And that meant David was two keystrokes away! She wracked her brain, trying to think of how she could contact him while she held the phone.

As if he'd read her mind, the soldier peered over her shoulder and demanded she hurry.

She typed in the password. Within seconds, her text message app dinged with a security code. She started to enter the number, but the soldier grabbed the phone from her and typed in the code himself.

Apparently satisfied he had what he needed, he walked away without another word to her, his boots crunching on the surface of the trail.

Natalie tried to make out her surroundings by the light of his flashlight, but her eyes had only begun to adjust when the light clicked off and she was left in utter darkness again.

Defeated, she burrowed back into the smelly sleeping bag. She'd prepared her mind and heart to accept that no ransom could be paid. She'd even imagined what she would do if Mom and Daddy offered to pay whatever they demanded. David would refuse. He had to. She understood that. If anyone was allowed to pay a ransom for her, no missionary or short-term mission group would ever be safe here. It was something they'd discussed more than once during their missions training.

And of course, her parents knew all that. She and Dad had even faced threats of kidnapping in the past—threats that thankfully had turned out to be idle.

No, as hard as it would be for them, Natalie didn't think anyone would pay.

She swallowed hard and squeezed back tears. It was one thing to be strong now, but if it came to her life being on the line, her resolve might not be so strong. For a moment, she was grateful they didn't have any money in their account. *Please, Lord. Help me. Give me your strength*.

Had David called her parents? Surely he would have let them know by now. Thinking of their sorrow—and of David's—was almost harder than thinking of the torture she might have to endure when her captors found out no ransom would be paid. She'd mustered courage with the sense of responsibility this babe in her womb brought. If she had to, she would die to save this child. It was the only thing she was certain of right now.

20

David paced on the patio of the Middleton's house. The young couple's living quarters and Hank's home office were behind the medical clinic where Meghan, an R.N., saw patients from Conzalez and a few outlying villages.

At this rate, *he* might need a nurse. His blood pressure had to be through the roof. And if ever he needed to be calm and clearminded it was now. It had been thirty-six hours since Natalie's abduction and still no ransom call had come in.

He and Hank had been on the phone to mission headquarters in the States every few hours until they'd finally been told, "We'll call you the minute we hear anything."

The old don't-call-us-we'll-call-you message. So, what was he supposed to do in the meantime? He could not just pace this concrete for days on end while who-knew-what was happening to his wife! But even Hank warned him against going back to the place where Natalie had been abducted, fearing guerrillas might still be in the area.

Hank's policeman friend had gone there with another officer from the National Police yesterday to take photos and scour the area for clues. But they found none and still had no real leads.

He and Hank did have clearance to go pick up the pontoon boat. He half expected it to be gone, but Hank didn't seem worried and said the police had kept an eye on it the first twenty-four hours, hoping Natalie's kidnappers might try to steal it.

Too many agencies were getting involved and too many of them in this part of the country couldn't be trusted. Never mind the fact that there were hundreds, sometimes thousands, of kidnappings in the Republic of Colombia each year. Many victims were never recovered, presumably sold into human trafficking or murdered when ransom wasn't forthcoming.

He took some comfort in the fact that they hadn't taken Lele. Because if Natalie's abductors were involved in trafficking, they surely would have taken them both. But if it was kidnapping for cash, how could he reconcile the fact that there still hadn't been a ransom demand?

He went inside where he found Meghan baking in the kitchen. Lele was perched on a step stool "helping." But Meghan didn't seem to mind and Lele seemed oblivious that anything was amiss.

Meghan looked up from mixing batter. "Are you hungry, David?"

"Not yet, but thank you."

"We're makin' a cake!" Lele said—in English, to David's surprise.

She licked a rubber spatula and grinned up at him, a dollop of yellow batter on her nose.

"Looks to me like you're *eatin'* a cake. And"—he reverted to Timoné—"before it's even baked." He managed a smile, even as he longed for Natalie to be here to laugh with him.

"Mr. David! That's only batter."

Meghan tilted her head, apparently not understanding.

David translated and motioned between her and Lele. "You doing okay? Seems like you're finding ways to communicate."

"We're getting along famously. Although sign language may

not be the best option when you've got a spatula full of cake batter." She winked and bent to wipe up a splatter from the floor near Lele's feet.

"Is Hank in his office?"

She nodded.

He walked down the hallway that led to the bedrooms and Hank's office and knocked softly on the door.

"Yeah, come on in."

He opened the door and found Hank talking on the landline phone.

"Oh, sorry... I'll come back later." But he raised a brow, wondering if the call might be about Natalie.

Hank motioned him in. "Yes, I understand," he said into the phone. He cradled the receiver between his shoulder and chin, moved a pile of overflowing folders from a chair, and motioned David to sit. "He's here right now."

David took the chair and leaned forward, senses on alert, trying to discern who he was talking to.

But Hank's expression remained enigmatic. "Yes sir. I will. I understand," he said again. He hung up and slowly turned. "That was Bob Richmond at headquarters. They got a call a few minutes ago. Natalie's kidnappers are asking for one million dollars. I'm sorry, David."

He sucked in a breath. "Okay. So it's the real deal then." It wasn't a question. "Did they give proof of life?"

"Nothing we'd accept...even if we did pay ransom. They sent a screenshot supposedly from Natalie's phone." Hank pulled up his e-mail program on his desktop computer and opened an image. "Is this Natalie?"

David rose and examined the image, bracing himself for a disturbing image. Instead a screen capture of her phone appeared on Hank's computer. "Yes. It looks like her phone screen, but that doesn't prove anything. Except that they have her phone."

He pulled up their bank account on his own phone. "No

surprise, it looks like they've cleaned us out. About four hundred dollars. You think they'll deduct that from the million they're asking?" He despised the bitter sarcasm in his voice.

Hank scoffed. "Bob said the FBI investigators think the dip into your account might be a case of an underling getting greedy. Whoever's demanding the ransom hasn't identified themselves yet, but they likely don't know about this transaction. And don't worry, your account is insured. The bank is working on securing your account going forward. And if you need funds in the meantime, I'm happy to—"

"We'll be fine. Our monthly support isn't dispersed until the end of the month. But... If some lone ranger soldier got into our account, does that mean Natalie gave him the password?"

"Probably," Hank admitted. "Bob said the transaction happened at two-thirty a.m. Transferred to a Venmo account."

"Yes. That's just after the call came through on my phone. That's traceable, isn't it? It had to be after that when they got the password."

Hank sighed. "It's probably traceable, but hackers can cover their tracks faster than they can be traced."

"I wonder if Natalie was somehow able to dial me? Why else would I have been able to overhear that conversation?"

"Is she pretty tech savvy?"

"More than I am. But that's not saying much."

"So, she was probably okay as recently as two o'clock this morning. Good."

He wished he could feel relief in that. But what if they got her phone and her password and now they didn't need her?

As if he'd read David's thoughts, Hank shook his head. "They'll find her. They're trying to trace that bank transaction now. If we're lucky, somebody screwed up big-time and we can get a ping on their location."

David nodded and sent up a desperate prayer for Natalie. "So, what's next then? Have her captors been told that we won't pay ransom?"

"I'm sure they have."

David scrubbed his face with his hands. "It's a good thing they didn't call me."

"I know, friend. It's easier when it's only a theory. Another thing altogether when it's *your* wife they're holding. And you might as well be prepared..."

"What?"

"They'll probably coerce her to make a plea for the ransom. It will look as if she's under duress—and she might be—but you know that won't change our policy."

He nodded. The thought of watching such a video sickened him. Even as desperate as he was for a glimpse of Natalie.

"It may not happen," Hank said. "Let's pray they find her and rescue her before it does. But I just wanted you to...be prepared."

He opened his mouth to reply, but his voice wouldn't let him. He gave a curt nod.

Hank put a hand on his shoulder. "What do you say we go pick up your boat?"

"Or at least see if it's still there."

Her stomach churned from the lukewarm, tasteless stew they'd brought her a few hours ago. The baby hadn't moved for several hours.

Natalie relieved herself in the covered bucket in the corner and lay back down on the sleeping bag on the hard wood plank floor, her backpack making a lumpy pillow beneath her head.

She attempted, without success, to ignore the awful stench that hung in the air and willed her baby to give her some sign that he was alive.

She imagined a warm shower, went through the motions in her mind, shampooing her hair, drying off with a warm towel. The sensation was so real it frightened her, but when she came to her senses, the stench was still there, the open bucket toilet was still in the corner, and despair blanketed her.

Unrelenting rain pelted what must be a metal roof and she stared at the rivulets of water forming muddy tracks in the dust on the skylight.

She tried to pray and instead was overwhelmed by the crushing weight of depression. The room she was in—or maybe it was merely a shed?—was constantly dim, the only hint of light coming from the filthy skylight overhead. It was just enough that she could see movement in the corners, on the walls. Lizards? Spiders? *Please, Lord, not a snake.*

She shuddered and forced herself to think of something else. She'd been careful to keep track of the days. By her calculations, this was Sunday morning—unless she'd been unconscious longer than she thought immediately after they'd captured her. It had only been three days, three nights. Yet it seemed like an eternity.

She thought of other missionaries who'd been abducted. Many had been held for weeks, or even longer, like a group of missionaries she'd read about recently. Two long months when they didn't know if they would be rescued or die in captivity. At least they'd had each other. And ultimately, miraculously, they'd escaped! They'd made it! Shouldn't that give her hope?

But two months? She didn't have two months! Her baby was due in two or three weeks. Maybe sooner.

She forced herself to concentrate, trying to remember *how* those missionaries had escaped and wished she'd paid more attention to the details of their story. She and David had prayed for them when it happened, never imagining the horrors of what they were likely going through.

Was anyone praying for *her* now? David was, of course. And her family back home in Kansas. It had only been three days. Of course, they were praying. But how long before even they gave up hope?

Another memory came. When she was just a little girl, two missionaries to the Philippines, Martin and Gracia Burnham, had been held captive by the Abu Sayyaf for more than a year. Martin had died during a rescue attempt. Before she'd come to Timoné the first time, Natalie had heard his wife speak about their ordeal at a Kansas church. That was the first time she'd begun to realize what her dad had actually gone through when he'd been held captive.

But she hadn't truly understood. Not until now. And Dad had been held for even longer than the Burnhams—two and a half years. She couldn't even fathom it.

She squeezed her eyes shut, remembering Mrs. Burnham's poignant account. An entire year of her children's lives lost to her. Her husband gone. Gone for almost twenty years now.

What if *she* was still in this dank room when it came time for her baby to be born? Could she forgive the same way the Burnham family had? Forgive, even if there was no apology? Forgive, even if there was no justice?

Please, God, don't put me to that test!

And yet, already, there was much to forgive. Could she even forgive the policy of Gospel Linguists to not pay ransom? Hadn't Jesus Himself died as a ransom? And yet, she understood the reason for the policy. And she and David had discussed it more than once. He'd made her promise that if he was ever abducted, that she would not agree to paying ransom. She honestly didn't remember if she'd asked him to promise the same in return. But she knew if he'd pressed her, she would have. They'd agreed it was the only sound policy. One that saved many lives in the long run, even if it might require a life in the short run.

She was already responsible for one life lost— *Oh, sweet, sweet Sara.* She truly didn't want to add all the other missionaries that might be put at risk of abduction to her list of liabilities if it was known a ransom had been paid for her release. But... Could it be done in secret?

No doubt, the news of her capture was already on the front page of *The Wichita Eagle* back home, and maybe even the nightly news. A wave of nausea came at the thought. She'd been the subject of news headlines before, after the accident that had taken Sara's life. She didn't relish having her name splashed all over the TV or even the little *Clayton County Courier* again.

Her eyelids grew heavy but she forced them open only to see the faint light from the stingy window fade and go dark. She fought for breath, not sure she could bear one more night of overwhelming gloom.

My help cometh from the Lord, which made heaven and earth. He will not suffer thy foot to be moved...

That Psalm again. What did it say about her that until now, she had not missed her Bible. But now she grieved the loss of that little New Testament as if it were a living, breathing being. And in a sense, it was. God's "living and active" word as the Bible called it. She'd committed Scripture to memory as a child. Where was it now?

"I will lift up mine eyes unto the hills, from whence cometh my help," she whispered. "My help cometh from the Lord, which made heaven and earth. He will not suffer thy foot to be moved..."

There was a beautiful lulling cadence to the King James version she'd memorized as a child. Almost like a lullaby. She repeated the verses, trying to remember what came next. She'd had to learn the entire chapter in her fourth grade Sunday School class. Psalm 121. She'd won a prize for reciting the psalm in front of the entire congregation. A little book of cartoonish angel stickers. She hadn't a clue what she was reciting then. What *keepeth* meant or *behold*. Wait... That was it.

"He that keepeth thee will not slumber," she whispered. "Behold, he that keepeth Israel shall neither slumber nor sleep."

She added the new snippet to the first verse and recited the words again, this time as a prayer. Her eyelids grew heavier. How could she be tired when all she'd done for hours on end was sleep? But what else was there to do? And her baby needed her to rest.

But God did not "slumber nor sleep." He kept watch over her. And over this child.

She splayed the fingers of her right hand over the mound of her belly. *Please move, Baby. Please don't leave me...*

Today was Sunday. When she woke again it would be Monday. She could make it one more day.

"I know our government won't pay and I know what the mission's policy is, but surely we could make private arrangements to get her out of there." Cole Hunter's voice wavered. "There has to be *something*..."

David understood how Natalie's father felt. In fact, he'd been oddly grateful that he didn't have the means to ransom Natalie himself, because he would have been mightily tempted to do so. But he and Natalie had discussed it—a distant possibility at the time—after one of their missions training sessions and they agreed with Gospel Linguists' policy and their reason for it: paying ransom would only put other missionaries and travelers at greater risk of abduction.

Natalie's mother, being a former missionary, no doubt understood better than Cole why that policy had been put into place. But it was one thing to talk about it in theory and another altogether when it was your beloved wife or daughter who was being held.

"I don't know what to tell you, Cole. I've wondered if there's a different angle we could take because of the baby. Not just that it's two lives, but also because Natalie is so close to giving birth."

"Well, that should carry some weight. The dangers for her

and the baby are greater than for the average healthy abductee. Surely that counts for something. The medical aspect, I mean."

Abductee. He'd gained a whole new glossary over the last three days. But even a linguist didn't relish having words like *captivity, hostage, ransom, terrorist*...and worse in his lexicon.

"Believe me, Cole, I'm as desperate as you are to find a way to negotiate her release. But it simply can't involve paying a ransom."

After a long pause, Cole breathed a weighty sigh. "Her mother says the same, even though I've never seen her so tormented."

"It must feel like a nightmare for her to be going through this all over again."

"Nightmare is an understatement. I mean how much is one woman supposed to endure? The news media is circling, wanting us to make a statement. Give interviews, even."

"But you haven't said anything yet?"

"Just that we covet the prayers of praying people. There was a blurb on national news last night so word is getting out and thousands are praying, David. Churches all over the state. The country even."

"We appreciate that. More than you can know."

"Yeah, well, prayers are great, but when does it end? If you two raise this baby in Colombia, what's to say we won't be right back here twenty years from now? Or ten?"

He cringed. "Yes, that's crossed my mind too. And I've wondered about that angle for negotiating—that the country owes this family some kind of compensation for all you've...*we've* been through. But of course, if the U.S. can't condone paying ransom, then a country like Colombia absolutely can't."

"But you and I both know they *have* paid in the past. It just depends on who you are. But I will sell the practice to raise the money if I have to. Just say the word."

"I know you would, Cole. And I appreciate that. I do. But you know the policy that—"

"As her husband, David, and the father of her baby, I think your request would carry a lot more weight than ours." Anger had crept into Cole's voice. "Are you sure you've made yourself heard?"

David sighed. "I've done everything I know to do, Cole, short of traipsing through the jungle searching for her. And between you and me, Hank and I are planning to do just that later this afternoon."

"Why? Do you have some leads?" Surprise—and hope—threaded his tone, making David regret not framing it more carefully.

"Only that I was there when she was taken. We would have gone sooner, but the FBI here wanted to thoroughly comb the area before the scene was contaminated."

"Well, it's something, I guess. I'm running out of consolations for Daria. Has anyone been in contact with them since the first ransom demand?"

David hesitated. "Just to reiterate our stance."

"And is there...a deadline on their demands?"

"According to Bob at Gospel Linguists, they've given us another week. From yesterday. October 21. Not that it makes a difference."

"But they must think there's a chance the mission will change its stance, right? Why else would they extend the deadline? You have to leverage that, right?"

David didn't like the false hope in his father-in-law's voice. Or the accusation that hovered just below the surface. "Cole, I hope I don't sound like an uncaring husband. But my hands are tied. I've been warned sternly about going rogue. The embassy here is working closely with the FBI and they've assured me that everything possible is being done to locate her. But I'm purposely being kept out of the loop. I don't know everything they have up their sleeve, and I'm not about to screw it up by interfering. And, I'm sure Daria has guessed this, but Natalie and I signed agreements with the agency about the risks we were knowingly taking to do what we do. Obviously, when you sign those things, you never think it's going to happen to you... Still, she and I have always been in agreement about not paying ransom."

"Yes, well... I wonder how she feels about that policy now. This is our daughter! And an innocent baby!"

He exploded. "You think I don't know that? This is my wife and *my* baby!" He dropped his head, trembling, struggling to control his anger. Natalie's dad was speaking from pain and fear. He understood that. Still, the incrimination in his tone cut deep.

He took a deep breath and blew it out slowly before speaking again. "I'm sorry. But we'd be signing someone else's death warrant if we paid. It would never stop. Natalie knew that. All I can tell you is that I'm trusting God for the outcome. I know she is too. And Cole... I'm listening to the counsel of our mission board and the authorities from each country. And of course, I'm considering the thoughts and advice of everyone who loves Natalie. You and Daria most of all, naturally."

Another long silence and David sensed the man was weighing his words carefully.

Finally Cole croaked out, "I'm sorry. I know you love her as much as we do. And you know we're praying. Constantly."

"I do know. Thank you. Please tell Daria too. I feel those prayers. And I know Natalie must feel them every bit as much."

"GOD? WHERE ARE YOU?" NATALIE WAILED, NO LONGER caring if anyone heard.

She'd read somewhere that your life flashed before your eyes just before you died. Maybe she was going to die, but there was no flash of her life's events. It was more like an unending, *s-l-o-w* crawl.

She paced the fourteen short steps from one end of the space to the other. Over and over again, just to keep her muscles from atrophying. And to keep her sanity. Though she wasn't sure that was working.

Confusion blurred the hours, but if her count was right—and if she hadn't missed a passage of the sun over the skylight in the roof—she'd now spent at least ten days in captivity. Surely they'd forgotten her. Not just David and her family, but her captors. No one had told her anything. There was no photo taken that she was aware of, no threats made, no video to persuade her family.

It was as if she'd ceased to exist for anyone who had the power to free her. If not for the soldiers who brought her bottles of tepid water, and occasionally tossed in a hard crust of bread or a green banana, she would have felt completely forgotten.

She'd lost her appetite, but she ate whatever they brought. For the baby's sake. Even so, the elastic on her skirt now clung low on her hips, despite her distended belly.

Her baby had moved only twice since she'd been locked into this space. And barely enough to make his presence known. Still, those flutters gave her hope and purpose.

She counted off ten more laps of the small room before lying back down on the clammy, fetid sleeping bag. The elastic she'd pulled back her hair with had broken a few days ago, but her hair was so grimy with oil and dirt that it stayed in a loose braid of its own accord. She would never again take shampoo for granted.

Her thoughts swirled and she tried to pray, but couldn't seem to get out more than *please* and *help*. Finally, she felt herself drifting into blessed sleep.

She didn't know how long she slept, but she woke to loud pounding on the door. She sat upright, her heart lurching into her throat. She stared at the door, torn between dread and hope.

"*¡Nos vamos!*" Two soldiers—one she hadn't seen before—stormed into the space. Behind them, light poured through the door and she soaked in the view beyond: a thick stand of bamboo and in front of it, palm leaves quivering in the breeze. Never before had they allowed her a glimpse of what was just outside her door.

She scrambled to her feet and scooped up the sleeping bag.

"*¡Déjalo!*" The taller man kicked the blanket into a corner. "*No necesitarás eso.*"

She wouldn't *need* the sleeping bag? Why?

Trembling, she grabbed her sneakers from the corner, tapping them hard on the floor to dislodge any possible critters. She quickly put them on, then reached for her backpack that had served as a paltry pillow. If they told her she didn't need that, she would know this was her death march.

But they said nothing and only strode through the door, leaving it wide open.

She stepped through the doorway and tilted her head to the sky above, instantly drenched in waves of euphoria even as she squinted against the daylight. Trying to be as unobtrusive as possible, she took in her surroundings, memorizing landmarks, trying to remember if anything seemed familiar.

The babble of the river came from a distance away, a sound she hadn't detected from inside. The rush of water had to be the Guaviare, didn't it? But nothing else around her gave a clue to where she might be, how far from Conzalez they'd brought her. Or even what direction the small city was from here.

Turning back to the door she'd walked through, she saw that her prison had been a simple garden shed, unpainted except by the mildew that tinted it green. Grasses and weeds grew up tall around it, nearly hiding the structure from anyone who wasn't looking for it. The dark metal roof blended in with the jungle's browns and greens.

She'd heard the sound of motors a few times while trapped inside, but that was usually when food and water had been delivered to her. There were no vehicles in sight now. And no road that she could see.

"Walk." The taller soldier swung his chin in the direction the sun was dipping. West. She clutched her backpack, remembering the two links of Lele's chain still tucked in the outside pocket. It killed her to think of letting go of that last memory of the little

Timoné girl she carried with her, but it might be her only chance to drop a "breadcrumb" to lead anyone who might still be looking for her.

Had anyone found the other links she'd left on the road? No. If so, they would have found her by now. And ten days of rain would have turned all but the paper clips to mush. It would be a miracle if those weren't buried in mud.

If she ever got out of here, she would see to it that Lele had all the art supplies in the world so she could make her a chain that reached from one end of their *utta* to the other.

The utta. Oh, how she missed the simple life they'd lived in Timoné. How often had she taken their pretty hut for granted? Or worse, complained because it didn't have some of the modern amenities she wished for. *Forgive me, Lord.*

Now that she might be on her way to her death, she so desperately wanted another chance to be grateful for all God had blessed her with. She wanted to raise this baby with her beloved husband. Watch Lele grow up. *Oh, please, Father. Please rescue me!*

She slid her hand to the zipper on the backpack. The soldiers seemed not to notice. She inched the zipper open.

But what if they caught her? This place seemed to be in the middle of nowhere, no road or even path that she could see. Maybe she should wait and see if they led her to a trail that would be more likely to be seen and followed.

But even if they led her to her death, she would soak in the bliss of the sun on her face and suck deep gulps of fresh air.

She took comfort in the thought that she might soon be with her baby in heaven, and even that their last moments on this earth would be spent in the jungle she'd grown to love. The place that had become home to her.

If only this one last time, her baby would hear the songs of the rainforest's birds, the *swish-swish* of the long-fingered mango leaves, and the rhythmic drip of the afternoon rains trickling from banana leaf to banana leaf. These were the only lullabies this child of David and Natalie Chambers had ever known on this side of heaven.

Taking two steps backward, she deftly separated the last two paper clips, making sure Lele's folded papers and decorated corn husks stayed attached to each link. Inhaling deeply, feeling as though she were leaving half of her heart behind, she shuffled two more steps backward and let the link fall onto the floor of the shed.

"What's the matter?" Tomás, the tall guard who'd been with her from the beginning, glared at her. "You'd rather stay here? That can be arranged."

"No. No, I'm coming."

He stormed past her and she didn't look back, but held her breath as the padlock clicked into place. This time with her on the other side of the door.

Pyxis:
The Compass

❧ 22 ❧

The sun was just coming over the horizon on Tuesday as David steered the boat out of the shallow inlet that served as a harbor for Conzalez and whispered the same prayer he'd prayed a thousand times in the past twelve days. "Be with Natalie, Father God. Strengthen her. Hold her up. Somehow, God, let her know we are looking for her, praying for her."

When he and Hank retrieved the pontoon boat last week, he'd been surprised to find the boat untouched. Surely they'd been observed as they disembarked that day. Hank believed that whoever David had seen on the opposite shore was likely who'd alerted Natalie's abductors that they were coming in to Conzalez by land.

Hank had driven him back to the site, and they'd taken the Jeep in as far as it would go, but with the rainy season ramping up, the rutted trails were impassable barely a mile beyond the point where she'd been abducted, and the trail seemed to end there.

A dozen days she'd been gone. The ransom deadline had passed two days ago. Was she even still alive? Given that they'd refused from the outset to pay the million-dollar ransom, there had been no proof of life offered. The video Hank had warned might come had never materialized. Unless the authorities were lying to him, there had been no further communication with Natalie's abductors. It was as if they—and Natalie—had dropped off the face of the earth.

He hadn't dared to voice it, even to Hank, but he was starting to fear that this was about the baby. That she had been taken, maybe from the very beginning, for an infant that could be sold for tens of thousands on the black market. And what would happen to Natalie after that? Would she be useless to them then? Or would they try to force her into their vile human trafficking racket.

He gripped the steering wheel till his knuckles turned white. He couldn't let himself think that way. If he'd known that fateful afternoon that she would still be missing almost two weeks after her abduction, that he would know virtually *nothing* about his wife's whereabouts...he wasn't sure he could have borne it. And if he had known, oh, how different his last conversation with his beloved wife might have been. Instead of giving mundane instructions, he would have assured her of his deep love and admiration for her. He would have promised her that he already loved their child and that he would have been the best father he knew how to be if only God would let them raise their son or daughter.

Sometimes he despaired whether she was even still alive. Mission headquarters in the States checked in with him every other day to report—pretty much nothing. Only that they continued to work with the FBI and local authorities.

Alejandro Moreno, Hank's policeman friend, had informed him two days ago that they'd swept the area where Natalie was kidnapped without finding more than tire and boot tracks. That meant Hank and David were cleared to explore the area without danger of contaminating the crime scene.

Today David intended to walk farther into the jungle, beyond where the trail ended, praying he'd find something they'd missed.

He would need to beat the afternoon rains though or risk getting stuck in a mudslide.

Hank had a plane coming in from Bogotá that needed maintenance on a quick turnaround, and he'd pleaded with David to wait until tomorrow so he could accompany him. "The last thing we need is for something to happen to you too, man."

"I'll be fine," he'd told Hank. "I'll take the sat phone and be back before noon. I need some time, Hank. Alone." It was an excuse intended to persuade, but it *was* the truth. He needed time to think and pray without the distractions of the comings and goings from Hank's office, the barrage of phone calls on three different phones, Meghan's well-intended solicitousness, and Lele's constant chatter.

That thought brought a smile. In truth, the girl had been a welcome distraction for all of them. He was grateful Meg had taken over Lele's care completely, freeing him to do what was needed and even to accomplish some of the translation work he could concentrate on now that he had access to the internet.

The trouble was, he *couldn't* concentrate. Thoughts of Natalie and the horrors she might be going through, took up every hour, every minute. And were followed by a thousand stabs of guilt: that he hadn't done enough before, that he wasn't doing anything productive to find her *now*, and that he wouldn't be able to do anything in the future if this dragged out for weeks.

The only good thing about everything that had happened was that he'd lost all fear for his own safety. He would gladly fight guerrillas in hand-to-hand combat, battle poisonous snakes, swim across a crocodile-infested river if it would bring his wife back to him. And he just might be walking into that kind of danger today.

He navigated the shallows where tree branches hung low over the dark waters of the Rio Guaviare. Natalie had always said the water looked like milky *cazho*, especially on mornings like this when a mist curled off the water before the sun rose to burn it off.

He steered the pontoon close enough to shore that he would see the opening to the inlet where they'd left the boat that fateful day. He intended to retrace every step Natalie had taken up until the point she'd been abducted. He felt certain she'd been oblivious to the danger that awaited. His last memory of her—before her screams as she was captured—was the smile she'd given him and Lele from across the road, thinking that Hank was approaching in the Jeep.

In his mind's eye, he remembered the road as a splayed Y— almost a T—with the truck coming around the bend from the east with Natalie on the north side of the road and him and Lele on the opposite. But it had all happened so fast.

For the first time since it happened, he felt unsure of his memories. What if his eye-witness testimony had skewed everything and prevented the authorities from seeing vital clues?

Maybe being on the trail again would give clarity. Better than sitting back at the Middletons' house doing nothing.

The river narrowed and he guided the boat into what Natalie called a tree tunnel— branches on one bank lacing with those on the opposite shore to form a shadowed passage, the air dead still, yet cool. Natalie always said it felt as though they were traveling back in time. Oh, that he *could* travel through time and make a different decision.

Once clear of the tunnel, the river looped south then back east again where it widened. He found the mouth of the inlet where they'd parked and retraced their route as exactly as he could, noting what the views were to the opposite bank where someone might have spotted them.

He cut the engine, lopped his backpack over one shoulder, and climbed into the tepid water to moor the craft.

The banks were still slippery from yesterday's rains and by the time he reached the trail his pant legs were caked in mud. Following the same route they'd taken that day, emotions rushed back. When he came to the spot where they'd grabbed her, his breath caught, and for the first time he got an inkling of what PTSD must be like.

He stopped and bent, bracing his hands on his knees, catching his breath, reliving that day. Tire tracks were still visible, even what looked like faint boot tracks. Wouldn't the rains have washed them away by now?

But of course this road was still used by some. And the police —and supposedly FBI agents—had been here since the abduction as well. Still, seeing the tire tread pattern in the sienna-colored mud made it all too real. His breaths came fast and shallow and he bent in the road, trying to steady himself, bracing his hands on his knees.

How awful it must have been for Natalie. It didn't seem like there was any way she could have endured the terror without going into labor and by now, her due date was near, terror or not.

He'd prayed for her and the baby as one, but now he prayed for them separately. Mother and child, pleading with God that the baby was still alive and that it was safe with Natalie.

"Please, God," he whispered.

At a break in the rainforest's canopy, he assessed the sky, then pulled his phone from his backpack and checked the time. He probably had another four hours before the afternoon rains began, but he would play it safe and give himself three. He had no desire to spend a night in the jungle.

Making note of the time, he set out in the direction the Silverado had gone. The tire tracks soon disappeared but the trail was fairly clear and still wide enough for a vehicle—barely.

He'd hiked for almost thirty minutes when the trail narrowed and appeared to end. There wasn't a clear fork in the road, but it would be slow going on foot, let alone for a truck. Peering into the undergrowth, what looked to be a trail came into view. Pushing aside large palm leaves confirmed that vegetation had been hacked to create a trail.

He'd learned enough in his years in this wild country to mark his way. Meghan had given him a couple dozen bright orange ties for that purpose. He fished them out of a pocket of his backpack now and tied one on a low-hanging branch where he would see it coming back, but not in such an obvious place that someone else might see it and trail him.

He'd been hyper aware on the river lest someone follow him, but he hadn't been as careful once on the trail. He stopped now, listening for a telltale snapping of twigs or the quieting of the forest's denizens.

As he forged into the undergrowth, picking out the trail, and keeping an eye out for reptiles underfoot, a flash of pink caught his eye. Thinking it was merely a blooming flower or maybe a bird foraging on the forest floor, he took another step, but something made him look closer.

He turned on his phone's flashlight and stooped to examine what looked like a large paper clip. Gingerly lifting one end, he inspected his find. It was, in fact two oversized paper clips, one lime green, attached to an aqua-colored clip like links in a chain. He'd used clips like these in his translation work. The second clip had a clump of something mushy and bright pink hooked to it. Wet paper maybe? It seemed incongruous to find a manmade object here. Probably just trash discarded by a hiker.

He wasn't the only one who'd passed this way. The machete-blazed trail testified to that, but still, finding objects as mundane as office supplies so far from civilization gave him pause. He started to pick off some wet vegetation that clung to the metal. But wait—

He smoothed out what he'd thought were soggy, dried husks. There was a primitive design inked on them. Writing maybe?

He shined the flashlight again and inspected the find. Few of the indigenous tribes in this part of the country had a written language, but these markings were primitive, as if a child had drawn them. And they were repetitive, like an artsy pattern, not part of an alphabet. Interesting.

He tossed the clips back onto the forest floor. Immediately it brought a smile as he imagined Natalie scolding him for littering. Just as quickly, his throat swelled with the reality of her absence.

He started to pick up the clips again, but he hadn't brought anything for trash except for the plastic baggie his sandwich was in. If he saw the trash on his way back, after he'd eaten his lunch, he would pick it up then. And if not, he prayed he'd have a chance someday soon to apologize to his wife.

He walked on, climbing as the trail ascended. He secured two more orange ties to the foliage as he went, but after ten minutes the path disappeared again. He paused, breathing heavily, and searched for clues to know which way to go.

He brushed vegetation aside in an arc ahead of him, and his breath caught when he spotted another clump of colored paper, bright aqua blue this time. He flipped on the flashlight again, checking that he still had plenty of battery power on his phone. The aqua mush was connected to a single paper clip, oversized like the one he'd found before. This one was missing the husks with the inked pattern, but no doubt they were from the same batch of "litter." But why would the two be so far apart?

He wished now that he'd picked up the other two linked together, but he didn't want to waste time going back. He put the recent find in a pocket of his backpack and followed the trail until it faded again.

Using the same method as before, parting the curtain of grasses and palms, he found what appeared to be the trail's continuation. Now he kept an eye out purposefully for more "litter." And was rewarded only a few steps forward on the trail.

Maybe a hiker had used the paper clips and colorful bits of paper the way he was using Meghan's ties. Breadcrumbs to find the trail back. They'd probably been clipped to branches only to wash off in an afternoon deluge. But they were proof a human had passed this way.

At the thought, a chill went through him. These markers might lead him to one of the guerrilla encampments. Or a gang hideout. Maybe the same men who'd taken Natalie? He turned a three-sixty on the trail, his senses on high alert.

Someone had passed here before. And it was in the general direction the Silverado had escaped to with Natalie. If they'd taken her this way, they'd have had to walk. And the distance would have been torturous for Natalie in her condition.

He forged on, careful not to make any noise louder than bird-song could cover.

❧ 23 ❧

"Get up! Time to go!"

Natalie stirred and opened her eyes. Long camouflage-clad legs stood over her and the butt of a rifle nudged her shoulder. Rubbing her eyes, she sat up on the hard earth, wincing, her spine like jelly.

"Please. I can't go any farther. I need to sleep." She'd decided not to let them see her weakness, but she couldn't stop the tears that came now. "I'm sorry. But *please*. Have mercy. For my baby's sake. Can't you see?" She placed her hand over her belly.

She detected the slightest softening of the guard's features, but he motioned again for her to get up. He swept a hand in the direction of the woods, speaking English with a heavy accent. "Toilet. Hurry."

She struggled to her feet, pulling her backpack up with her and picked her way into the jungle and behind a veil of branches that afforded privacy.

Five soldiers in the mismatched camouflage uniforms of the guerrillas had escorted her from her prison yesterday, but after only an hour, three of them parted ways leaving her with Tomás and another soldier she simply thought of as "the quiet one."

She'd asked his name once, and he'd merely grunted with a derisive sneer.

They'd not treated her unkindly, and for that she was grateful. If anything, they'd handled her as they might have handled a package to be delivered. One whose outer wrappings weren't as important as what was inside. And that was what worried her. Where were they taking her? And why?

She wrapped her arms around her midsection, praying her baby would kick, somehow let her know he was still alive. It had been so long since she'd felt him move.

Before finally stopping to sleep last night, they must have walked for three hours, part of it slogging through mud in heavy rains. If she hadn't been in such pain, she would have relished the "shower" the deluge provided.

At times she could have sworn they were going in circles and she'd lost all sense of direction. As if her swollen ankles and blistered heels weren't enough, she'd been awakened every hour or two by a searing pain low in her back. Already this morning, her spine screamed for relief.

When she returned to where her guards waited, Tomás handed her a bottle of water and immediately set out walking. She had no choice but to follow, praying for strength and stamina.

She'd eaten a banana and some bitter berries the guards picked on the trail yesterday, but her appetite was gone, vanquished by the pain that had been her constant companion since she'd been freed from the shed. Cradling her belly, she lifted, trying to ease the weight of the baby and take some pressure off her back. But the action did little to alleviate her agony.

She stumbled behind her captors, every step torturous, wondering where they might be taking her—and why her baby hadn't moved in such a long time.

❧

CLOUDS WERE MOVING IN FAST. HE'D BE LUCKY IF HE HAD AN hour before the rains began. But he couldn't turn back now. Not after finding yet another paper clip with the same clump of soggy paper as the others.

He felt certain now that he was following a trail. And as much as he wanted to believe that Natalie had left it, he couldn't think why on earth she would have had access to paper clips. The only thing she'd had with her was her backpack, and they surely relieved her of that. But *someone* had left a trail, and it seemed purposeful.

So he climbed on, even as the trail became less obvious with every step. He watched the ground as he walked, his eyes on the lookout for another flash of neon-colored metal. He marked his own route with the orange markers Meghan had given him, but he half expected to break through the foliage and find a main road. Why else would someone have come this way? It didn't make sense.

He trudged on, losing the trail more than once, but always finding a splintered branch or once, a faint boot print that let him know humans had passed this way.

Racing the clock—and the weather—he lost the trail yet again and debated whether he could afford to go on. He'd almost decided it wasn't worth getting caught up here when he came to a small clearing. The sky darkening and clouds heavy with the coming rain, he peered through a gray mist to see the sharp lines of some sort of structure.

Pulse pounding, he started across the clearing, but halted when he noticed an overgrown, moss-covered shed on the opposite side. The structure was void of window on the side facing him. Still, he felt exposed and vulnerable. If anyone was inside and saw him, he was a sitting duck. He forced himself to stop and waited in the shadows, watching for signs of life.

He checked the time and waited five long minutes—minutes he could ill afford—before creeping into the open space. Heart in his throat, he circled the structure, searching for an entrance.

No windows at all, only louvered vents at the roof's peak. A small metal door was padlocked shut. The shed was likely storage for grain or wood. But why up here, so far from the city? And why the metal door? Drugs, weapons, or other contraband came to mind as possibilities. As did the likelihood that if anyone found him here, they'd be inclined to make sure he never made it out of the jungle.

And a good hiding place for contraband also made a good hiding place for a kidnapping victim.

Heart hammering, he pounded on the door. "Natalie? Natalie, are you there?"

The deafening silence of the rain forest answered back, and the sky spit a sprinkling of rain. A final warning before the clouds opened as they did every afternoon. Calling her name again, he beat on the door with a closed fist.

Why hadn't he thought to bring tools with him? He searched the perimeter of the building for something to break the lock. Finding nothing, he scrambled back down the trail a hundred yards where he remembered climbing over a small stone outcropping. He dug out a heavy rock and lugged it back up to the shed.

Holding the rock in both hands, he struck the padlock over and over until finally, one side of the hasp latch gave way. Breathing hard, he renewed his efforts until the whole latch came loose and he could lever the door open.

He peered through the opening. The interior dark, the only light filtered through a small skylight in the center of the roof. He stepped inside. A skittering sound joined the light patter of rain, and he quickly turned on his phone's flashlight and scanned the room.

A many-legged insect scurried into a corner, but the shed was empty. Except for a mound of rags in one corner. Holding the flashlight high in one hand, he kicked at the rags, then gingerly lifted the wad, expecting some jungle critter to run out.

Nothing did, but the "rags" turned out to be a small sleeping bag. Filthy and damp, but it looked like it had originally been an olive shade of green.

He dragged it outside and unzipped it, looking for some clue as to who it belonged to. Although given that it was the same color as the guerrilla soldiers' uniforms, he had little doubt. The thing stunk like body odor and was no doubt flea-ridden—or worse. But if he got stuck out here, it might offer some shelter from the downpour.

He checked the sky. It was barely sprinkling. If he hurried, he could get back on the water before the rains hit. He'd call Hank from the boat so he and Meghan wouldn't worry.

Debating whether to replace and secure the hasp, leave everything as he'd found it, he decided he couldn't afford to waste the time. He had no intention of returning, and since the shed was empty, he wouldn't be putting anyone's belongings at risk.

He went inside and gave one last sweep of the flashlight. Nothing. Even the critters seemed to have vacated. He stepped one foot onto the ground, tapping the button on his phone to turn off the flashlight, when the beam caught something just to the left side of the doorframe.

He turned on the light again, alarmed at how low his phone's battery was. He aimed the beam at the spot where he thought he'd seen something. He bent closer. His breath caught.

Another paper clip. This one dry as toast. What had been shreds of wet, colored paper in the others was a folded square of bright green paper with some kind of husk threaded through it. He slid it from the paper clip and unfolded it.

Disappointment deflated his hope when the paper proved to be blank. But when he started to refold the square of paper, he realized it was sticky on one end. A sticky note. Like the ones he and Natalie used that had gone missing from his desk. Along with a box of oversized paper clips.

Gabrielle? Was it possible Lele's mother had been here? Had left this trail. He and Natalie felt sure she was the one who'd stolen the items from their *utta*. Had her guerrilla boyfriend brought her here? Had she been held here against her will?

He folded the decorated husk back inside the sticky note as he'd found it and stashed the whole thing into a dry pocket of his backpack. The soggy pieces he placed in the plastic baggie from his sandwich with the clips.

First thing in the morning, he'd bring Hank back here—hopefully with his policeman friend, Alejandro—and retrace the trail he'd left with Meghan's orange ties, see if they could make some sense of this mystery.

The steep descent to the inlet and his boat went twice as fast as the hike up, mostly because he turned the events of the day over and over in his mind, trying to connect dots that refused to be connected. He couldn't imagine why the paper clips he'd found were significant, and yet he felt certain they were. It seemed too much of a coincidence that the little paper clip "crafts" had been made from the exact same materials stolen from his and Natalie's desks.

And if they *were* somehow connected to Gabrielle, why would she have left them here, so far from Conzalez?

He unmoored the boat and guided it out of the shallows. As the river widened and he was certain he was alone on the water, he punched it, trimmed up the motor, and headed full throttle toward Conzalez.

❇ 24 ❇

She slept under the stars that night, under the watchful eyes of Tomás and two other soldiers. And though she was bone-weary and the ground damp and cold, Natalie relished looking up at the night sky sans the barrier of a dirty skylight. After so many nights locked in the shed, it was a wonder to peer through the cavelike openings in the trees above her, all the way to the stars. She could almost imagine she was free.

The jungle's tumultuous night music rose and fell in cadence with the breeze, and she remembered Mom telling her how Dad had studied the constellations of the Southern Hemisphere and knew the names for many of the stars. Before he'd left to go to the far-off village where he'd ultimately been left for dead, he and Mom had agreed to watch a star named Spica in the Virgo constellation, so that even though they would be separated by the miles—for what they thought would be a few short nights— they would still be connected, knowing they were both looking at the same star in the night sky.

She squinted and focused on the largest star she could locate. Was that Spica? Little had her parents known what their lives would become after that final night together. Oh, how she missed them both. She wondered if Dad, from his eternal home in Heaven, knew her situation. Could he be praying for her even now? She hoped so.

And David, her precious David. How she longed to feel his arms around her. Oh, what regret she felt for the foolish arguments they'd had. Would she ever see him again? Ever have a chance to make amends?

A tune wove its way through her thoughts, bringing to mind a kids' movie she'd watched as a small girl about a little lost mouse named Fievel. The popular theme song had always made Mom cry because it reminded her of those months when, unbeknownst to her, Dad *was* alive and they had indeed been sleeping beneath the same big sky. Wishing and praying under the same bright star.

The haunting melody of "Somewhere Out There" continued to play, full and rich, and she let the tears come, weeping for everything her parents had endured, and lost, and for everything she and David were going through now.

It did help to remember that even though she and David had been separated by locked doors and walls and guards—and miles —they *had* been sleeping beneath the same southern sky every night. And tonight she knew without a doubt that the same God was holding each of them in His loving arms, giving hope, comfort, and a peace that made no sense under the circumstances, yet was more real than anything she'd ever known.

⁂

HER BACK SPASMED AND NATALIE STOPPED TO RUB AWAY THE pain that had grown worse after a night of sleeping on the ground.

They'd been walking for nearly two hours when the trail widened and her guards snapped to alert. Tomás gave a shout and trotted ahead. A large pickup—maybe the same one her abductors had driven?—pulled onto the road from its hiding place in the foliage and crawled toward them.

As terrified as she'd been to see that truck a few weeks ago, an equal degree of elation raced through her veins now. She sank to the ground, her legs giving out. She didn't care if the truck was hauling her to her execution. That would be a mercy now.

The two guards lifted her into the bed of the truck. They tied a scarf over her eyes and ordered her to lie down. She complied willingly, and at Tomás's command, the truck's engine revved. They bounced along the rutted road for what seemed an eternity, until she almost wished to be walking again. Every jolt brought agonizing pain and Natalie forced herself to recite the verses that had brought such comfort over these days.

I will lift up mine eyes unto the hills, from whence cometh my help...

She'd set the psalm to a tune late one night and now she sang softly. She couldn't hear her own voice over the roar of the engine and the crunch of tires on gravel, still she sang. She gave a little gasp of pain with every bump in the road, but she sang. And she thanked God for whatever was ahead. Whether her release from captivity or...a more final release. Tears rose at that possibility, yet a still small voice deep inside whispered to her in a language without words, quieting her soul. *Help me, Lord. Go with me.*

Unexpected joy replaced the fear and uncertainty inside her, and she knew a closeness to God she'd never known. Oh, to have back all the hours she'd spent questioning *why?* If she could, she'd turn all those *whys* into *thank yous.*

The truck bumped onto mercifully smooth pavement and slowed. Gradually she became aware of the sounds of a city. Children playing, people laughing. Dogs barking. A donkey brayed and someone honked a horn. Oh, how she'd missed the simple sounds of life. But a city? She hadn't expected that. She'd assumed they were driving deeper into the jungle.

Oh, please, God. Maybe there was yet hope. Maybe her baby would know life on earth after all. Did she dare believe someone had negotiated for her return? That they were taking her to David? Or flying her back to the States?

No. She couldn't let herself hope. Not if those hopes were only to be crushed. She lay on the hot, dusty bed of the truck and relished the smooth road, listening for familiar sounds. Anything that might tell her where she was. Snippets of conversation she overheard were in Castilian Spanish, not a dialect. Having no idea how far they'd traveled or even which direction, she couldn't guess how far Bogotá was. Or any other city.

The truck took half a dozen turns and finally stopped. The driver cut the engine and two guards lifted her by her arms and carried her a few paces.

A door opened and closed behind her, then when she struggled to support her own weight, they carried her again, not letting her feet touch the floor. They walked down what must be a narrow hallway, judging by how closely they pressed against her on either side. Another door opened and the guards' steps became clumsy and halting as if they were going down stairs. Yes, that must be it because the air grew instantly cooler and dank-smelling.

They stopped and set her down. A door closed behind her and they yanked the scarf from her head. A strand of hair caught in it, and she cried out, rubbing her scalp.

She looked around and gasped. Her eyes were still adjusting, and the windowless room was dim, lit only by a single light bulb hanging from a rafter by a cord, but she was in a room twice the size of the shed. There was a bed. A desk with a small lamp and a chair. A pedestal sink with a mirror that looked like it might hide a medicine cabinet.

Tomás crossed the room in three strides and opened a small door. "Bathroom."

"Oh, thank you, Jesus." She hadn't meant to say it aloud.

Tomás barely concealed a smile. He pointed to the bed. "Rest."

She nodded, trying not to imagine what she was supposed to rest up for.

He left and the deadbolt clanked in the heavy metal door. She was still in a prison, but there was a strange comfort in the change. She explored the space. The bathroom was separate from the bedroom with a flushing toilet, filthy though it was. And a sink where she could wash up. She felt almost giddy.

They'd left a change of clothes for her, ill-fitting though they looked—a long gathered skirt and an oversized floral blouse that looked like it might have belonged to someone's great-grand-mother. But they were clean and dry. Even a small stack of cotton underwear, each piece still sporting a price sticker.

The medicine cabinet revealed a toothbrush still in the pack-age, and toothpaste, a bar of soap, and a comb. She'd never been so grateful for basic hygiene and wasted no time shedding the outfit she'd worn for days on end.

She closed the cabinet and found a stranger staring back at her from the mirror. Dark crescents formed shadows beneath her eyes, her cheeks were sunken, her hair matted and lifeless. The outline of her ribs was stark, her skin pale and ashy. Only her breasts and belly bore any sign of her youth. Tempted to cry, she was too grateful to be alive. And *here*.

She bathed at the sink as best she could, the water tempera-ture never getting past lukewarm, yet it felt heavenly. She dried quickly with the worn, dingy towel that hung from a hook, moving quickly, not knowing how long she had or if someone might walk in on her.

She pulled on the new clothes and placed her old skirt and T-shirt to soak in a sink full of soapy water. She was tempted to throw them away, having worn them for two solid weeks. But merely having the mundane tasks of washing and hanging clothes to dry—something with purpose—lifted her spirits. And this way she would have a clean set of clothes to change into.

She went to the bed and pulled down the worn, but clean covers. There was even a top sheet under the thin blanket. And a pillow. She'd never seen anything so beautiful. Feeling weak in the knees, she crawled onto the mattress.

Breathing a prayer of thanks, she curled on her side and imagined David in the bed beside her, his strong arms around her, his long fingers splayed protectively over the belly that held their child.

⚜

HOW MANY HOURS SHE'D SLEPT SHE COULDN'T GUESS, BUT SHE awoke as if from a drug-induced coma. When she finally shook herself awake, she swung her legs over the side of the bed. Her bare feet met cold concrete, but she spotted a small basket of food on the desk. It hadn't been there before. Someone had been here.

Despite having grown accustomed to her guards entering the shed at random hours, it still unnerved her to think of someone coming in while she slept. She rose to inspect the contents, trying to rub away the now constant throbbing in her lower back. She prayed these back issues would go away before she went into labor. She wasn't sure how much more she could bear.

The basket held cheese and salami wrapped in waxed paper, a sleeve of store-bought crackers, and a pint carton of cow's milk. They were definitely in a more populated area. Someplace with a proper supermarket judging by the package of polvorosas. The kind dusted with powdered sugar. She opened the wrapping and ate one of the buttery sugar cookies. Her appetite seemed to still be on hiatus, but the cookie was the first thing that had actually tasted good to her in many days. She ate another, then broke off a hunk of cheese and ate it with a cracker. She would eat if only for her baby's sake.

The room, the lightbulb, running water... It all felt surreal. But the question dogged her: Why had they moved her from the shed? Were they finally going to ask for ransom. Were they merely fattening her up, cleaning her up to prove she was still alive? And why else would they have brought her clean clothes and toiletries unless something had changed. She just didn't know *what*.

           ℋ   25   ℋ

David combed his hair and beard in front of the mirror over the small powder room sink across from the guest room where he'd slept for thirteen nights now. He crept quietly to the kitchen not wanting to wake Meghan or Lele, but hoping Hank was already up. The earlier they got on the trail, the better.

He brewed coffee and made sandwiches for him and Hank to take with them.

His eye caught the plastic baggie he'd emptied late last night while he told Hank and Meghan about his discovery. Meghan had used her blow dryer to dry off the soggy clumps of paper that had been stuck to the paper clips. She and Hank seemed skeptical that the whimsical pieces had anything to do with the missing office supplies back in Timoné, but once the paper was dry, she'd folded each sticky note and tried to piece them back together to match the dry one he'd found inside the shed.

The paper had dried crinkly and smudged, and the design on the corn husks had faded almost to nothing, but when Meghan attached all fifteen of the paper clips he'd found together into one long chain, it made a cheery, child-like chain. The corn husk strips were missing from a couple of the paper clips but she'd made those the top and bottom links so it was hardly noticeable. The colorful chain twirled from the light fixture over the kitchen table even now.

"Hey! Where did you find that?"

He turned to see Lele standing in the hallway, eyes wide. She pointed to the paper clip chain.

"Shh... Don't wake up Miss Meg. Come here." He pulled out a chair at the table and sat.

She pattered over and climbed onto his lap, but immediately bowed her head and mumbled, "Are you mad, Mister David?"

"Why would I be mad, honey?"

"Because. I stole your things. Miss Natalie said that was bad."

"Miss Natalie?" He was starting to think she wasn't quite awake. She must have dreamt about Natalie. Poor girl. He turned her around on his lap and tipped her chin to face him. "Look at me, Lele? What are you talking about?"

Meghan came down the hallway. "Good morning."

"Good morning. Sorry if we woke you up."

"No, Hank woke me. He's almost ready. Good morning, Lele. You're up early."

"Did Miss Natalie give *you* my wind chime?" She pointed to the chain, using the English words for wind chime.

"*Your* wind chime?" David arched an eyebrow. "What do you mean, Lele?"

Meghan knelt in front of her. "These wind chimes are yours, honey?"

Lele shook her head adamantly. "No, it was a *sorpressia* for Miss Natalie. And Mr. David. I made it!" She puffed her little chest out, but then her face fell. "It's all messed up though."

David rose, unhooked the "wind chime" from the light fixture, and squatted on the floor beside Meghan. "This is important, Lele. *When* did you give the wind chime to Miss Natalie?"

"She found it when we went to get my shoes."

"Back home, you mean? In Timoné?"

She nodded solemnly, her frown deepening. "She wasn't supposed to find it yet. It's not finished. But she said we had to talk to you. She was a little mad."

"Do you mean before we came on the boat? This trip?"

"When we went for my shoes," she repeated.

"At your abuelo's house?"

She nodded. "But we had to hurry to get on the boat because you were waiting for us. Miss Natalie almost left it in my loft, but then she put it in her backpack."

David exchanged a look with Meghan. "Lele, did she bring this with her on the boat?"

She shrugged her slim shoulders. "It was in her backpack."

"Meghan..." He could hardly breathe. "Natalie dropped these! I know she did. That shed I told you about? It's where they were holding her!"

"*Were?*"

"The shed was empty. But she'd been there. That's where I found the last link, the dry one. But she dropped these. I know it. She left us a trail! But we must have missed something."

He pointed to a design on the strip of corn husk that hadn't gotten wet. "Did you write this, Lele?"

She nodded.

"Does it mean something?"

"Mean?"

"Were you trying to write something? Words?"

She looked at him like he'd lost his marbles. "I can't write words, Mr. David. I'm just little."

He couldn't help but laugh, even as his mind went a mile a minute about what this all meant. "So, it's just a...design. To look pretty?"

"I copied Miss Natalie's fuzzy shirt."

Ah. He understood now. He turned to Meghan. "I thought it looked familiar. It's like the pattern on a sweater Natalie sometimes wears on cool days."

"A *jacket*," Lele added, using the English word. "She wears it to school."

"That's right." David nodded. "Meg, we've got to—"

"I'll get Hank!" Meghan jumped up and raced down the hall.

David squeezed Lele so tightly she cried out. "You did good, Lele. You did good. We're going to find Miss Natalie." *Please don't make a liar out of me, God.*

He'd prayed that prayer too many times in the last days. But God had smiled on them today, And for the first time in a long while, he felt true hope!

NATALIE WRITHED ON THE BED. THE PAIN HAD WORSENED over the last few hours, and she feared something was wrong with the baby. What else could it be?

She forced herself to recite a litany of thanksgiving aloud, something that had made the suffering tolerable in those eternal days in the shed. Only now she had so much more for which to be thankful.

"Thank you for this bed, Father. Thank you for a sink and soap. And"—she breathed through the pain—"running water. Oh thank you for the water, Lord. Thank you for a comb, a toothbrush... Thank you for a real bathroom with a real toilet. Ohhh—"

The pain in her abdomen was almost unbearable. If she didn't get—

Without warning, a warm gush of fluid wet the sheets beneath her. "Oh! No!"

She'd read about a woman's water breaking just before delivery started in a book Mom had sent her. Was this *that*? She didn't think she'd peed the bed. She would have given anything to be able to search online, find out what was happening to her, what she should be doing.

But if her water had broken, contractions would likely start soon. She couldn't have this baby by herself! She needed help. *Oh God, please... Send somebody...*

She climbed off the bed and half-crawled to the bathroom. She cleaned up as best she could and, on her knees, situated the sheets so she wasn't lying in the damp spot. Her back screamed for relief and no position she tried offered it.

She looked over to the desk. No one had brought her food yet today. Whenever they showed up, she had to convince them to get her to a hospital. The thought brought distress. They'd shown no favoritism toward her because of the pregnancy. Except for the fact that they hadn't killed her yet, despite no ransom being forthcoming. That had to count for something.

But would they be persuaded that she needed to get to a hospital? If, as she suspected, they were waiting for the baby to be born, then she needed to convince them that the baby was in danger.

She tried to sleep. To rest up for the labor that was certainly impending. The only thing that kept her from crying out in pain was to continually change positions. She would get a few minutes of relief before another spasm hit. Then the process would start all over again. How would she manage if true labor pains started on top of this agonizing back pain? This was so different than how she'd imagined her first baby's birth would be.

Deep sadness welled up inside her. If she died in childbirth, what would happen to her baby? Would David ever know he'd had a child and whether he'd had a son or daughter?

Moaning, she'd just changed positions again and found a bit of relief when footsteps sounded outside the door. The now familiar *scritch-scritch* of the key in the lock, and the door opened.

Tomás entered and closed the door behind him.

"Please! Tomás! I need help! I think the baby is coming. El bebé." She held a hand over her belly.

He set the small basket he carried on the desk and studied

her as if trying to decide if she was telling the truth. "How do you know?" he asked in English.

"I think...my water broke." Did he even know what that meant? She was embarrassed to share details with him, but how else could she convince him?

"When?"

"A couple hours ago. And I have pain. Terrible pain. Please. I need help."

He pointed to the basket on the desk. "Eat something. You'll feel better."

"No! You don't understand! My baby is coming... Please! I need to be in a hospital."

He backed toward the door. "Rest. We'll see how you feel later. First babies take a long time."

She stared, disbelieving. First, at his callousness. And second...how did he know that? Was Tomás a father? She'd never considered the possibility, but she milked it now.

"Tomás! Please, don't leave me. I can't have this baby alone. Please..." With great effort, she slipped from the bed and staggered toward him.

He turned and opened the door, waving her off.

"I'm begging you, Tomás! Please!"

He stared at her. Was that alarm she detected in his expression? But then he pulled the door closed behind him. The latch clicked and the key turned again.

After that, the only sound was her own anguished keening as a tsunami of pain brought her to her knees on the hard concrete floor.

＊ 26 ＊

David paced the Middletons' patio, watching the sun rise behind the ridge of mountains. Another day gone. Two full weeks since Natalie had been abducted, yet it felt like they were no closer than they'd been to finding her than they were that first devastating day.

Yesterday, he and Hank had led Alejandro Moreno to the shed. The policeman helped them search the area for other links or clues that might tell them where Natalie's captors had taken her after they'd left there. Judging by boot prints, discarded cigarette butts, and other evidence, Moreno surmised there'd been two or three men guarding her.

Somewhat troubling was the fact they hadn't found any *solid* proof Natalie had been there, for instance, no smaller tracks with the imprint of the tennis shoes she'd been wearing. But Lele's "wind chime" being there was proof enough for him. No other way that could have gotten there.

"But perhaps she's light enough that her footsteps didn't make an impression that would withstand the rains," Moreno told David. "Or they carried her."

That gave him little comfort. Why would they be carrying her unless she was injured or bound and unable to walk? Having made the strenuous trek to the shed twice now, he couldn't imagine her making that climb in her advanced stage of pregnancy, but neither could he see someone *carrying* a pregnant Natalie up the trail. It had been challenging enough for him alone with only a backpack to haul.

He plopped into an Adirondack chair feeling utterly defeated. He'd prayed so hard that they'd come back with Natalie yesterday. That he would be able to call Daria Hunter and tell her that her precious daughter had been rescued. But that they hadn't come back with so much as a new clue, let alone with Natalie, had thrown him for a loop. *God what are You doing here?*

Two weeks they'd been searching for her. She had to be close to delivering by now. Since they'd never had a sonogram or even seen a doctor other than consultations with an ob-gyn in Kansas who'd kept tabs on Natalie's pregnancy via sat phone conversations, it was difficult to be sure about her due date. Her doctor had estimated it would be somewhere between the last week of October and the first week of November. Dr. Davis hadn't seemed too concerned with narrowing the window further since the pregnancy had been so free of complications.

He needed to call Cole and Daria today—before they called him. He hadn't spoken with them since Monday morning and they'd be anxious. They didn't yet know about the trail of Lele's wind chime, and it almost seemed worse to call with news that had led to a frustrating dead end than to call with no news at all. Then again, if the shoe was on the other foot, he would want to know.

"Mr. David, can I get up?" Lele peeked through the sliding screen door.

He rose and quietly slid the door open. "Good morning. It's early, honey. You sure you're ready to get up?"

She nodded.

"Did you sleep well?"

She nodded again, then frowned. "I had a dream."

"A good one or a scary one?" He'd taken Meghan's lead—and what he remembered from Natalie—on how to speak to Lele. He had to admit that this whole ordeal had been good for his relationship with the child. Even though she adored Meghan, she'd clung to him tightly. Preferred him. And he felt honored.

"My dream was kinda good, kinda scary."

"You want to tell me about it?" He motioned her to the chair he'd just vacated and sank back into it, pulling her onto his lap. Oh, how he wished Natalie were here to help him know what to say.

Lele sniffed and leaned back against him. She was so tiny she seemed breakable, though her escapades in the jungle said otherwise.

"So, what happened in your dream?"

She looked hard at him. "Miss Natalie was hanging up the wind chime in the kitchen."

"Here? At Miss Meg's?"

She shook her head. "No, at our *utta*. In the village. But she hung it over the *fogoriamo* and it caught on fire and flames shot everywhere!"

"Was that scary? Did you get hurt? In your dream?"

"No. Miss Natalie was cheering and telling you, 'Come look!'"

"Did I come look?"

"Uh-huh. And you got mad. Very mad. You were yelling."

"At Miss Natalie?"

Lele burst into tears. "No! At me! I'm sorry, Mr. David. It's my fault that we lost Miss Natalie!"

"Lele? Shhh... It's okay." He pulled her closer. "Why do you think it's your fault?"

"Because! I stole Miss Natalie's markers. And I stole your paper clips." She used the English word for markers—because there was no Timoné word—and for paper clips, she said *kadina*, the Timoné word for chain.

"No, of course it's not your fault." He waited until her cries quieted, then turned her to face him. "It was wrong to take our things, but that's not why they took her, Lele. You had nothing to do with it. In fact, your wind chime might even help us find her."

"Help?"

"Because she left a trail for us to follow." He explained how he'd found the links of the chain at each fork in the road.

"But why did she throw it away? She didn't like it?"

"I'm sure she loved it. But she needed something to mark the way so we could find her. You understand?"

Lele nodded solemnly.

"I know you won't ever take anything from our *utta*—or anyone else's—again. And Miss Natalie has already forgiven you. You understand what forgive means?"

"She's not mad?"

"No, she's not. I'm sure she understands that you're sorry and that you'll try very hard never to steal anything again. So she won't be mad at you about it."

Lele took in a shuddering breath. "I wish *she* could tell me."

"She will. As soon as she can, she will."

Oh, Lord Jesus, please let it be soon.

Meghan slid open the door and held the coffeepot where he could see it. "Are you ready for coffee?"

"That would be wonderful."

She disappeared and emerged a few seconds later with the heavy pottery mug he preferred.

"Lele! I didn't hear you get up." Meghan spoke pidgin Spanish to the little girl.

The two had somehow managed to communicate quite well.

She wriggled off of David's lap and went to hug Meghan's legs. "Careful, honey. I've got hot coffee." Meg held the carafe high.

Lele sniffed the air. "*Cazho.* Miss Natalie *loves cazho.*" She drew out the word. "With goat's milk. That's how she likes it. I hope those bad men give her some."

David and Meghan exchanged a look. They'd hoped since

Lele hadn't spoken of the abduction that maybe she hadn't seen the worst of what happened, hadn't been traumatized. But of course, she'd been in the Jeep with him and Hank while they desperately searched for Natalie. The poor child. She had likely imagined even worse than the truth—if that were possible. They needed to reassure her that God had Natalie in the palm of His hand. Because he did believe that. Hard as it was not to think of the worst. But even if what happened to Natalie ultimately *was* the worst, even if she'd suffered greatly, for her that meant gain. Gain of the best kind. *For to me, to live is Christ, and to die is gain.*

Meghan filled his mug then set the carafe down in the middle of the picnic table out of Lele's reach. "Are you hungry, sweetie? Ready for some breakfast?"

Lele's eyes brightened.

"Let's go find something to eat." She slid the door open again. "I'll leave you the pot, David."

"Thanks, Meg. I'll save Hank a cup or two."

"Take what you need. I can make another pot when he gets up."

"Let him sleep. He's carried a heavy burden for us for far too long. You have too. I'm so sorry, Meg."

"David. Don't you dare apologize. We only wish there was more we could do."

"No matter how this all ends, I'll never be able to thank you enough for going through this with us. Especially with that one." He winked at Lele.

"Am I *that one?*" Lele wrinkled her nose, repeating the English phrase.

David and Meghan laughed.

Lele's face fell. "Is *that one* bad?"

"No. No, sweet Lele." He pulled her into a hug. "It is good. Very, very good."

Her quizzical look made him want to weep, but he was wrung out. And he didn't know how much more they might endure before this was all over.

$$\approx \quad 27 \quad \approx$$

The room spun and Natalie gripped the lumpy pillow, waiting for the agonizing wave to pass. She was in labor. She was sure of it. She didn't have a watch or a clock to time her contractions, but she'd counted through three of them now as best she could and they seemed to be coming at regular intervals. Every five or six minutes. And had been for the last few hours.

The pain in her back had eased up slightly. At least between spasms. But those in-between times were getting shorter as the contractions grew longer. She carefully surveyed the room that had become as familiar to her as her the *utta* at home. But now she looked with different eyes, searching for anything that might help her with this birth—and after the baby came.

She didn't need the blanket herself since the nights were warm. It was still relatively clean and would keep the baby warm and cushioned. She had running water but no way to boil it.

Oh, how she wished she'd read more about labor and delivery. But knowing that they were coming to Conzalez with plenty of time to spare—and an Internet connection—she'd planned to do her research after they arrived, and with Nurse Meg to answer any questions she had.

Mom had warned her to be careful what she read online. "There are horror stories that have nothing to do with your pregnancy, and I know you well enough that you would take them all to heart." Mom was right, and of course, in Timoné those stories were easy to avoid since they rarely got online. But now, alone in this windowless room, she would have given anything for information about what was happening to her.

The contraction eased, but it seemed only seconds before the next one started. She bit back a moan, though she didn't think anyone could hear her, since she'd only ever heard distant sounds of traffic, dogs barking, and occasionally voices shouting from a long way off.

She didn't know how breathing exercises helped with labor pains, but lay back on the bed, taking slow, even breaths and blowing them out in short puffs the way she'd seen women in the movies breathe through a contraction.

It did little to stop the pain, but soon the contraction eased. When another one didn't start in a few minutes, she got up and used the toilet. She washed her hands and splashed water on her face, then turned out the light and climbed back into bed, dreading the onset of the next contraction that was sure to follow.

She must have drifted into a restless sleep, but the knock on the door brought her bolt upright in the bed. No one had ever knocked before entering this room.

"Hello? Come in?" She didn't know if they could hear her, but she was too frightened to get out of bed and open the door, especially when a contraction was likely to debilitate her at any moment. But what if someone had come to rescue her? What if they'd found her?

"Come in!" she squeaked, unable to make her voice any louder.

She stilled at the familiar sound of the key turning in the lock, and watched as a patch of light from outside the door silhouetted someone backing into the room, carrying what looked like a large cardboard box. The figure moved gracefully like a woman, but before she turned around, the door closed and the room went dark again.

"Who's there?" Natalie strained to see in the dark.

No response, but the commotion near the door roused her curiosity more than it frightened her. The rustle of paper and the soft *thud* of items being laid out on the desk almost made her forget the building spasms of another contraction. But then the pain built to a crescendo and she almost forgot there was anyone in the room with her. The intensity of it made her cry out against her will, yet she was powerless to stop it.

"Help!" she breathed when momentary relief finally came. "Please, help me. Please... I'm in labor!" She struggled to remember one word of Spanish. "*Por favor*, I'm having a baby! I need a doctor. *El doctor*." She pronounced it dock-*tore* and prayed this person would understand what she was asking for.

Shuffling footsteps approached her bed, as if the person was feeling their way in the dark. "I will try to help you. *Onde está luzára?*"

Natalie sucked in a breath. The feminine voice spoke Spanish, but had used the *Timoné* word for light, not the Spanish *luz*.

She replied in Timoné as best she could remember. "There's a switch on the wall over the desk."

"*Egracita.*" Timoné again. More shuffling steps and then fumbling near the desk. Finally the light overhead came on.

Natalie squinted, waiting for her eyes to adjust.

The slightly built woman went to the sink and deftly pulled her dark hair into a bun before washing her hands. She wore the green camouflage pants of the guerrilla soldiers and a dark olive T-shirt. "You have pain?" she asked over one shoulder. "Many pains?"

The quiet voice seemed familiar, confusing Natalie.

"Or pain all the time?" The woman probed.

Natalie started. The young soldier's inflection was definitely —and uniquely—Timoné. Natalie tried to see her face, but another contraction bowled her over. Squeezing her eyes tight, she tried not to scream. When the pain finally subsided and she lay panting, exhausted, she felt the warmth of a gentle hand on her forehead.

"Your baby will be here soon. I will help."

Hearing the Timoné accent flooded Natalie with a sense of well-being, and the gentle touch moved her to tears. It had been so long since someone had touched her with kindness.

"How long have the pains been coming?"

"I don't know for sure. It seems like several days. But there's no clock here, so I'm not sure."

"Babies pay no heed to clocks." Even the soft chuckle held the musical lilt of the Timoné dialect.

For some reason, she thought of Meena. She would have happily trusted Lele's grandmother to deliver her baby. She imagined her warm presence now and it brought comfort. "You're from Timoné? How did you know I was here?"

"Shhh. Quiet." She said the word in English, but the distinctive accent remained. She would have bet a small fortune on it.

"Where am I? Who are you?"

"Hush. Do not worry about that. We will get this baby out of you."

The phrase seemed odd, even given Natalie's relatively small Timoné vocabulary. As if the baby was a tumor that needed to be excised. Did this woman know something she didn't? Panic surged through her veins and she fumbled for words. "Is my baby alive? Are you...a doctor?"

Soft laughter. Not cruel. More like self-deprecating. And oddly familiar. "I am not a doctor. But I will help you."

The woman leaned over the bed and plumped the pillow behind Natalie's neck. A whiff of heavy perfume masked a hint of body odor.

Maybe it was her own. She'd perspired heavily and it had been hours since she'd washed up at the sink.

The woman straightened. "Can you sit up in the bed?"

"I'll try." She forced herself to her elbows but before she could sit upright, another contraction started. "Oh... Oh! Another pain is starting."

"It's okay. You won't die."

"What?"

"You won't die. I thought I would, but I did not."

Natalie held tightly to those words until the waves passed. When they did, she struggled again to sit up. "You have a baby?"

The woman didn't seem to hear. Natalie repeated the question, trying to meet the woman's gaze. Maybe she could befriend her and somehow get out of here. "Do you have a baby?" she asked again.

A shadow passed over the woman's face. The lightbulb overhead caught the thick bun atop her head, the smooth bronze complexion and full lips. And as if a veil had been lifted, the woman's features shifted to become inimitably familiar.

"Gabrielle! Is it you?"

But she knew it *was*. This was Lele's mamá. Jamos and Meena's daughter. There was no doubt.

❧

"Do not use my name."

Gabrielle said the words matter-of-factly, but Natalie sensed an urgency to the command.

"Why? Gabrielle, did your father find you? Have you talked to him?"

"My father is dead."

"No! He's searching for you, Gabri—" She cut off the syllable at the girl's warning glance. She lowered her voice. "Please... He's been looking for you ever since the day you left the village. He misses you desperately!"

"My father is dead." She repeated the words in that same wooden tone.

A tone Natalie took to mean that Jamos was dead *to her*. That she'd written him off. And then it struck her: Did Gabrielle know that her mother was actually dead? She did *not* want to be the one to bear that news. Besides, now was not the time. For Gabrielle's sake, but more for her own. She didn't have the strength it would take to comfort the girl.

As if to verify that, another contraction began. She fought it, feeling an urgency to reach this lost young woman. It seemed Gabrielle had hardened herself to what waited for her in Timoné. But maybe she would listen to reason where Lele was concerned. "Your daughter needs you." She wanted to tell her that Lele, too, missed her desperately, but that wouldn't have been the truth.

It bothered Natalie deeply that the little girl seemed to hold no affection for Gabrielle. Had her mother's rejection done permanent damage. And yet, there was no doubt she'd loved Meena and Jamos. And that she'd carved out a space for David and her in her heart. So she told Gabrielle only what was true. "Lele needs you. Please, come back to the village."

Gabrielle's smile was almost a sneer. "Lele has my mother. There is nothing for me there."

So she *didn't* know about Meena. *Oh, dear Lord. Be with her. Comfort her. Open her eyes to the truth.* But she couldn't tell her now.

Right now *she* needed Gabrielle. Because this baby was coming and there was no one else to help.

The contraction swelled and took control of her body, stronger even than the one before.

28

Alejandro Moreno's brow furrowed, and he propped his beefy hands at his belt. "Is there anything else you remember from the first time you came up here?"

The moss-covered shed looked untouched since he'd been up here three days ago. Three days. If this was how the authorities defined "getting right on it," they were sunk.

But what if he'd blown the best chance they had of finding Natalie by taking things into his own hands?

"Anything at all?" Moreno pressed. "Tracks? Smells? Anything that might give us a clue…"

David looked to Hank, as if his friend might be able to jog a memory loose. But Hank hadn't been here when he'd followed the paper-clip blazes of Natalie's trail.

He tugged at his beard, trying to think what he might have failed to mention. And came up blank. He stared at the shed where Natalie had certainly been held. Where would they have taken her from here? And why?

As if reading his thoughts, the policeman eyed David. "And when did you say your wife's baby is due?"

"We don't know for sure, but early November was her best

guess. Any day now really." It startled him a little to realize that the first of November was less than a week away. "That could be off a little either way though. Natalie hadn't seen a doctor yet. We planned to see one first thing after we got here. Why are you asking?" But before the words were even out, he knew the answer.

Hank apparently did too because he put a hand on David's shoulder. "Let's don't go there, David. Not yet."

Ignoring Hank's obvious hint, the policeman went on matter-of-factly. "If your wife was targeted because of her pregnancy, they might have taken her to a clinic or even a local hospital to deliver. Especially if there were complications."

Even though he wasn't surprised by this news, it chilled him to think of Natalie in labor with only strangers surrounding her. And yet it gave him a whiff of hope too. "If that's the case, someone at the clinic—or hospital—would report it, right? To the police?"

Moreno's frown deepened. "The more likely scenario is that someone will pose as her husband, she'll be threatened into silence, and they'll leave the hospital as soon as the baby is delivered."

"Without any proof? That can't be right. Especially when they know about the kidnapping."

"We've put out bulletins to all the local hospitals with your wife's photo. With any luck, she'll be recognized if she winds up in a hospital."

With any *luck*? It was all he could do to keep his voice steady. "If that happens and they...*sell* the baby, will they let Natalie go then? If it's only the baby they want?"

Moreno shook his head. "Not if they think they can still rustle up some ransom money."

"But the mission hasn't heard anything from the kidnappers since they refused to pay."

"They're in no hurry. If it's the infant they want, they

wouldn't turn her over until she'd delivered anyway. So no reason to ask again for the ransom. Not yet."

"Why the first time then? You think they had no intention of giving her up? Even if we had paid?"

"They likely knew the mission would turn them down. They just needed you to know they had her. Give you or other family members time to come up with the money."

"But you *do* think they'll contact the mission again?"

"More likely you. Or her family in the States. They may already have done that."

"No." He gritted his teeth, at the very end of his patience. "Not unless it was in the last fifteen hours. I talked to her parents just last night."

"You're sure they didn't pay and just aren't telling you?"

He shook his head. "I don't think so. Nothing seemed...amiss when I talked to them." It hadn't crossed his mind that Cole and Daria might try to take matters into their own hands. And that if Natalie's kidnappers contacted them, they might pay a ransom in secret. The possibility sent a strange surge of hope through him. He wouldn't blame them. This was their beloved daughter. Maybe more importantly for Daria, this was Nate's *only* daughter.

"Okay," Moreno conceded. "You know them better than anyone else."

"I knew them too." Hank looked to David as if asking permission to continue.

He nodded.

"Natalie's mom was also a missionary," Hank continued. "Her birthfather was held hostage at a village a couple days from Timoné. I don't think they would go against the mission's policy."

Moreno looked from David to Hank and back again, as if David might confirm. Finally he said, "We don't know what we'd do—or not do—until our own son or daughter is involved."

David's anger rose swiftly. "My son or daughter *is* involved, *sir*. Not to mention my wife!"

"David..." Hank put a hand on his shoulder and squeezed.

David shrugged out from under it. Did Moreno fault him for not being willing to pay? Was the man looking for a bribe? Surely he, of all people, understood why the mission had the policy they did. Moreno and his men's work would be tenfold what it was now if every organization paid ransom. It was bad enough that corporations and wealthy individuals paid millions of dollars to get their spoiled kids or spouses back from kidnappers.

Moreno walked away a distance to speak with one of the deputies he'd brought with them.

Hank pulled David aside and spoke under his breath. "I know you're frustrated, man, but we need Moreno on our side. There's nobody else I trust."

"Sorry. I shouldn't have..." He didn't finish the sentence, but paced a few steps back and forth, forcing himself to take deep breaths, to let the anger go.

After a few minutes, Moreno came toward them, his men behind him. "We've followed her trail as far as we can. There's no sign of tracks any direction except back the way we came. I don't know what else we can do up here."

"Thank you, Alejandro." Hank extended a hand.

"Yes, thank you." David gave a curt nod.

Moreno glanced up at the clouds overhead. "We'd better get moving. Don't much feel like spending the night up here." He hollered at his men, motioning them to head down the way they'd come.

David didn't want to spend the night up here either, but he felt like if he followed Moreno and the other officers back down to Conzalez, that would be the end of the search for Natalie. The police officer had as much as said that they'd done all they could do. This was the end of the line.

How was he supposed to live with that? How could he just let it go at that?

He couldn't. And if they were calling it a day, then he was done toeing the line. Till now, he'd tried to stay out of their way, follow protocol. Let them take the lead. But he couldn't mess up their investigation if nobody was investigating.

Now, all bets were off.

Carina:
The Keel

29

Natalie grabbed Gabrielle's arm in a panic. Unable to stop herself, she squeezed until the girl cried out.

Gabrielle's obvious pain took Natalie's mind off her own agony, if only for a few seconds. "I'm sorry. I'm so sorry. But please! I can't do this anymore. I need help."

"I am here to help. You're doing fine." Gabrielle spoke in a calm and quiet cadence. "The baby will be here soon."

The contraction abated, but they'd been coming one on top of the other for several hours now. She braced for the next one, not sure she could survive even one more. Not that she had a choice.

"What day is it?" She breathed out the question she'd started to ask several times but had, until now, been interrupted by another unrelenting contraction.

"Today? It's October 26. Your baby's day of birth." A shadow passed over Gabrielle's face.

Something was wrong. Natalie opened her mouth to ask what was troubling Gabrielle, but another spasm arched her back and hardened her belly. How much longer? Why was it taking so long? She moaned through the interminable pain, too exhausted to scream any more. Had anyone outside these walls heard her? Surely they would have come to check on her if they had.

As if in answer to her thoughts, a knock sounded at the door.

Gabrielle smoothed Natalie's matted hair away from her forehead. "I'll be right back."

"No!" Panic gripped her at the thought of being alone. "*Kopaku*! Don't leave me!"

"I'm just going to see who's here. I won't leave you. I promise." The girl hurried to the door.

Something had changed drastically in Jamos and Meena's daughter. There was a sadness in her demeanor, yet it translated to a gentle kindness and a maturity Natalie had never seen in the young woman when she'd lived in Timoné. Natalie grieved that Lele had not been the recipient of this new attitude. Grieved that Meena had not known this daughter. She prayed for a chance to talk to Gabrielle about Lele. And Meena.

The door creaked open and a yellow glow from the hallway spilled in. It was strange to have lived in this room for three days now, yet not know anything about what was beyond these walls. Natalie blinked against the light, and when the door closed again, Tomás stood at the end of her bed.

He and Gabrielle had spoken briefly at the door as if they knew one another. Now he swept off his billed camouflage cap and worried it between his hands. He studied her, but said nothing.

Instead he turned to Gabrielle and spoke to her in Spanish. Something about *el bebé*.

Natalie didn't have time to wonder how Tomás knew Gabrielle before the next wave of pain rolled over her. She bit her lip, not wanting him to see her agony.

But he turned away from her and started toward the door. "Gabby? Can't you do something?"

"Like what? I don't have a clue what I'm doing," she snapped, using a mixture of pidgin Spanish and the Timoné dialect. "I'm not a nurse."

"*Hablar español.*" He obviously didn't want Natalie to hear what they were talking about.

Another contraction started and Natalie called Tomás's name. "*Por favor.* I need a doctor, Tomás. Please. Something is wrong!"

He looked to Gabrielle for confirmation.

She shrugged. "I think it's taking too long. But it was the same for me. Maybe everything will yet be okay."

"No! No, it won't be okay. I need a doctor. Something is wrong."

Gabrielle regarded her, then turned to Tomás. "Give us a couple more hours. If nothing has happened by then, we need to find a doctor."

He gave a sharp nod, placed his cap back on his head, and strode to the door.

Natalie wilted at the words.

But Gabrielle hurried after Tomás and grabbed his arm, tiptoeing to whisper something in his ear. The way she cradled his cheek and drew his head down toward her spoke of intimacy.

Was *Tomás* the soldier Gabrielle had followed away from Timoné?

He left, closing and locking the door behind him.

A little jolt went through Natalie. One completely unconnected to labor pains. The relationship between Gabrielle and Tomás couldn't be a coincidence. Had Gabrielle been involved in her kidnapping then? Had the girl betrayed her to the guerrillas? That might explain why Lele had been untouched. But how had Gabrielle known their plans?

A rising contraction kept her from examining the possibilities too closely. The pain quickly became excruciating. "I can't... I can't do it," she moaned.

"Yes, you can. I know you feel like you're going to die, but you won't. You can do it."

Gabrielle spoke with such assurance. How did she know that it felt like she was going to die? Was that how it'd been for her, giving birth to Lele. It seemed strange that this young girl had more experience than she did when it came to childbirth.

The pain escalated, and a primal urge to push overtook her. She gave into it and let it carry her, let her body do what God had created it to do.

But what must have been an hour or more passed, and she was still pushing, completely at the end of her strength. She was free-falling with no one there to catch her.

Gabrielle performed a rudimentary examination. "I don't see the baby, but I don't know what to look for. I've never been on this end of it."

"I need a doctor, Gabrielle."

"Tomás will be back soon. We will see what he says."

"But you told him 'a couple of hours' so he won't be back for at least another hour." Her voice rose at the realization. "*Kopaku*, Gabrielle? I can't go on like this. I need help."

The urge to push returned. But again with no progress that she could determine. Exhaustion took over, and she fell into a troubled slumber. Contractions continued to rouse her every few minutes, but she simply did not have the strength to push with them. Mercifully, she'd begun to feel almost numb to the pain. It was all she could do to draw in her next breath.

She wasn't sure how long she slept, but she was vaguely aware of Tomás returning, a hushed conversation with Gabrielle at the door, then he was gone again.

She felt an urgency to beg him again to get her help, to call a doctor or take her to an emergency room. But she had no strength left. Not even to speak his name.

She longed for David's presence. For Lele's cheer. For her mom and for Daddy.

And Dad. She would see him soon!

For to me, to live is Christ, and to die is gain.

Tears welled at the remembered Scripture. Yet she knew it was true, even if she longed with everything in her to remain this side of heaven.

She thought fondly of each of the beloved people God had placed in her life. In these last moments on this earth, she would pray that God would somehow allow them to know what had happened to her and the baby. Pray that, if by some miracle, the baby lived, that he would be found and someone would take him to David.

In her mind, she wrote a final letter to him. Her beloved David. If she'd had the strength, she would have asked Gabrielle for paper and pen, but since she didn't, she imagined her words scribbled across a white page. She prayed that somehow God would make the heart of her thoughts known to David.

Despite the tragedy that marked her early years, God had given her a wonderful life. God had been merciful when she deserved shame and punishment. She realized she had lived a redeemed life, even as her heart broke that it was ending without her getting to hold her baby, to raise a family, grow old with David, have some adventures. Oh, but they *had*. She and David. God had used them to heal each other. *Help him through, Lord. Cradle our baby in your arms whether he comes with me now or later, in your timing.*

Suddenly, inexplicably, a remarkable peace fell over her, along with the certainty that God would see David through just as he'd seen her through. They could both rest knowing heaven held everything that truly mattered. She was at the finish line and God would carry her the rest of the way home.

"Thank you, Father," she whispered and closed her eyes.

"HAVE YOU SEEN THIS WOMAN?" DAVID HELD OUT THE PHOTO of Natalie, keeping his eyes on the nurse's face, watching her expression for any telltale hint of recognition.

"No. *Lo siento*, I have not treated an American woman."

"You're certain? She might have been with a Colombian man. She is very pregnant. About to deliver." He shaped his hands into a mound over his own flat belly. He didn't think the woman was lying to him, but this clinic was his last chance.

The nurse smiled softly. "*Lo siento*, sir, I would have remembered such a beautiful blond woman. Especially if she was here to give birth, since we don't deliver babies. We would have sent her to Santa Lucia's up the street. Have you checked there?"

"Yes. I've checked all the hospitals."

"*Lo siento*," she repeated, her tone dismissive, "she was not here."

His shoulders slumped, matching his spirits. "*Muchas gracias.* I'm sorry to have bothered you." He repeated the apology in Spanish, since the woman's English seemed minimal. "*Perdone la molestia.*"

"*Está bien.* I'm sorry I could not help you." The woman put a hand on his shoulder and guided him toward the waiting room.

He thrust the slip of paper with Natalie's photo and his name and cell phone number underneath, into the woman's hands. He'd left six such "wanted posters" with other nurses in the various hospitals and clinics around Conzalez, asking them to please call him if a woman matching Natalie's description was admitted. "*Por favor*, you will call me if she should show up?"

"I will call you." The woman gripped his upper arm, more forcefully escorting him to the front desk where he'd persuaded the receptionist to give him entrance.

Outside the building, the sun beat down, searing his already sunburned skin. He wiped his brow with his sleeve and willed himself not to collapse. A sense of hopelessness moved over him in that moment, almost worse than the day, more than two weeks ago now, watching the truck drive away with Natalie screaming. At least that day, he'd had hope. Hope that it was all a mistake. Hope that she would find a way to escape. That God would intervene.

Today, he had exhausted everything he knew to do—at least everything that wasn't foolish and dangerous.

$$\maltese \quad 30 \quad \maltese$$

"I can't! I can't!" Natalie wailed, confused—and furious to be awake, alive, still in a battle she no longer had the will to fight. The pain had returned and it was worse than ever. Unbearable.

Gabrielle patted her cheek over and over. "Stay awake. You have to help me. Miss Natalie, listen to me. *Kopaku.* If you want to live, you have to push this baby out now! Push!"

Sucking in a breath, she tried. But nothing. It was as if she was paralyzed. A sob of anguish rose in her throat. Her baby was going to die and it was her fault because she simply didn't have the strength to push any more.

"If you can cry, you can push!" Without warning, Gabrielle slapped her hard. "Now push!"

Her cheek stinging, Natalie sobbed harder. But fueled by anger and determination, she tried to obey. She filled her lungs, then pushed with all her might. *Oh, God...* It was the purest prayer she could utter.

At the foot of the bed, Gabrielle shouted, "Again! Good... Oh, I see the head. Push again, Miss Natalie!"

She pushed until she had nothing left. Then pushed again, feeling as if every blood vessel in her face was bursting. She pushed once more, and suddenly a gusty wail filled the room. This time, not her own, but a newborn's.

"You did it! It's a girl! A little girl!" Gabrielle hustled around the bed. Doing what, Natalie couldn't tell, but the baby's wailing continued.

Natalie tried to lift her head, to see her baby...her *daughter*. But she couldn't. "It's a girl? Are you sure?"

Gabrielle chuckled. "I think I recognize a *chica* when I see one. Now you rest. I'll bring her to you. Let me clean her up a little."

"Is she okay? Is everything okay? Please let me hold her."

"She is *perfecta*." Gabrielle's voice lilted over her shoulder with uncharacteristic joy.

"Thank you. How can I ever thank you, Gabrielle! You did it!"

The lilt turned to laughter. "I did nothing but cut the cord. But the baby is here. That is all that matters."

She turned away and Natalie rested, listening to the water run in the sink, Gabrielle moving efficiently about the space, cooing to the baby in a tone that, strangely, Natalie had never heard her use with her own daughter.

A few minutes later, Gabrielle returned the baby to her. The tiny girl wore nothing but a too-big disposable diaper and the blanket that swamped her. Overwhelmed with love for her daughter, she explored the fringe of pale hair and the round, dimpled cheeks with her fingers.

"She'll need some clothes. It gets a little chilly in here at night sometimes. Can you—"

"Don't worry. She'll be taken care of."

"I wish Mr. David could know about her. Do you know how far we are from Conzalez?"

She'd tried, without success, to get some clue out of Gabrielle about where they were and what the plan was for her. But the girl had been close-mouthed so far, and ignored her question now.

"You should try to nurse the baby right away."

She nodded, eager for the experience, and relieved that Gabrielle was encouraging her to bond with her baby. The baby latched with only a little persuasion. Natalie stared down, already so in love with this little angel in her arms. She knew her milk wouldn't come in for a couple of days, but the baby was getting at least some sustenance.

She caressed the soft cheek. "Happy birthday, sweet girl," she cooed. "October twenty-six. That's a good day for a birthday."

"Oh, no, Miss Natalie." Gabrielle came to her side, smiling. "You labored all day and all night October twenty-six. This little one did not come into the world until October twenty-seven."

"Today is October twenty-seven?"

"Yes, and the day is almost over."

No wonder her labor had seemed interminable. "I wish I could have a calendar. And a clock. Do you think you could get those things for me?"

"We'll see."

Gabrielle was as noncommittal as she'd been with each of Natalie's requests and probing questions. The girl had obviously been warned not to give her any information. Which was disturbing since it pretty much confirmed that Gabrielle was complicit in her abduction.

David must have told Jamos that they planned to travel to Conzalez for the baby's birth. That was the only way Gabrielle could have known. And that must mean Jamos had found his daughter and mentioned their travel to her. He would have known Lele would be with them. Maybe he was attempting to reunite his daughter and granddaughter. Who could blame him? He likely didn't realize how deeply Gabrielle was caught up in the guerrilla activity.

Natalie would probably never know exactly how it had all happened. And she didn't want to waste these precious early days with her newborn mulling over questions without answers. As the baby nursed, contractions started again. They were much milder than before, and while she cradled her baby, Gabrielle helped her deliver the placenta—an almost painless task compared to what she'd been through with the delivery.

Gabrielle wadded up the rags she'd placed under Natalie's hips during the delivery and smoothed the damp, wrinkled sheets as best she could. Gabrielle tended to her while the baby drifted to sleep at her breast.

When Natalie woke again, the baby was tucked in beside her, nestled in a cocoon formed with the blanket. Gabrielle was gone, but a small package of newborn-size diapers sat at the foot of the bed. She took one and changed the baby.

She lifted the sleeping infant into her lap, marveling at her tiny pink fingers and toes. As Gabrielle had declared, she was perfect, flawless. This baby needed a name though. Nathan Cole David or any combination thereof would not do for this princess. But they'd barely settled on a boy's name, let alone discussed the possibility of having a girl.

A deep yearning for David overwhelmed her. It seemed so strange that they had a daughter and David didn't even know it. He should be cradling her, helping her choose a name. But she wanted a name to call their precious daughter. If she chose something David didn't like, they could always change it later.

Now that the baby was here she *had* to find a way to escape. She couldn't raise this child in a dark, windowless room where she never knew whether she would get food to eat or the supplies she needed. She had to build up her strength and find a way to get to David.

Natalie touched the tiny rosebud lips, needing proof that her baby was still breathing. The rhythmic rise and fall of her little chest convinced her that all was well, and watching the baby sleep, she fell head-over-heels for this precious child she'd carried through such difficult circumstances. Two long days of labor! But now, only the blood-spotted, clammy sheets remained as a reminder of the agony she'd been through. But what she'd always heard was true. The pain was almost forgotten. She was elated that her baby was safely here, alive and thriving. And she had survived when she thought death was certain. The nightmare was over.

But a shadow obscured her joy. She tried to nudge it aside but the knowledge remained: Her ordeal wasn't over yet. She had a daughter to protect now, but was still captive. Wasn't she?

She trained her eyes on the door. Hoping against hope, she carefully placed the baby back in the nest of the blanket. The infant scrunched her tiny red face into a scowl and gave a little shudder, but then relaxed into stillness. Natalie eased her legs over the edge of the mattress and tested her legs.

Her knees buckled as if they were made of jelly. But she held onto the bed until she gained her balance, then reached for the wall and felt her way along it toward the door. The concrete floor was like ice, yet it invigorated her to be out of bed for the first time in days.

Halfway to the door, she made an urgent detour to the bathroom, then washed her hands and face at the sink. She didn't recognize the woman staring back at her from the mirror. Gray pallor, sunken cheeks, thin skin draped over a protruding collarbone. The image frightened her and made her wonder if she had indeed almost died. But she was still alive, and now that the baby was here, she would fight to stay that way.

She reached for the door handle and turned. Locked. As she'd expected. Even so, her spirits deflated.

Now what?

Her brief jaunt around the room exhausted her, but the pangs of hunger were welcome. It was a sensation she'd almost forgotten. She glanced at the desk to see a few half-eaten packages of the food Tomás had left each day. Maybe that's what Gabrielle had been subsisting on?

Her stomach rumbled, and she chose some nuts and crackers and a bottle of tepid water and returned to the bed. She ate as much as she could stomach, but didn't have the energy to return the leftovers to the table. She nursed the baby, then settled back to try to sleep.

She must have drifted off again because she didn't hear Gabrielle come in, but when she opened her eyes, the young woman was standing over her, watching her as if assessing.

She instinctively reached for the bundle beside her, reassured when the baby stretched and settled back to sleep. "What time is it?" She tried to sit up.

"You sleep. I'm going to take the baby so you can have the whole bed."

"Take her?" Her pulse quickened. "Take her where?"

"No, I just mean I will hold her so you can sleep." She pointed to the chair at the desk by the door. "You need to get your strength back."

Something about Gabrielle's tone held an urgency that made alarms go off for Natalie.

"You're right, but... I can sleep better if she's with me." She pulled the baby closer and closed her eyes. But there was no way she would sleep now.

❧ 31 ☙

Meg set a plate of scrambled eggs in front of David. "Can I make you some toast too?"

"Thank you, but this is plenty." He took a bite but only to humor her. "Hank is already in the office?"

She nodded. "He has a Zoom meeting this morning."

David eyed her, hope welling inside him. Maybe the mission had gotten some news. Or even a new ransom demand.

The sympathy and regret in her eyes told the story. "I'm sorry. I should have said right away. This is something for work. We would let you know if we heard from headquarters. You know that, David."

"Of course. I guess…hope springs eternal."

"I know. For me too."

Lele's chattering floated in from the patio out back and Meg smiled.

He looked past her to the patio, but his gaze landed first on Lele's battered little "wind chime." Meghan had hung it over the sliding door that led to the patio where Lele played now. He'd spent too many hours staring at her wilted creation looking for some new clue it might hold that would lead them to Natalie.

"I hope Lele's not been too much trouble, Meg. I can't thank you enough for everything you've done for her...and making it possible for me to keep up the search. You know my offer still stands to find an apartment for the duration of our stay. I know you must be wondering how much longer we're going to be invading your space."

She waved him off. "I don't want to hear another word about that, David Chambers. And you know I would happily care for Lele even if she was a complete brat, but on the contrary, she is a delight."

"She seems to be weathering this surprisingly well. I give you all the credit in the world for that, Meg."

"Well, she has been a balm for our souls, David. She truly has, so please don't apologize again. And believe me, she is about half as much work as Teo and Matthias. Not to mention, I much prefer making paper dolls to playing soldier."

He smiled up at her. "Natalie would feel the same, I know."

"I wonder if your baby is here yet." Meghan's voice held an edge of testing.

"I've thought of little else. And wonder if I may have to live without ever knowing. I'm not sure I could bear that."

"Hank and I pray every day that you won't have to, David."

He had been in a pit of despair since striking out at the last medical clinic. He'd returned to each hospital and clinic yesterday, hoping a different staff member would be working on Sunday—someone who might remember if Natalie had been there or who would be willing to contact him if she did show up.

But if anything, he met with even more resistance from the weekend staff. No one had seen her—or so they claimed—and no one would even agree to take the flier with Natalie's photo. He didn't blame them. If their suspicions were correct and Natalie was being held because of the baby, then anyone who tried to get in the way was putting themselves in danger.

He took a few more bites of the eggs for Meghan's sake, then pushed the plate away. "Thank you for breakfast."

"You're most welcome. But I wish you'd eat more."

He ignored her chiding and scraped back his chair. "I told Lele she could go to the grocery with me today. Apparently, Hank paid her a few pennies for helping him in the hangar and they're burning a hole in her little pocket."

Meghan laughed. "I won't apologize for Hank, but I do hope the salary he's paying Lele doesn't end up *costing* you money."

David grinned, grateful again for these friends who had been such a blessing in this ordeal. "I hope you can take the rest of the day off and do something you want to do."

"Quit worrying about me. I am not suffering in the least." She punched his arm lightly.

Her playful affection reminded him in that moment of Natalie, and he feared he might collapse with longing for her.

Meg must have seen something in his expression, for she turned serious. "It has been our honor to do what little we've been able to do, David."

"What you two have given us is anything but little." He dared not say more lest he break down.

"We'll get out of your hair. And hey, we'll bring supper home tonight. You relax."

"Aww, I just might take you up on that."

"Please do. We'll see you later this afternoon."

He slid open the door and motioned to Lele. "Are you ready to go shopping? Run and get your *zapatos.*"

"Can't I go barefoot? Why do I have to wear *zapatos?*"

"Lele..."

"Okay...okay... I'll get them. Don't leave!"

"I won't leave without you."

Lele had started using a little English, but more of the Castilian Spanish that Hank and Meg usually spoke. Of course, that was the variety he spoke here in Conzalez as well, so it was pretty much all the child had heard for more than two weeks now. He was impressed with how quickly she'd picked up the dialect. Quicker than Natalie had, although that was usually the case with children.

Lele emerged from the little storage room that had become her bedroom on this trip. Without help, she'd put on the little sandals Meghan had bought her. She carried a little purple purse over her shoulder.

"Is that yours?"

"Miss Meg gave it to me."

"That was awfully nice. I hope you said *gracias*."

"Of course, I did."

He tousled her hair, but she swatted his hand away. "Don't mess up my pigtails, Mr. David! It took Miss Meg all morning to fix them!"

"Sorry...sorry." He tried to smooth her hair back down.

She swatted at his hand and ducked out, heading for the front door.

She'd grown up so much in just two weeks. It was hard to tell how she was handling the situation with Natalie. He felt bad that he'd mostly left it to Meghan to deal with her, but he simply couldn't handle everything involved in the search for Natalie and playing counselor to Lele too. Not that he would have had a clue how to speak to her about what had happened. Meghan seemed to think she was handling it well, but the poor child had been through a lot in one short year of her life.

She'd lost—in one way or another—every member of her family, and now Natalie too. Of all the people in her life, he was the last one who should have been charged with her care. He didn't take the responsibility lightly.

They strolled in the direction of the grocery store, which was half a mile from the mission compound. Lele skipped ahead, but he called her back, keeping an eye for vehicles, remembering how quickly life could change. He offered his hand and she slipped hers into his, keeping pace with him for a few minutes, then skipping ahead again in her excitement. Finally, he just kept up with her. It was easier that way.

He'd sometimes fretted about what to talk about when he was alone with Lele. Strange how a four-year-old could intimidate him. Now, he didn't know why he'd ever worried because Lele had no trouble filling the silence. And he was getting a little better at carrying his end of the conversation. But oh, what he wouldn't have given for Natalie to be here with them, enjoying a trip to the colorful market.

"So, what are you planning to buy with that *fortuna pequeña* Mr. Hank paid you?"

She gave him a look that said *You need to ask?* "Candy, of course."

He laughed. And for the first time in two weeks, life felt a little bit normal. He quickly squelched the thought. As much as he was enjoying the moment, he did not want this to become his new normal. *Normal* without Natalie was unthinkable.

32

"Mmmm... So good." Natalie stabbed another potato and put it in her mouth. Leaning back against her pillow, she forced herself to savor it. They must be close to restaurants because Tomás had brought warm food in styrofoam bowls for her and Gabrielle—David's favorite *ajiaco* with slices of avocado, capers, and sour cream. For the first time since she'd been taken, food tasted delicious to her. She gazed down at her baby, sleeping peacefully on the bed beside her.

Gabrielle had also brought clean sheets, which she was savoring even more than the meal. She'd been so sure that she would never hold this baby in her arms on this side of heaven. Now that she had, a strange euphoria held her in its grasp. And she gave herself permission to bask in it for a while. Because if she let herself think too long about her reality—that David wasn't here to share it all with her, that their future was one big question mark—despair crushed her.

Gabrielle pushed her half-eaten bowl aside and rose from her seat at the desk. "Let me take her while you eat."

"No. Sit. *Kopaku.* I'm almost finished and you've barely touched your plate. Is everything okay?"

Tomás hadn't stayed to eat with them, and something about the furtive conversations he and Gabrielle had gave Natalie a sense that something was about to change.

"Everything is fine." But Gabrielle didn't sit back down. Her bowl sat forgotten while she flitted about the room, rinsing out the already-clean sink, straightening the few items on the table, and avoiding Natalie's eyes.

Something was going on. Something Gabrielle apparently couldn't confide to her. But the way she was tidying up the place made Natalie wonder if they planned to move her to yet another location. Maybe this room had only been for the birth of her baby. But surely they wouldn't take her back to a remote place like the shed when she had a baby to care for. She needed access to diapers and wipes. She would need a few changes of clothes for the baby—and for herself, since her clothes had been spit up on and worse. She also needed a better way to wash their clothes and bathe the baby.

She let the mundane thoughts occupy her mind because if she didn't, grim possibilities took their place. The most unthinkable of all that they might try to separate her from her baby. But they wouldn't do that as long as she was nursing, would they? Her baby needed her. She shook her head. She couldn't survive if she let herself entertain such horrors. She was still overwhelmed with gratitude that childbirth hadn't ended in tragedy for her or her baby. It was time to focus on what God had already accomplished: Her baby was here, safe and healthy. She had survived an agonizing birth.

She'd feel better when they'd both been examined by a doctor, but she was healing slowly and regaining her strength. Her milk had come in last night and the baby nursed gustily every two or three hours and seemed to be thriving. Every hour, she fell further in love with her daughter, even as she grieved how much David had already missed of these early newborn days.

Troubled, she finished eating and lifted the baby onto her lap, the blankets there still warm from the bowl of *ajiaco*. "I wish I could sleep as peacefully as you do, Baby Girl."

"You have no name for your baby?" Gabrielle met her eyes for the first time since Tomás had left.

"I want David to help me choose her name."

"You didn't have a name in mind? Before?"

"We had a name for a boy. I always thought it was a boy." Smiling, Natalie seized an opening. "How did you choose Lele's name? When she was born?"

Gabrielle tensed almost imperceptibly, then merely shrugged. "She needed a name, so I chose one. If Mr. David does not like the name you choose, you could change it, no?"

"I guess that's true." She paused, then pressed on. "Do you know what they plan to do with us, Gabrielle? Will I see Mr. David again?"

"You will see him if you do everything they say."

"Then...they have asked again for ransom?"

She stiffened. "Why do you ask me? I don't know the answers."

"*Kopaku*, Gabrielle... I need to know what will happen to us. Tomás doesn't tell you what they are planning?"

"Tomás tells me what he chooses to tell me."

"But, of course, you know where we are now. What city we are in. Are we in Conzalez? Can you just tell me that? David is looking for me. In Conzalez."

Gabrielle eyed her with suspicion. "Why do you think we are in...a city?"

"I hear the sounds sometimes. The cars, shouts. And where else could Tomás find warm *ajiaco*? Please tell him *egracita* for me."

"*You* tell him *gracias*." Her demeanor had cooled considerably. "He will be back."

"Yes, *gracias*. I will."

Gabrielle seemed intent on banishing Timoné from her

vocabulary and transitioning to Spanish. It told Natalie that the girl had no intention of returning to the village.

Natalie lay back on the pillows and looked at the dingy ceiling. "I miss seeing the sky. Even at the shed, where I was first, I had a skylight. At least I could tell what time of day it was. It's hard not knowing if it's day or night."

Gabrielle followed her gaze to the ceiling. "I'm sorry," she said simply. "It is morning."

"Morning? And we had *ajiaco* for breakfast?" She shook her head and gave a teasing smile. "Is Tomás *trying* to confuse me more?"

Gabrielle laughed. "Tomás will eat *ajiaco* any time of day or night."

"Ah, David too. It's his favorite."

"It is morning, Natalie." Her expression turned pensive. "Probably about nine o'clock. But I like to see the evening stars as well."

Gabrielle warmed to her again, and it filled Natalie's heart with affection.

"My father—Dr. Nate, I mean—loved the stars and could point out all the constellations." Speaking Dad's name brought a lump to her throat.

"My papá also loved the stars. Tomás knows the constellations too. But they are his map, not his pleasure like they were for Papá."

"His map? You mean he navigates—" She struggled for the Timoné word.

"Yes, *el recorrido*. He *navigates* by the stars." She tried out the English word. "They give him a route to follow." Gabrielle traced a finger along the palm of her hand, as if it were a map, then looked heavenward again, even though the only views were water-stained ceiling tile. "Tomás is teaching me the constellations. So I can navigate too."

The revelation surprised Natalie. "Why do *you* need to navigate?"

Gabrielle looked away, suddenly intent on a hangnail. "He showed me a constellation last night that is the home of Canopus, the brightest star in the night sky, second only to Sirius."

She nodded. "I've heard of Sirius."

"The constellation is called Carina. Tomás says the word means *amada*."

Almost without thinking, Natalie translated to English. "*Beloved*... Carina. What a beautiful name." She stroked her sleeping daughter's cheek with the back of her hand. "That's it. I will call her Carina. Carina Grace."

"Ah, yes. It fits her. She is beloved. Carina." Gabrielle spoke the name with the musical Spanish R and reached to touch the baby's foot. "Carina, where your brightest star shines."

"Second only to Mr. David." Natalie echoed. She smiled at the thought, then brushed away sudden tears.

Would he ever meet his daughter? How was he faring with Lele? She was tempted to tell Gabrielle that Lele was with David —something she suspected Gabrielle already knew. But if not, she didn't want to put the child in danger. And it didn't seem right to use Gabrielle's own daughter as a pawn, even if it was to save all of them.

She cradled her baby close. "Carina Grace," she whispered. "How do you like your new name?" She thought David would approve, especially when he knew how her name came to be.

She briefly touched Gabrielle's arm, grateful at how God had been working in the girl's life. And aware that what she was about to say wasn't completely candid. But if she was to find a way of escape, she would need Gabrielle's help. To get back to David. "I couldn't have done any of this without you, Gabrielle. You brought little Carina safely into the world. Thank you so much. God sent you to me, I have no doubt."

"God didn't tell me to come."

"Ah, but sometimes He uses us without our knowing."

"Ah, that is what Mamá and Papá said." Gabrielle's gaze turned pensive.

Natalie smiled. "Your papá is wise. Your mamá was a very wise woman too." Heat rose to her face, realizing she'd slipped and used the past tense. She'd been waiting for the right moment to tell Gabrielle the difficult news about Meena, but that moment was not going to come unless she created it. "Gabrielle, do you remember reading the Bible when you came to the church with your parents? That is where their wisdom is from."

"Bible?"

"Sorry. *Nuevo Testamento.*" There was no Timoné word for Bible. David referred to the Bible as *Yahweh's Logos.* And the New Testament translation he was working on as *Nuevo Testamento.*

"Like the book Mr. David was writing?"

"Well, he's not *writing* it. He's translating it. *God* wrote it."

"God?" Gabrielle looked skeptical. "God cannot write."

"Yes, he wrote through the hands of men He created. And gave us a book so we would know how to live."

She nodded. "That's what Papá and Mamá said. But Papá could not read the book. Not like Mr. David and Tados."

"Mr. David will gladly teach your papá to read it. When the Timoné *Nuevo Testamento* is finished."

She shook her head, a shadow darkening her face. "No. Papá is dead."

The statement startled her. "Do you mean...he really died? How do you know?"

"The soldiers killed him. He would not stop coming to take me back. Even when they warned him. Tomás told him. But Papá would not listen."

"No. Are you certain?" What if they'd only told her that to coerce her to stay with them?

"I am sure. Tomás saw him die." She bowed her head and her voice broke. "Lele will be heartbroken."

"Oh, Gabrielle, I'm so sorry." Natalie spoke over a huge lump in her throat. "And yes, Lele will be heartbroken. *I* am heartbroken. Your father was a good man. Your mamá too. They loved you very much."

"You will tell Mamá that he is dead?"

She froze. *Give me the words, Lord.* "Gabrielle," she whispered. "Come here." She laid little Carina on her lap and patted the edge of the mattress. "Sit down. There's something I need to tell you…"

33

Gabrielle tilted her head as though trying to absorb the news. "*No!* Not Mama! Not Mama too!"

Natalie reached for her hand, feeling her way around the Timoné words, wanting to get this right. "I am so very sorry. But oh, sweet girl... Your mamá is in heaven. With your papá. She was very sick for a long time. And finally, she died."

"No! Not Mamá? Not Mamá too!" Gabrielle moaned and wailed as if her heart had broken.

Natalie could imagine how she would feel if she lost her own mother. Just thinking of Mom and Daddy filled her with longing. Would they ever get to meet their granddaughter?

As Gabrielle's wails grew louder, Carina flinched. She put a hand on the baby in her lap to quiet her, then put an arm around Gabrielle's shoulders.

But there was no quieting her.

"I am so sorry, Gabrielle. Your papá was with her when she died. And your mamá died with a sweet smile on her face. Lele was there with her too. She noticed that smile. Your mamá knew she was going to heaven. She had no doubt."

"You also had no doubt." Gabrielle stated it matter-of-factly.

Natalie frowned. "I don't understand."

"When you almost died. When Carina was coming."

"Did you think I almost died?"

"You did." Gabrielle nodded. "When my baby was born, I thought I would die. But I did not. Even so, I was certain that you *would* die. The pains went on for so many days...and still the baby didn't come. Your color was that of *la muerte*."

So she'd been right when she'd thought she was near death. Grateful all over again, she pushed the thought to a far corner of her mind. "You still remember Lele's birth so well?"

"No, I don't mean Lele." She dropped her head briefly. "I mean my other baby. The boy."

"You had another baby? But...where is he? I don't understand."

She closed her eyes. "I don't know where he is. Tomás told me he died. But I don't believe him. Why did we not bury him?"

"You never saw your baby...after he died? When was this, Gabrielle? When was your baby born?"

"His birthday was the same as mine. September five." She stared into some unknown distance. "He came too early. Too small to live, Tomás said."

September five? "*This* September?"

Gabrielle nodded.

Less than two months ago. Had Jamos known his daughter was pregnant? Was that why he was so desperate to bring her home to Timoné? "I'm so sorry, Gabrielle."

She didn't seem to hear and stared past Natalie, speaking as though to herself. "He was so tiny. And yet I nursed him for five days and he grew content. And happy. I know he was! Tomás said the baby was still at my breast when he died. I fell asleep, and when I woke up, Tomás had already taken him. He didn't want me to see him *muerto*."

An alarm went off in Natalie's head. "But...you had no funeral? No burial? Why?"

"Tomás said there was no time."

"Why?" What could have been so urgent that there wasn't time to bury a tiny son? "Then where did they put him? The baby's...body?"

"Tomás wouldn't tell me. He said to forget about the boy. That we would have other babies." She shook her head. "I don't know. I feel he is still alive. In my heart, you know? But Tomás says—"

"That's not right, Gabrielle. He should have let you say good-bye. He should have let you see your baby. Give him a proper burial." Even as she spoke the words she knew what had likely happened. And it sent terror through her. She pulled Carina closer.

"It is in the past." Gabrielle came alert as though snapping out of a trance.

"Gabrielle, this is important. Listen to me, *kopaku*. Are you free to go?"

"To go?"

"Is Tomás holding *you* prisoner? Same as me?"

She drew her forehead into furrows, as if trying to figure out the answer to a difficult question. "I don't know," she said finally.

"Listen to me, Gabrielle." She clutched the girl's forearm, determined to make her see reason. "It is not right that we are not free to go."

"When your ransom is paid, then *you* are free to go."

"But what if they won't pay my ransom? And what about *you*? Who will pay yours?"

"I will stay with Tomás."

"Even though you believe he lied to you? About your *son*?"

"I love Tomás. I told Papá. And you will be free...soon. They may yet pay?" It was a question.

"No, I don't think they will, Gabrielle. But...even if they do not—" She paused, the profound truth washing over her. "My ransom has already been paid..." Her voice broke as she realized the absolute truth of it. "My ransom—and yours if you will accept it—was paid more than two thousand years ago. Jesus

Christ paid the ransom for me. With His death on the cross. That is what your mamá and papá believed, Gabrielle."

She nodded and Natalie could tell she had heard Jamos and Meena speak of this before. "Do you think they are in heaven? Truly?"

"I *know* they are. They believed. And you can too."

"No." She shook her head and refused to look into Natalie's eyes. "You don't know what I have done..."

"Gabrielle, listen to me. There is nothing you could do that Jesus cannot forgive. It is His free gift. All you have to do is hold out your hand and take it. Do you understand?"

"No... It is too late for me. He cannot forgive me."

"Oh, if you only knew the things God has forgiven me."

She shook her head more adamantly. "No. But will you tell Lele? Before it is too late for her?"

"I think Lele already believes. At least as much as she can at her young age." She told Gabrielle what her daughter had said about Meena's smile even in death. "Your parents—and Lele—they would want you to accept this gift that Jesus offers. So you can walk with Jesus here on earth, and then be with him—and them—in heaven when you die."

"But Tomás. He does not believe."

"But maybe someday he will. The ransom was paid for him too. For anyone who accepts. If he turns from his evil ways and—"

"Tomás is not always evil. Sometimes he is very kind and good. Like Papá." Her voice broke again. "It is only the soldiers that make him do evil things."

"He must be strong and do what is right, Gabrielle. And even if he doesn't, *you* must do what is right—what you *know* is right. Do you understand me?"

Gabrielle slid off the bed and went to the sink. She scooted from sink to table, into the bathroom, then back—avoidance tactics.

She scooped up the woven market bag she used for supplies.

"I need to go to the market. The baby needs diapers and formula and I will bring you something to eat."

"What? Carina doesn't need formula. I am nursing her. Gabrielle, listen to me. You don't need to leave. We have enough diapers for a while. And I have enough *ajiaco* in my belly to last me all day. Please stay and talk to me."

"No, I can't. I told Tomás I would have everything ready."

"Ready for what?"

She sucked in a breath as though realizing she'd said something she shouldn't have.

"Ready for what, Gabrielle?" she repeated, alarm rising. "Tell me what they are planning."

"It will be all right. You will see."

But Natalie didn't miss the false note in the girl's tone. She was hiding something.

"I will be back." Gabrielle hiked the empty bag up on her shoulder, slipped on her sandals, and left the room without another word.

❧ 34 ❧

"**Y**ou have enough for three pieces of strawberry taffy or one chocolate bar."

"But I want both, Mr. David. Hey, I know!" Lele's voice rose hopefully. "I could have one piece of taffy and one chocolate bar?"

"No, I'm sorry. The chocolate bar costs more. You have enough for three pieces of taffy *or* one chocolate bar. Or you could buy one piece of taffy and you would have money left over."

"Enough for a chocolate bar?" A gleam lit her eyes.

He leveled his gaze. "Enough for two more pieces of taffy." Several women shopped among the aisles, and he was no doubt providing great entertainment as he tried to reason with this clever child. "Make up your mind quickly or we'll still be deciding when the owner closes shop. Then you'll be out of luck."

"What is luck?"

He chuckled and tugged on a braid. "I'll tell you later. You need to decide about the candy. Now."

Her shoulders slumped. "How am I supposed to decide when I like taffy *and* chocolate bars?"

"I don't know, Lele, but I'm going to go find the tea Miss Meg asked me to get. It's right over there, you see?" He pointed to the end of the aisle where tea and coffee were displayed. "It'll take me thirty seconds, and when I'm finished, you need to have your decision made. Understood?"

"Yes, Mr. David."

He searched for the brand Meghan had written down, glancing back every few seconds to make sure Lele was still there. She was, hands on hips, features in a thoughtful frown. He had an odd flashback of the items she'd stolen to make the wind chime *sorpressia* for them. Maybe she would be tempted to steal again, especially since she was having such a hard time deciding. But he felt sure her remorse was genuine and maybe this was a good test for whether or not she'd learned her lesson.

He finally found the right tea and picked up two tins, then turned. "Lele, have you—" His heart stopped. She was gone. "Lele!" He ran past where she'd been standing to the next aisle, pulse racing.

There she stood in the middle of the aisle, still clutching the taffy in one hand and a candy bar in the other. Thank God.

The side door squeaked open, then slammed shut, and the proprietor shouted angrily from behind the counter. David looked up in time to see a flash of yellow as someone dashed around the corner. Shoplifter, most likely. But that didn't stop his heart from thumping like a drum.

"Lele! Don't ever leave my sight like that again, do you hear me?" He inhaled deeply, fighting to steady his quavering voice. "Now, you need to decide or we're going to leave without any candy at all."

She turned to face him, looking dazed.

"Hey. It's okay. I'm not angry. You just scared me." He knelt to her eye level, and quickly realized there was more at play than his reprimand. "What's wrong, Lele? Is everything okay?"

"I saw Mamá."

He followed her gaze to the store window. "*Your* mamá? Gabrielle?"

She nodded.

"Just now, you mean? Where?" His gaze panned the aisles of the store.

Lele motioned toward the sidewalk where the shoplifter had fled. "She ran outside."

"Are you sure it wasn't just someone that looked like her?"

"No, it was Mamá. I know it was."

"Did you talk to her? Did she see *you?*"

"She was walking over there"—she pointed to the end of the aisle—"but when she looked at me—" Lele burst into tears. "She ran away! She threw down her groceries and ran away when she saw me!"

He dropped to one knee and pulled her into his arms. "Oh, sweet girl. I'm so sorry. I don't know why. Maybe she...didn't really see you. Or maybe it was just someone who looked a lot like her." But the very fact that whoever Lele had seen turned away when she spotted Lele made it more likely that it *was* Gabrielle.

For Lele's sake, but more importantly, for Jamos's sake, he should probably pursue this. Not that it would do any good, but how could he ever face his friend and tell him he'd been that close to Gabrielle and had done nothing?

"Here... Give me the candy. This once, we're going to buy both the chocolate and the taffy. But we need to hurry."

He urged her toward the counter, stepping over a small pile of packages in the middle of the aisle. It looked like someone's shopping bag had broken.

"There. Mamá dropped those." Lele pointed to the pile. "When she ran."

"These things on the floor?"

She nodded.

Looking closer at the jumble of items on the floor. A bottle of over-the-counter pain medicine, some red-and-white peppermints, a now-dented bottle of Coca-Cola, a package of disposable diapers, and a tin labeled *Fórmula Infantil*. Not likely Gabrielle.

He gathered up the items and took them to the counter. "Someone must have dropped these."

"*Sí*, I saw her." The clerk rolled her eyes and scooted the items to one side.

David put enough pesos on the counter to pay for Lele's candy and told the clerk to keep the change. Then he picked up Lele and strode toward the door. "Which way did she go?"

She pointed west.

"You're sure?"

"*Sí*. I'm very sure."

He hurried in that direction, hiking Lele up to his shoulders on a street filled with noon-hour shoppers. "You keep an eye out for her up there, okay? What was she wearing?"

"A shirt like Miss Natalie wears to fit her baby. Stretchy."

"A T-shirt?"

"Yes. T-shirt," she repeated.

"What color? Do you remember?"

"Um...yellow. But like mustard, not like corn."

The flash of color he'd seen. "Good girl. Keep your eyes open and holler if you see her."

He went two blocks and stopped. "Anything?"

"No. I don't see her."

The next block was a dead-end, so he took a wild guess and turned left, hoping Gabrielle—if it was her—had done the same. "Do you see anyone?"

"Just a man with a crazy hat."

David saw him too. A lanky man in a hat like a court jester's. And the guy wearing it looked pretty strung out. Things were starting to feel a little sketchy at this end of the narrow street. Not a place for Lele.

He turned back and quickened his pace, feeling conflicted. Gabrielle had made her bed. He had more important things to worry about, Gabrielle's daughter, for one. But Natalie was his first priority.

Still, if it really had been Gabrielle—and he wasn't completely convinced—maybe there was some purpose in Lele seeing her. If he couldn't have a happy ending, maybe Jamos could.

"You keep watching, okay?"

"I am."

Two blocks and still no sign of Gabrielle or anyone else wearing a yellow T-shirt.

"I'm sorry, Lele, but I think we missed her."

She was silent for a minute. Finally, her voice a whisper, she said. "I don't know why she wouldn't talk to me."

"I'm so sorry, honey." He didn't know what else to say.

Nor did he know what to do with the anger that seethed toward Lele's mother. How could someone abandon this sweet child? And for a mercenary soldier? Likely the same ilk that had kidnapped Natalie. There was no making sense of it.

But a singular thought niggled at him: What if Gabrielle had connections to the same guerrilla faction that had taken Natalie? The girl might have information that could ultimately lead them to Natalie. At the very least, she might know some of the guerrilla encampments and hiding places.

He lifted Lele from his shoulders and set her on the sidewalk in front of him. "Let's go back to Miss Meg's, okay?"

She nodded, sorrow clear in her gaze.

He took her hand and headed back toward the Middletons' compound.

A plan had begun to form. But not one he could share with anyone else. Still, it filled him with a sense of hope—and purpose—that he hadn't felt in weeks.

❧ 35 ❧

David quickened his steps as he got closer to the bodega where Lele claimed she'd seen Gabrielle. He'd come here every day since, thinking surely she would come again. For the third day in a row, he took a table at the outdoor café catty-cornered from the bodega where he could see the entrances from both streets.

He ordered coffee and sat there with his laptop, ostensibly working, but always with an eye on the little shop.

Lele had told Hank and Meghan about seeing her mamá when they got back to the Middletons' house that day, being far more matter-of-fact in her account to them. So much so, he was starting to believe it really had been Gabrielle she'd seen. Then again, it was still possible the girl had been mistaken. But just in case Lele was right, he'd trimmed his beard shorter than usual and purchased a newsboy cap unlike anything he ever wore in Timoné. He felt a little silly in his "disguise," as if it could hide his Caucasian features, let alone his six-foot-five stature, from anyone who was keeping an eye out for him.

But something he couldn't stop thinking about... The items that had been dropped on the floor in the bodega. A package of diapers. The disposable kind. At least that's what it had looked like. And baby formula.

He didn't know anything about Gabrielle's life since she'd left Timoné. He guessed she'd been gone probably close to a year now. It was possible she had an infant. After all, she'd left to follow a soldier, one she claimed to love, according to Meena. That might explain why she hadn't wanted to speak to Lele. And too, Lele had grown a lot in a year. Natalie'd had to sew her new clothes. Maybe Gabrielle simply hadn't recognized her. He wished he'd thought to tell Lele that. And he would if she asked again.

If Gabrielle had spotted him in the bodega, or the first day he set up shop here at the café, she'd probably picked out a new market to shop at by now. If she didn't show up today, he wasn't sure what his next move would be.

He'd made excuses to Hank and Meghan about needing to get some work done, and Meg graciously offered to watch Lele as long as he needed. But the truth was, he'd accomplished little except to keep up with emails from supporters and other well-wishers who were following the story of Natalie's abduction.

And he was running out of things to say to them. And to Natalie's parents. Every road seemed to lead to a dead end. Still, he couldn't shake the feeling that if he found Gabrielle, he might get some answers. Maybe not for himself, but at least for Lele. And maybe for Jamos, too. At least now, he could tell his friend that he'd done everything in his power to find Gabrielle.

A young woman—dark-haired, petite—rounded the corner, and David's radar went up. But when she looked up, it wasn't Gabrielle. He settled back in his seat.

He would make one more round of the local hospitals tomorrow. Five days had passed since he'd contacted the last one. Five days during which Natalie could have gone into labor and had the baby. It had been three full weeks now since her abduction. *Surely* her due date had come and gone by now. And if she still hadn't shown up at a hospital or clinic, then he was at yet another dead end. So many dead ends. At what point did everyone just give up? In some ways it seemed like they had.

But he couldn't. Not ever.

§

CARINA WRIGGLED AND ROOTED IN THE BLANKET, whimpering as if in pain. The baby had been fussy all day, nursing every two hours or more, but never seeming satisfied.

Exhausted, Natalie placed her daughter across her lap and patted her tiny back in a rhythmic motion. Surely her milk supply wasn't drying up. She'd found it disturbing that Gabrielle had talked about buying formula. No doubt, a command from Tomás. And the possible reasons behind his request turned Natalie cold inside.

She cleaned out the sink and filled it with lukewarm water. Undressing the baby, she inspected her tiny body for signs of what might be causing her discomfort. Finding nothing, she bathed her in the too-small sink and after a few minutes, the warm water seemed to relax Carina a little. She was five days old today, the first of November. The age Gabrielle's baby boy had been when she lost him. Natalie couldn't even fathom something happening to Carina.

Her imagination conjured a barrage of frightening scenarios. What would she do if Carina was sick? Could she convince Tomás and Gabrielle to take her to a hospital? Or would they let her die the way Gabrielle's son supposedly had, without a burial or funeral or even a chance to say goodbye? She had her suspicions about what had actually happened to Gabrielle's baby. And the thoughts paralyzed her.

What if they took Carina, but wouldn't let Natalie go with her? She would not let that happen.

She remembered her mom telling Nikki, when her sister was struggling to nurse her newborn daughter, that a baby could sense its mother's stress. That was probably all that was wrong with Carina.

Forcing a calm she didn't feel, she sang one of the psalms she'd learned as a child in Sunday School. *Bless the LORD, O my soul: and all that is within me, bless his holy name.*

At the first soft note, Carina looked up at her, so much trust in her deep blue eyes. Sometimes, like now, with the quirk of a tiny eyebrow or a crooked half-smile, Natalie would catch a glimpse of David in their daughter's face. A wave of longing for him rushed over her. Her voice broke, but she kept singing. Her daughter didn't seem to mind her wobbly voice as Natalie choked back tears.

She finished the bath and wrapped Carina in the towel they shared. She cuddled her daughter close before diapering and dressing her, then nursed her again. Carina struggled to nurse at first, but finally settled in and, after a few minutes, fell asleep at the breast.

The psalm played over and over in Natalie's mind, calming her. She placed Carina on her chest, covering them both with the single blanket, and had just begun to drift off when the key turned in the door.

She started to sit up to greet Gabrielle, but hearing Tomás's voice too, she pretended to be asleep.

Tomás hadn't been here since Monday, and if she hadn't lost track of a day, it was Thursday now. From their hushed conversations and Gabrielle's sour mood, Natalie suspected the two were fighting. At least something was going on that Gabrielle wasn't telling her.

"I don't care what you tell her, just be ready. One hour." Tomás's voice rose.

Gabrielle shushed him, and Natalie strained to hear, praying their argument wouldn't wake the baby.

The room was still bathed in darkness, with only the light from the small desk lamp illuminating their silhouettes. Natalie watched them through hooded eyes, trying to figure out what was going on.

They spoke in rapid whispers, and though she couldn't hear most of what they said—and couldn't understand most of their rapid Spanish—but judging by their furtive glances in her direction, they were talking about her. And whatever they were discussing, it was clear they were in sharp disagreement. Usually, Gabrielle deferred to Tomás as if she feared him. Now, her harsh tone matched his, and Natalie prayed they didn't come to blows.

She lay frozen in the bed, her senses on high alert. The baby slept on her chest, her uneven little breaths making it even harder to hear the conversation.

Finally, Tomás stormed out, but Natalie didn't miss his final words: "Have everything ready. I'll be back in one hour. You hear me? One hour. No more."

They must be moving her again, but why?

Gabrielle leaned against the door for a long minute after Tomás left. Natalie thought to get out of bed and ask her what was wrong, but something made her stay quiet.

The soft shuffle of footfalls told her Gabrielle was pacing the short span of the room.

After another minute, the lightbulb flashed overhead and Gabrielle shook her shoulders. "Miss Natalie. Get up. Hurry. We must go. Quickly!"

She pretended to squint against the light. "Go? Where?"

"I don't know. Just hurry. I'll get the baby's things. Get your shoes on and pack your things." She tossed Natalie's empty backpack on the bed. "There's no time."

"What's going on, Gabrielle? Are you okay?"

"Just hurry. We must get away from here."

"Is Tomás coming with us." He'd said he would be back in one hour.

"No. Tomás is—" Gabrielle bordered on tears. "He is coming for Carina. Less than an hour. We must hurry!"

"Coming for Carina? Why?" But she knew why.

Gabrielle's voice turned hard. "They've sold her."

"Sold her? No! To who?" Her blood ran cold. She didn't want to know the answer.

"Can you walk?" Gabrielle yanked Carina's extra onesies from the footboard where they were hanging to dry. She stuffed them into the market bag along with a handful of disposable diapers.

"Of course. But where will we go?"

Adrenaline kicked in. She climbed out of bed and swaddled Carina in the blanket, then stuffed her extra change of clothes and underwear into the backpack. Her hands trembled as she tied her shoes.

"I will carry the baby, but we must hurry. We must leave *now*."

"Where will we go?" she asked again. "Where *are* we, Gabrielle?"

No reply, as Gabrielle raced about the room, gathering everything she could fit into the woven bag. She grabbed the scarf they'd used as a blindfold the day they brought Natalie here. She lobbed it onto the bed. "Cover your head."

Natalie gathered her hair on top of her head and quickly wound the scarf like a turban. Her blond head would have been a beacon for anyone looking for them.

Realization dawned. Could this be the escape she'd prayed for? *Please, Lord!*

They were leaving this place. Or would die trying.

❦ 36 ❦

"Wait here." Gabrielle opened the door, revealing a concrete hallway that angled left ten feet ahead. She crept to the end and peered around the corner before motioning to Natalie. "All clear."

Knowing Tomás's plans, Natalie insisted on carrying Carina herself. She'd tied the baby snugly to her chest in a sling made from the thin blanket. Still weak from the birth and weeks of captivity, she felt woozy and braced a hand against the concrete wall to steady herself.

"Follow me. And don't speak to anyone." Gabrielle led her through a maze of cinder block hallways, then up a steep stairway into an alley.

Natalie blinked at the brightness of the day and choked up, realizing that her daughter was five days old and had never seen the sun. She shielded the baby's eyes with the scarf, then realized Carina was fast asleep.

Exhaust fumes and the rank smell of trash wafted toward them, but Natalie breathed deep, welcoming the smells compared to the dank cellar-like room. How absurd that she'd slept here all these days, not knowing what was above her, all around her.

As her eyes adjusted to the light, she took in her surroundings, trying to put landmarks to memory.

An elderly man stood in an open doorway smoking a cigarette, watching them. He showed no surprise at seeing the odd trio emerge from the belly of the city. Gabrielle ignored him and led the way down the alley.

The signs on buildings they passed were all in Spanish, but nothing looked familiar.

"Where are we, Gabrielle? Is this Conzalez?"

The girl hushed her and turned down a narrow street lined with small, dilapidated houses. "*Darse prisa*. And don't speak to *anyone*," she warned again.

Hugging the alleys and keeping to the shadows, they walked quickly for many blocks. The buildings grew fewer and farther between, and the paved streets turned into pea gravel and then dirt. Natalie struggled to keep up. Thankfully, Carina slept peacefully, lulled by the motion of their journey.

After half an hour, she begged Gabrielle to stop. "I need to rest. Just for a minute. Please."

"*Sí*, but only for a minute."

"Carina will wake soon and want to nurse."

"She might have to wait."

"Where are we going? If you can take me to a phone, I can call David. He can come and get us and take us to safety."

Gabrielle scoffed. "You don't know what you are saying."

"What do you mean? Of course he will. Just tell me where we are and I can—"

"*¡Callarse!* Shut up!" She repeated herself in English, and the venom in her voice took Natalie by surprise.

She forced herself to remain silent and followed Gabrielle, who'd apparently already forgotten her need to rest. Every step felt like one step farther from anyone who could help them. And one step closer to a situation worse than she'd just escaped.

Another ten minutes of walking, and the city was swallowed by the jungle. The sun was sinking fast.

"Where will we sleep tonight?" she risked.

"I do not know. I only know that we need to get as far from Tomás—from the city—as possible." Raw fear sparked in the girl's dark eyes.

"Gabrielle, the rains are coming, and we don't want to be out here at night. It's dangerous. Especially after dark, and we're not—"

"Dangerous?" she spat. "Don't talk to me about danger. I risked my life for you. I gave up Tomás for you—" Her words were lost in a convulsion of sobs and she turned and forged ahead on the trail, leaving Natalie in her wake.

"Gabrielle! Stop... I'm sorry!" She started after her.

Gabrielle turned and stormed back toward her, expression fierce. "*Shhh!* Quiet! You will get us all killed!"

"I'm sorry," she whispered, sick with remorse. "And thank you! I know you risked much to help me. To save Carina. And I'm truly grateful, Gabrielle."

"Then you will follow me and keep your *brihacho* mouth shut. Tomás will kill us both if he finds us."

Natalie answered with a curt nod and trudged after Gabrielle, praying Carina wouldn't wake up.

The fear in Gabrielle's eyes was real, and Tomás had already killed Jamos, so Natalie had no doubt he would kill them too. There was money at stake. Someone had paid him for an infant —for Carina! Even so, spending a night out here would be a death sentence too.

The crack of thunder split the air and an instant later, sheets of rain cascaded over them. Instinctively, she pulled the blanket tighter around the baby and hunched over to keep her dry. Another few minutes and the trail would be impassable.

EYES DOWNCAST, DAVID CLOSED THE DOOR OF THE CLINIC, the last on his list, and headed back toward the Middletons'.

What now? He could spend the rest of his life searching hospitals and clinics or sitting at the café across from the bodega waiting to see if Gabrielle showed up.

He would never give up hope on finding Natalie and their child. *Never.* But he had some hard decisions to make. First of all, Lele. She'd thrived with Meghan and Hank, but they'd already turned down one placement for a foster child because he and Lele were taking up the extra bedroom space.

The Middletons had been nothing but kind and generous, assuring him they were welcome to stay as long as needed. But he couldn't remain with them indefinitely. In addition, he worried that Jamos would return to Timoné and find Lele gone. Of course, he'd left word with Tados and others in the village who would let Jamos know what had happened.

If he stayed in Conzalez, he needed to find a different place to live. And a job to pay the rent. He couldn't expect their supporters, however generous-hearted and concerned by the situation, to pay while he searched for her and the baby. They entrusted their donations so he would translate the Bible for the Timoné people. Show them the love of Christ.

But if he went back to Timoné, he *couldn't* continue his search for Natalie. And giving up on her and the baby wasn't an option. Any minute he wasn't actively searching for them, he felt like a failure, as though he was shirking his most sacred duty as a husband and father—protecting his family.

It was a twenty-minute walk back to the compound and he spent the time praying, asking God to show him what he should do next. Hearing no clear answer by the time the Middletons' place came into view, he committed once again to trusting God. That was all he could do. It was the *most* he could do.

"David!" The front door flew open and Meghan came running. "Hurry!" she shouted, urgency in her voice.

He took off, his long legs quickly closing the gap. "What is it?" he yelled.

"There's been another ransom call! About fifteen minutes ago! We tried calling your cell but you didn't answer."

"What?" His chest ached. He'd silenced his phone in the clinics and had forgotten to turn it back on. "Is it serious? Is there proof of life?"

"Oh, David. Yes! Come see!"

She led the way inside where Hank sat at his computer. He turned when they entered, but David couldn't read his expression.

Hank motioned to a stool beside him. "Sit down, David. Gospel Linguists called a few minutes ago. They received this photo and a new demand for ransom early this morning. It looks like Natalie." He eyed David as if making sure he was ready to see something difficult.

Taking a deep breath, David nodded and straddled the stool.

Hank clicked on a link and a color image appeared on the screen. He waited a moment before enlarging the photo.

The image had been shot in a darkened room and the colors were muted, the image a little blurry, but it was her. David had no doubt. Glad he was seated, he swallowed hard against the ache in his throat. The photo was of Natalie lying on her back in a narrow bed, her eyes closed as if in sleep. Peaceful sleep. Her arms cradled a bundle on her chest. Part of a round head with a haze of pale hair was visible. It looked like an infant, but he supposed it could have been a doll, a prop. The image wasn't sharp enough to be sure.

Hank zoomed in closer. There was another person in the photo—a shoulder and part of an arm looming to one side of the bed—but no identifying features. It was hard to tell even whether the person was male or female.

Natalie's left hand overlapped her right on the baby's back and her tattooed wedding band was clearly visible. He lifted his own left hand, comparing the patterns. They were a match. It was Natalie.

But what *wasn't* clear was whether the photo had captured her sleeping—or posed in the peace of death.

❧ 37 ❧

"**D**o you think she's alive?" David turned to Hank, hating the tremor in his voice.

Hank frowned. "I don't know, brother. I'm praying so. Meg feels sure she is."

David swiveled on the stool to look into Meg's eyes, hoping to find the truth there.

She smiled softly and nodded. "Maybe it's wishful thinking. And if she is...gone...she is at peace. Look at her face. But I think she's alive. And I think that's your son or daughter she's holding, David. The look on Natalie's face..."

He rose. "What do we do next? What is the mission saying?"

"I've forwarded the image to Moreno," Hank said. "He has his forensics guys working on it. They'll extract any information they can get from the digital image. There's no time stamp or anything, and unfortunately, it came as a .png file—a screen shot —so that tells us when the screen capture happened—last night at 7:57—but that doesn't mean it's the date the actual photo was taken."

"Was it Bob Richmond at headquarters who called?"

Hank nodded. "He's forwarded everything to the FBI and

the other local U.S. agencies that have been working on the investigation."

"No change on the ransom, I assume?"

"No. I'm sorry."

David nodded. He understood. And yet, the stakes were *so* much higher now. "So, that means they didn't give any details about where we were supposed to make the drop or get Natalie back?"

Hank nodded, looking solemn.

"Can you zoom in any more? Or lighten the photo?"

"I've tried several different settings. This is about as clear as it gets."

David returned to the stool and Hank enlarged the photo until it was nothing more than a mass of pixels. The third person in the photo bothered him deeply. "Why would they have needed this person"—he tapped the disembodied shoulder and arm on the screen—"if Natalie was alive? And how could she and the baby—if that really *is* an infant—have slept through a photo shoot?"

"Well, it's obvious they didn't use flash," Meghan said. "It wouldn't have taken more than a split second to shoot a photo like this since no one is posing. I just assumed that person was helping with the baby, a midwife maybe?"

"Or one of the kidnappers."

"They could be one and the same."

"I know." He raked a hand through too-long hair. "That's what scares me."

Remembering his phone, he fished it from his pocket and turned it back on. Several emails flowed in, notification bells dinging. He scrolled quickly through the list. He'd been copied to the one Hank had shown him from Gospel Linguists. He opened it quickly, just to verify it was the same email and that he hadn't missed any part of the message.

But when the photo loaded, something clicked. That flash of yellow—the small, feminine wrist and sleeve of the mystery person in the photo. *Yellow...like mustard, not like corn.* "Oh, dear God... Can it be?"

"What is it, David?"

He looked up from his phone to meet Hank's worried frown.

"I think I know who this is." He tapped the yellow sleeve on his screen.

Meghan came to look over his shoulder, and he told them in more detail about Lele seeing her mother in the bodega that day, and how she'd been wearing a mustard-colored shirt, that she'd dropped a package of diapers. And baby formula.

Hank pivoted in his chair. "You think she's involved in Natalie's kidnapping?"

"She must be. How else would she be in this photo *with* Natalie?"

"It's kind of a long shot." Meghan looked skeptical. "Identifying her by a T-shirt and a few inches of arm?"

"I realize it wouldn't hold up—even in a Colombian court—but I think it's her, Meg. I just have this feeling. And I think I know where to find her."

He needed to go back to the café by the corner bodega. No, it wasn't God's audible voice that told him... He wouldn't have bet his life on it, but it was stronger than a hunch. He tried to explain it to Hank and Meghan.

"I'll go with you," Hank said, scraping back his chair.

"No. I need to go alone. She got spooked before. I can't afford to lose her this time."

Hank sighed. "Keep your phone with you then. I'll alert Moreno and his men."

David nodded. "Just tell them to stay out of sight. Let me talk to her first."

"Be careful, David." Meghan put a hand briefly on his shoulder.

Hank did the same. "Don't do anything foolish, man. It's not worth getting killed over."

"Yes, Hank. It is."

❧

Natalie looked out from the "perch" where they'd spent the night. The three of them had climbed another five minutes until the rain and the muddy trail made it impossible to go farther. But they'd landed on an outcropping shadowed by a rock overhang—essentially a "cave" with open sides. They'd spent a miserable night, drenched and shivering but at least protected from the rain and mud.

Taking inventory this morning, she realized that the sound they'd taken for heavy rainfall all night, was instead a natural waterfall trickling musically beside their open-air cave from high overhead.

Gabrielle still slept, her back against the wall of the cave, her clothes, like Natalie's caked in mud. Her shuddering breaths sounded as if she'd cried herself to sleep. The girl had sacrificed everything to save Carina. To save them both. Natalie would be forever grateful.

The baby stirred, and Natalie nursed her, holding her as close as possible, trying to warm her little body. She had only one clean diaper left and she would wait until the little onesie, drying on a rock in the sun now, was warm and dry before she changed her.

The sun was high in the sky when Gabrielle finally awakened. She sat up and stretched, looking around as if bewildered.

"Good morning. I was beginning to think you were going to sleep all day."

"The baby is okay?"

"She's fine. Not as fussy this morning. And she nursed well."

Gabrielle rose and went to the edge of the outcropping. She turned, looking behind her, then panned the forest canopy above. "I know this place."

"This very spot?" Natalie patted the stone surface she sat on. "You've been here before?"

She nodded. "Come. Look!"

Natalie struggled to her feet with the baby in her arms, then followed Gabrielle to the edge of the outcropping. Gabrielle turned and pointed overhead. "*El campanario.*"

"Ah, yes. Steeple." The rock formation above their cave did, indeed, look like a steeple with a bell tower rising to the sky.

Gabrielle climbed down some twenty feet from where they'd slept and parted some palm branches. "You see?"

Natalie gave a little gasp. "That's Conzalez!" Below them, the town twinkled in the morning sun, a few small boats slicing through the Guaviare's brown waters, morning traffic clogging the narrow roads. Natalie didn't think she'd ever seen anything so beautiful. She turned to Gabrielle. "It's where we've been all along?"

"Yes," she admitted. "But it's not safe to go back."

"But Gabrielle, David is there. And our friends, Hank and Meg. They can help us." She pointed below to where the river curved into a bay. "Our friends live right at the entrance to that small bay. We're *so* close."

Distance was deceptive in the jungle but they'd only climbed for about an hour yesterday. The trip back down to the city would go even faster. Joy flooded her. If David was still in Conzalez, he was less than an hour away! "Oh, Jesus, thank you," she whispered.

But Gabrielle frowned. "You think Tomás doesn't know where your friends live? He'll have men waiting there even now."

"Then we'll go somewhere they don't expect. And call David from there."

Gabrielle stared out over the town. After a long minute, she turned to Natalie. "I know where to find David. A place Tomás does not know. I will go. You stay here with Carina until David comes for you."

"But how will he find us? Shouldn't we go together?"

"There is a target on your back. And a price on Carina's head."

"I will show him. I promise." She looked back to where they'd stashed their soggy belongings. "Have you eaten?"

"Not yet."

"You need to eat. For the baby."

"You need to eat too, Gabrielle. For the journey."

They sat together and ate the nuts and dried fruit they'd brought from the basement room in Conzalez. But Gabrielle ate in silence, clearly troubled. The girl was grieving Tomás and no doubt feeling deeply betrayed, but Natalie suspected there was more to it. Maybe just that she was completely alone in the world now. And if she had been involved in the kidnapping, as Natalie suspected, there would be consequences. Despite her heroic actions now, Gabrielle would likely serve time for her crime.

Natalie prayed for a way to encourage her. "You will come with us to Timoné?"

Gabrielle shrugged. "We will see."

"Lele will be so overjoyed to see you."

Gabrielle didn't respond so Natalie tried again. "Gabrielle, I know it's painful now, but you can make a new life—you and Lele —in Timoné. David has taken care of your family's *utta* for your father so it will be ready for you."

Without speaking, Gabrielle rose, brushed off her hands, and climbed down to stand in the spot where she'd shown Natalie the view of Conzalez. She looked above her, then back down toward the city, as if gauging where they were on the mountain.

"You stay here. Do *not* try to come down on your own. They will kill you and take Carina. I will send Mr. David to get you. You wait for him."

"But you'll come with him. You said you would bring him to us."

"Yes, I will show him where you are."

She didn't like Gabrielle's rewording of her promise, but she didn't argue. She'd grown more fluent in the Timoné dialect during her time with Gabrielle, who'd gradually reverted to her native tongue as she and Natalie spent time together, but perhaps something was lost in translation.

"I will go now." Gabrielle bent to touch Carina's head. She smiled when the baby squirmed under her touch and opened her eyes.

She turned to leave, but Natalie pulled her into a brief hug. "Thank you, my friend. I owe you my life. I can never thank you enough."

"Oh, but you've done nothing *but* thank me since Carina came into the world." She gave Natalie a crooked smile. Then, seeming uncomfortable at the affectionate exchange, she turned and started down the hill.

Natalie watched her go, exhilaration and foreboding warring within her.

38

David ordered his third cup of coffee, one eye always on the bodega entrances at the street corner. He paid the cashier at the window and took the coffee back to his table on the café patio. He sipped slowly, not willing to risk missing Gabrielle because of a full bladder.

He kept his laptop open, pretending to work, but watched the street through dark sunglasses. One man—a native, judging by his appearance—had walked past the bodega at least three times. One of Moreno's plainclothes deputies, no doubt. But otherwise, it seemed to be business as usual on this Friday in November.

Two hours ago, he'd been so certain God had led him here, but with each passing minute, his confidence waned. He tapped out a message to Hank on his phone: *Still waiting.*

The reply came back immediately: *Still praying.*

How would he ever repay these dear friends who'd come alongside—

A rustling in the alley at the side of the building caught his attention. Some animal foraging in the rubbish bin probably. He bent to type on the open document, keeping up the pretense of working, but inclining one ear to the alleyway, senses on alert.

A minute later, footsteps approached from that direction, and he glanced up to see Gabrielle standing by his table, looking down at him. Her dark hair was piled in a knot on her head, but she looked the same as he remembered. So young. She looked scared too.

His heart hammered, but he forced himself to appear calm. "Gabrielle. *Hollio.*" He scooted out the chair beside him. "May I...buy you *cazho?*"

"No." Her face was like stone, no indication that she knew him. She spoke so softly he could barely hear. "You need to go get Miss Natalie and your daughter."

"What? You know where they are?" His pulse stuttered. They were alive. And he had a daughter. *Oh, dear God. Thank you!*

"Go quickly and tell no one."

"I...I can't pay ransom, Gabrielle."

"No ransom. Miss Natalie is hiding with the baby. But they won't be safe for long."

"Yes, I understand. Where do I find them?"

"Leave Conzalez by Martinique Street. By foot. Be sure you aren't followed. Look for *el campanario* halfway up the hill. They are—"

"Gabrielle!" A deep, angry voice called her name from the street in front of the café. "Back away!"

Her eyes went wide, as if she recognized the voice. "Tomás!" she whispered. But without turning to look, she flew off the patio, dropping to all fours and crab-crawling until she disappeared around the corner of the building to the alley.

David looked up to see Moreno's man standing in the street, his stance wide, pistol drawn and aimed toward the alley.

"No! Don't shoot!" He raced around the side of the café, keeping low to the ground.

"Don't shoot!" he yelled again. But before the words were out of his mouth, a gunshot split the air, and the *zing* of a bullet screamed by his ear. He hit the ground and lay prone, then raised his head enough to look down the alley.

Twenty feet in front of him, Gabrielle lay on the ground in the same position as he. "Stay down, Gabrielle! Stay low!"

The street in front of the café came alive with gunfire, people screaming and taking cover in the stores and the doorway alcoves. David risked lifting his head again and watched the first gunman crumple to the pavement.

David crawled on his belly to Gabrielle. "Are you okay?"

Her hair had come undone and now shielded her face, but her arm twitched in a way that frightened him. He looked over his shoulder to the street, trying to assess the threat. Half a dozen uniformed policemen had surrounded the felled man, their guns silent now.

David scrambled on his knees to Gabrielle's side. He shook her, alarmed when there was no response. He rolled her gently on her side and brushed the hair away from her face. His hands came away bloody.

"Gabrielle?" He couldn't see where she was bleeding from, but a pool of crimson spread underneath her. "Stay with me!"

She looked up at him with glassy eyes. Her chest rose and fell as she struggled for a breath, but it came on a gurgle of blood. She clutched his arm. "Tell Lele I love her... And... Mr. David—" She pulled in a hollow breath. "Tell Natalie. Tell her I believe."

"I will. I'll tell them. I promise. Where is Natalie?"

"*El campanario*. They—" She tried to speak again, but the spark vanished from her eyes, extinguished forever.

His heart sank, thinking of Jamos. His friend would be devastated. And Lele. *Oh, precious girl...* How would he tell them?

Placing a hand gently over Gabrielle's cool forehead, he closed her eyes. "God bless you," he whispered. "God go with you, Gabrielle."

He struggled to his feet, feeling disoriented. Not waiting to speak to Moreno, he ran in the direction of Martinique Street, scrambling to remember exactly what Gabrielle had said.

El campanario. Steeple. But she'd used the Spanish word, since there was no Timoné word for something that didn't exist in the village. There must be a church on Martinique where Natalie was hiding.

He came to the intersection and halted. Gabrielle hadn't said which way to turn, which direction to go on the street. *Go by foot*, she'd said. He surveyed his options. The street narrowed to the north. It would be more difficult to drive that street. But there were more buildings to the south.

Which way, Lord? Please. Show me.

There was no time to waste.

He started north, choosing the narrow way.

I will lift up mine eyes unto the hills, from whence cometh my help. My help cometh from the Lord, which made heaven and earth.

I will lift up mine eyes unto the hills... Look up, David.

The thought startled him, but he obeyed without hesitation. And there it was. *El campanario*. A perfect bell tower steeple, halfway up the hill, just as Gabrielle had said, and carved by God's own hand into the side of the green hill.

THE SUN BURNED DOWN THROUGH A CLEAR BLUE SKY, painting the floor of the shelter with yellow light inch by inch, until Natalie sat with Carina in one triangle of shade beside the waterfall. She wished she'd somehow marked the minutes—or hours?—since Gabrielle had left. But maybe she would have given up hope if she knew how long it had actually been since she'd disappeared down the path toward Conzalez.

Gabrielle had warned her to wait for David. That she and the baby weren't safe in the city. And even if they had been, she wasn't sure she had the strength to carry her daughter safely into Conzalez. But she would not spend the night here alone with her baby. There couldn't be anything in Conzalez that posed any more risk than a night alone in the jungle with a newborn baby.

She had rinsed off last night's mud as best she could,

splashing in the freezing waterfall. She'd dressed the baby in the last remaining diaper and the clean, sun-dried onesie.

She collected a small pile of heavy stones and a sturdy sharp branch as weapons against wild animals, but she couldn't carry those and her baby too, if she decided to leave. But if Gabrielle didn't return with help—hopefully with David—by the time the afternoon sun was halfway to the horizon, she would head down the hillside with Carina alone.

If she died trying to get down to Conzalez with Carina, she would still thank God for the many prayers he'd answered during these trying weeks. That Carina was here, healthy and strong. That God had sent such an unlikely friend in Gabrielle. That she'd grown so much in her faith and in—

A twig snapped in the trees in front of her. Holding Carina closer, she reached for two of the stones, gripping one like a baseball, ready to throw, the other waiting at the ready.

"Natalie?"

She sucked in a breath. "David?" She could barely get his name out.

He called her again. And then, the palm branches parted and he was standing in front of her, just the way she'd dreamed so many times these last weeks without him.

"Oh, David, is it really you?"

He scrambled up the rocks to her as if their lives depended on it. He knelt beside her, gathering her and the baby into his arms.

He drew away to look into her face, then gathered her to himself again.

Words caught in her throat and she couldn't seem to make them form into anything that made sense.

But then, no words were needed.

They wept together, and she somehow knew he was feeling the same sense of utter disbelief. Could this really be happening? After all this time, had God really answered their prayers and restored them to each other, healthy and whole, and with their daughter sandwiched between them?

Their daughter!

"Oh, David! Look at her." She held the sleeping baby up for him. "Your daughter, David. Your beautiful daughter."

He swept a new torrent of tears away with the back of his hand and took Carina in his arms. "I was so afraid we'd lost her. That I'd lost you."

"I hope you don't mind…I named her Carina. We can change it if you don't like it."

"Don't be silly. It's beautiful. She's beautiful. Like her mother."

"Oh, David—" Her voice caught on a sob. "The last time I looked in a mirror I was far from beautiful."

He cradled the baby in one arm like a quarterback and tenderly cupped her cheek with his palm. "*Mi carru.* I have never seen such a beautiful sight."

She placed her hand over his, then pulled it to her lips and kissed his fingers. She drew back just to look at him—to be sure he was really here in the flesh.

What she saw was blood on his shirtsleeve. Lots of blood. She gasped. "David… You're hurt."

He followed her gaze to his sleeve. "No. I'm fine. It's…it's not my blood."

She tilted her head. "Whose then…?"

"Oh, Natalie. I'm so sorry. Gabrielle was killed. She came to find me. To tell me where you and the baby were."

Tears came in a flood as he told her what had happened after Gabrielle found him at the café.

She told him then how Gabrielle had helped her deliver the baby and then escape before Tomás could take Carina from her.

"Tomás?" He stopped her mid-sentence. "Gabrielle spoke that name just before she was shot."

Natalie nodded. So much to catch each other up on, so much to process and grieve. "Lele? Is she okay?"

David's quiet laughter answered the question in the best way. "She is going to be over the moon about this baby."

"She might change her mind when she sees how much attention Carina takes away from her."

"I think Lele can hold her own."

It was a blessing to laugh together, despite the profound sadness.

They sat wrapped in each other's arms, their tiny daughter between them, for several minutes, whispering words of love, and thanking God again and again for this sweetest answer to prayer.

A shadow passed over them as a cloud hid the sun. David looked up and startled. With Carina still in his arms, he rose and checked his phone. "I don't have a signal, but we'd better get down the mountain before the rains come. Or worse, before Hank comes looking for us."

She laughed at his joke, then quickly turned serious. "Is it safe to go back?"

"I think so." He told her about Moreno's men shooting Tomás. "It'll take a while to get to the bottom of things. But we'll have Hank pick us up on Martinique Street. You won't have to walk far, and I'll carry our daughter."

She rose and stood beside him "Oh, David. I was so afraid you'd never get to meet her. That we wouldn't get to raise her together. Like Mom and my dad." She wept then, understanding at last the depth of sorrow her parents had suffered.

But David pulled her close. "No doubt your dad is looking down from heaven with joy right now. And your mom and Cole are about to get the happiest phone call of their lives."

"And Lele. Just wait till—" She stopped, realizing that David probably didn't know about Gabrielle's father. She sighed, tearing up again. "It's all too much to take in."

"One day at a time, *mi carru*. One day at a time. We have the rest of our lives to sort it all out."

He gathered her backpack and motioned for her to follow him. "Let's go home."

EPILOGUE

Timoné, Colombia, South America

"**S**ee? See, sister? I told you! My *colibrí* has come to meet you! Lele's laughter wove together with Carina's giggles as a colorful hummingbird flitted between them in the shade of the *utta*. Natalie couldn't help but join in the giggles.

These precious girls were her joy. And Lele took her responsibilities as a big sister very seriously.

Reaching for the elusive bird, Carina took two wobbly steps and promptly fell on the soft earth. Not even a year old and she was already walking. Natalie sighed. How would she ever keep up?

Carina started to fuss, but Lele hurried to her side and tugged her up by her pudgy hands.

"It's okay, 'Rina. It's okay, *bebé*. Get right back up. Remember what Papá and Nattía say?"

It still thrilled Natalie to hear Lele call David Papá. They'd settled on Nattía for her—a combination of her name and tía or auntie, not wanting to diminish Gabrielle's memory, since Lele had called her Mamá.

Hank and Meghan would be coming for a visit next month,

bringing two little girls they were fostering—and hoped to adopt. David was already bracing himself for the "invasion of frills." But he held his own just fine despite being outnumbered three to one in their *utta*. He had, however, begun hinting that it might be time to start trying for a boy.

Now she was the one holding out for a little more time. But she wouldn't let it turn into an argument. Oh, the things they'd fretted about *before*.

The girls heard his footsteps coming up the trail before Natalie did and hurried to meet their Papá.

David laughed and scooped up a girl under each arm, tossing them over his shoulders like two wiggly sacks of potatoes. They squealed with delight, and the smile he threw Natalie as he closed the gap between them said more than any words he could have spoken—in any language.

A note to my readers:

It has been more than twenty years since Natalie and David, Nate and Daria, Cole, Tados, and all the other characters from the Camfield Legacy Novels first made their way into my mind and heart. I've had so many requests for a third novel in the series over the years—the rest of Natalie and David's story—that I knew someday, when my deadlines allowed, I would finally write this story.

Some of the scenes have simmered on a back burner all these years and fell into place just as I imagined they would. Others, like little Lele and her family, and even the stinky monkeys, walked into the story more recently and seemingly of their own accord. Welcoming these new characters and playing with these details is my favorite part of the writing process.

As with the first two novels in this series—*Beneath a Southern Sky* and *After the Rains*—the villages, peoples, and dialects of Timoné and Conzalez are fictionalized as portrayed in *Breath of Heaven* and are purely products of my imagination. The historical and political journeys of the more than eight hundred real indigenous tribes of South America are complicated, varied, and ever-changing, and I can only write with authority about peoples of my imagination.

I pray these characters carve a place in your heart and memory as they have in mine. It feels odd to say that imaginary people have enriched my life, but it is absolutely true. I'm so grateful that one of our Creator's gifts to each of us is creativity. Whether in writing, music, art, invention, or the myriad other creative endeavors, they are all a reflection of who He is and how much He loves you and me.

So many thanks go out to those who've been part of bringing this story to life.

- My long-time (long, *long* time!) writing critique partner, Tamera Alexander. I'm not sure I could write a book without your discerning eye! Thank you, dearest friend.

- My editor/proofreaders, Vicky, Tobi, and Tavia. Your sharp eyes (and encouraging words!) are such a gift.
- Thank you, Pastor Ben and Pastor Josh. When I'm taking notes on the bulletin in church, it's *sometimes* because you gave me a great idea for adding God's truth to the fiction I write. After all, as Emerson famously said, "Fiction reveals truth that reality obscures."
- And as always, Ken Raney, love of my life. Couldn't do this without you, babe, (and wouldn't want to try.)

For more information, or to contact me, please visit my website: www.deborahraney.com. I love hearing from my readers!

Deborah Raney
May 16, 2022

DEBORAH RANEY's first novel, *A Vow to Cherish*, inspired the World Wide Pictures film of the same title and launched Deb's writing career. Forty books later, she's still creating stories that touch hearts and lives. A RITA Award, Carol Award, and National Readers Choice Award winner and three-time Christy Award finalist, Deb is a recent transplant to Missouri, having moved with her husband, Ken Raney, from their native Kansas. They love road trips, Friday garage sale dates, time with their kids and grandkids, and breakfast on the screened porch overlooking their wooded backyard.

Visit Deb on the Web at www.deborahraney.com.

For other books
by Deborah Raney

To learn more, visit:
deborahraney.com